THE CHOSEN
Breaking Bonds

BY
MICHAEL WILLIAMS

Copyright © 2019 by Michael Williams
Published in the United States by

ISBN-978-0-9974766-2-0

This book is a work of fiction. Any references to real people, events, establishments, organizations, or locales are intended solely to provide a sense of authenticity and are used fictitiously. All other characters, incidents, and dialogue are drawn from the author's imagination and are not to be construed as real.

Cover Art by: Michael Williams
Database Art by: Michael Williams

DEDICATION

I would like to dedicate this book to my family for always believing in me. I dedicate this to my friends for the support, and finally to you; the reader. Always strive to reach your goals no matter how hard it may seem. Embrace the hero in you...for you have been Chosen.

Table of Contents

Prologue

Within the dark corridors of an old steel mill, which sits firmly in Regal, Nevada, a faint flicker of a light bulb can be seen in the darkness. Directly underneath the light sits a man beaten within an inch of his life. The blood on his face has begun to dry signaling he had been there for some time. Slowly he regains consciousness. He manages to lift his head and takes a quick glance at his surroundings.

His eyes are met with nothing but an overbearing darkness. He panics and tries to get up, only to realize that his hands and feet are bound to the floor by industrial strength chains found at the abandoned steel mill. As he wraiths in place, his sweat soaked hair flings wildly.

Suddenly, he stops to listen as he hears footsteps. Along with the footsteps, the faint sound of something scraping across the floor can be heard nearby. "Who's there?" he shouts while he continues to try to escape. The sound of the footsteps gets closer and closer, the sound gets heavier with each step. Without warning a female body comes bolting out of the darkness and lands on the ground in front of him. "Eva, no!"

As he struggles to reach her, a voice from the darkness mocks his attempts. "Save what little energy you have left as you and I still have one last task that needs to be taken care of." In the dimly lit room all that can be seen of the mysterious person are his deep red eyes that are slightly illuminated.

"Do not worry, she still lives for now. Her fate solely depends on your level of cooperation. So, tell me Hotstreak, how much do you really care about her?"

"You won't get away with this. Someone will be sent to free me and take you down."

"So young and still so naïve, Hotstreak calling for help is exactly what I had in mind. So here is the plan. If you want her to live, you are going to call back to your precious base. Tell them you have a code red and need immediate assistance!"

"You're sick, you mean to slaughter them all. I won't do it, there is no way I would ever betray Atlas."

"Tell me Hotstreak, what is more important to you, this woman or your orders?"

Hotstreak looks down at Eva; tears begin to fill his eyes. "I am so sorry Eva." Hotstreak can see the shimmer of a blade in the dim light. "Wait, ok...ok I will do it. Just please leave her alone!"

"I have taken your communicator and set it to record. You have thirty seconds."

"To anyone that gets this message...this is Operative Hotstreak. I am calling a code red...I repeat code red. I require immediate assistance. Please...this is not a drill nor a joke, if you get this message please send help to these coordinates-"

"Times up, very convincing."

"I did what you asked, now please, do what you promised and let her live!"

"I am well aware of our previous conversation." However, he thrusts the blade through the back of the chair and into Hot-streak. "I never said anything about you." He snatches the blade out and slowly backs away as Hotstreak begins to pass away.

Across the country in a field just outside Savanna, Georgia, Burner waits for an STC to land. The wind from the turbines glides right over his baldhead. He gently rubs the scar across his nose as the back hatch of the STC opens. Out walks a man in his mid-thirties. "It's been a while, Burner."

"Well look who it is, Scott. Man, I am always so busy I hardly have time to hang out anymore. How have you been?" Burner states while wrapping his muscular arms around Scott for a hug.

"I'm doing well; how about you and I grab a drink when we get back and catch up." Scott invites Burner onto the STC where he sits in the pilot's chair. Burner takes a seat in one of the chairs mounted to the wall of the aircraft. "So how are Melissa and Jack doing?" Scott asks as he starts the engine.

"Melissa is doing great and Jack is getting bigger by the day. Can you believe he is two years old now?" Both Burner and Scott abruptly stop to listen to their communicators. "I guess the reunion will have to wait Scott, seems like Hotstreak went and got himself into some trouble. I just hope this is a problem we can handle…it's not every day that a code red is called."

Within seconds the STC was in the air. It takes a little over two and a half hours to get to Nevada. They land about a mile away from Hotstreak's coordinates. As the back hatch opens a gust of wind rushes in. Burner slowly turns the ring on his finger; he takes two deep breaths before standing. "You know, something doesn't feel right about this."

"What's the matter Burner?"

"This, what we are doing, it doesn't feel right.

Listen if I am not back in twenty minutes I need you to take off. I don't want you risking your life…you still have a job to do. I will go in and find Hotstreak and whoever else answered the call and get out of there."

Scott gets up and takes Burner's hand and gives him a firm handshake. "Good luck in there my friend." Burner turns and exits the STC, where he makes his way to the steel mill.

Trapped inside the old steel mill, Burner rests on both knees. Bodies were thrown around the room. Burner stumbles to his feet but falls back down due to an injury to his ribs. Amidst the moaning of a dozen injured men, Burner could hear a slight beeping. With all of his strength he crawls over to a corner of the room.

Once there he finds a lunchbox size electronic device mounted to the wall. Using one hand to cup his injured ribs and the other to slowly lift himself up off the ground, he stands upright and begins to pant excessively. *It is a concussion bomb, most likely intended to bury this place and us with it. Doesn't look to be any way to stop it…crap, so be it then*, he thinks to himself. Burner sets his communicator to record, "cough…cough, this is Operative Burner. To whoever gets this message, we were set up. It was a trap right from the beginning; Nova captured

The Chosen: Breaking Bonds

Hotstreak and Slipstream and used them to call code red to lure us all here to be slaughtered. They set concussion bombs to try and bury the evidence. I am all that remains, one lone operative and yet I am not enough to stop this from happening. Upon my arrival, most of our operatives were already engaged with Nova forces. We fought till the end; it is now that I realize we never stood a chance. Do not send any more reinforcements. Consider this place 'ground zero.' We have lost!"

Burner takes a big sniff as his eyes become watery. "My name is Mark Titus…I have done a lot of wrong in my life, but the one thing I did right was my son, Jack. Make sure he knows how much I love him and wanted to see him grow up. Tell him not to hate people just because they are different. Tell him to listen to his mother and…and that I will see him again someday. There is not much time left and I am almost out of energy, but I will still fight till my last breath for the safety of this world. Stay strong my friends and never lose sight of what part we play in this fight."

Burner turns off his communicator and turns his attention to the bomb. He ignites his body one last time. With what he had left, he superheated the wall around the device. The bomb as well as the charred remains of the wall falls out, down three stories to the ground. The fire slowly fades off of Burner as he watches the bomb plummet. But before he had a chance to celebrate, the bomb went off, bringing the entire steel mill down on top of Burner and the others.

Chapter 1

Awakening

One week later at Atlas Headquarters, which is located just outside the city of Lynnex, West Virginia.

Outside the Atlas base of operation stands two gentlemen; one rests his arm on the roof of a car. He moves to the back of the car and puts a suitcase into the trunk. The other man who appears to be much older extends his hand and says, "I am sending you to speak with a friend of ours. He lives in Mercury, North Carolina; I hear he owns his own school now so that is where you will find him. So, for now, you will have to use your real name… David. I have pulled some strings and secured you a suitable cover while you are staying there."

David looks content as the other man finishes speaking. "Remember to keep me informed regarding the status of your assignment. You know I would have gone myself but ever since we lost three/fourths of our operatives at the hands of Nova, I can't afford to be away for any reason. As it is I have to contact Newman about clean up. Our people are scared, Nova managed to take out a lot of our top operatives with ease."

David takes a firm grip of the man hand and shakes it; "I'll do my best Commander, but to be clear my assignment is to find Dennis Tavern, CEO of the Liberation Charity. You said he owns a high school, most likely Mercury High School. Once I contact him, inform him to speak with the board about the incident in Regal, Nevada."

"Correct, it is very important that the board is made aware. We also need him to put together a special package for the families of those lost in the attack. Watch yourself and report in periodically." David gets into the car and drives off east.

Later that night, in the city of Mercury, North Carolina, the back door of a modern suburban home slams shut. A teenage African American male no older than eighteen grabs a basketball from off the ground. He starts to slowly bounce it; his face was riddled with a combination of anger and sadness.

Moments later he starts to shoot the ball at the nearby basketball goal.

About an hour goes by and his watch now reads eleven fifty-five. Sweat pours from every inch of his body; his shirt becomes very damp. He stops to catch his breath as he runs his hand through his hair. *No way I can't be tired already, I am just getting started*, he says to himself. Just then he starts to feel sick to his stomach; a burning sensation as well as an unsettling sense of dizziness shoots through his whole body.

He fights to stand up right but can't fight it any longer. As he falls to the ground, he throws the ball skyward. A stream of fire erupts from his hand, propelling the ball into the air. As the ball sub-comes to gravity, it makes a thud on impact. Smoke left by the unsuspecting flame fills the air above.

Just around the corner at a greenish-blue house, the sound of water running can be heard through the window. Inside at the kitchen sink stands another African American teenager. He hums the lyrics to his favorite song while he washes the dishes. The ends of his braided hair protrude from the bottom of his wool hat. He abruptly stops humming and turns around to see his grandmother standing in the doorway.

"Devonte, baby do you know what time it is? You need to be heading to bed; you have school tomorrow."

He smiles, "Ok Nana, I just have a few more to wash." She walks closer and says, "Are you sure? You look like you are going to fall asleep any minute now. Ok. If you insist, but don't forget to clean up this water on the floor so you won't slip and fall."

She kisses him on his forehead, and then turns around and heads back upstairs. Devonte returns to washing the dishes but stops again as he notices his vision becoming blurry. A cold chill crept down his spine and went all the way down his arms. The once steaming hot dishwater froze into a mass of ice. Devonte panics and tries with all his might to free himself from the frozen mixture of ice and dishes. He can lift the block up out of the sink and hoist it over his head.

It was at that moment that Devonte blacks out, his body fell to the ground, and on impact the dishes shattered into tiny pieces.

Next door the crash can be heard through the open window on the second floor. A boy sticks his head out of the window; he is African American with shaggy hair that leans slightly to the left.

He turns his attention from the house next door over to a computer screen. He casually walks over to it and takes a seat in the chair in front of it. He types, "Environmental Science Term Paper by Xavier Evans." As he types up his paper, he can hear thunder in the distance.

After about a half an hour goes by and Xavier

puts the finishing touches on his paper, then he prints it out. The howling of the thunder can be heard clearer than before, and it is happening more frequently now. Xavier walks over to the window where he rests his hands on the windowsill. A bright flash of lightning makes his heart start to race.

This causes him to back away from the window. With each step, he grabs his chest as if he was trying to stop his heart from pounding. After a couple of minutes, his heart continues to race. He starts to make his way to the door but suddenly stops.

The lights in his room begin to dance off and on, at which point his entire body goes numb. An electric discharge abruptly springs out of his hand. It hit his computer and blows the screen out. Unfortunately, by this time, Xavier was already laid out across his bed.

The next morning, back at the house around the corner, the door to the backyard swings open. A voice called out to the boy on the ground, "Marcus…Marcus wake up you have an hour until school! Did you fall asleep out here?"

Marcus abruptly sits up, "What…oh yeah I must have gotten tired last night and just slept right here. Sorry dad let me go get ready for school." As Marcus gets up, he constantly stares at his hands, then rushes past his father inside the house.

The constant buzzing of an alarm clock jolts Xavier back to reality. He sits up on his bed and examines his room. His eyes widen at the sight of his computer with the hole in the screen.

Xavier leans over to the clock and checks the time; moments later he was up and off to the bathroom. About thirty minutes later he was heading out of the front door, "See you guys later, I'm running late, sorry I don't have time to talk." Both of his parents' wave goodbye to him.

Not too far from the neighborhood sits the local high school. Xavier rushes down the sidewalk paying no attention to anything or anyone around him. Right outside the front door, Xavier comes to a sudden halt as he collides heads with Marcus.

As they get up, Marcus grabs Xavier by the collar, "What the heck was that, are you blind?"

Xavier powers out and snaps back saying, "Hey I'm sorry; I'm kind of in a hurry. I didn't mean to run into you."

"Whatever; next time just pay attention and watch where you are going. Better yet, watch where I am going," Marcus says as he walks into the building.

Xavier watches as Marcus storms off and punches a locker as he makes his way through the hallway. Xavier hurries on to class making his way past the remnants of students in the hall. As he comes to the door of room two-fourteen, he sees the teacher approaching him. The teacher looks at Xavier and says, "Good morning Xavier, nice of you to join us." Xavier walks past him and sits down by himself at a table in the back of the class.

The unsuspecting sounding of the school bell startles Xavier as he unpacks his backpack. Moments later, the teacher puts the daily instructions on the board. Almost as fast as they were put on the board, Xavier copies them down on his own paper. It doesn't take him long to finish his work; afterwards he pulls out

a blank sheet of paper. Xavier starts to zone out and draw random lightning bolts on his paper.

The only thing that was able to break his concentration was the sound of the door opening and closing. He stops drawing as his attention shifts to the front of the room. Up at the front of the class stands a girl about average height with bluish color hair. The very sight of her made Xavier's heart skip a beat. Xavier watches as the teacher motions for the girl to sit next to him. As she approaches the table, the light dances off her caramel colored skin giving her a graceful appearance, almost as if she was walking on air.

Xavier takes a deep breath as his eyes meet hers. "Hi, my name is Jessica Martinez." Her smile was a soothing sight to Xavier; he extends his hand to her. She shakes his hand and takes her seat.

"Nice to meet you Jessica, I am Xavier…so are you new here?"

She puts her bag next to her and pulled out some paper and a pen; "Yeah, I just moved here over the weekend. My mother and I came to live with my grandmother who is very ill and needs some extra help around the house."

Xavier says, "Well then Jessica, welcome to Mercury High." There is a long period of silence between them and Jessica watches as Xavier continues to draw. "That's a pretty cool picture. How long have you been able to draw?"

Her Hispanic accent makes Xavier smirk and reply, "I learned how to draw about six years ago."

Jessica looks content; moments later the bell signaling the end of class echoes through the entire room. Most of the students rush out of the room leaving a handful of kids packing up. Xavier stands up to leave when he is tapped on the arm. He turns around to see Jessica holding a folded piece of paper, "Xavier, do you think you can show me where this next classroom is?"

"No problem follow me." Xavier escorts Jessica across the building to her next class. He waves goodbye as he turns around and walks away.

Meanwhile down by the lunchroom, Marcus is standing at a vending machine with a friend. The boy casually hands Marcus a soda and says, "So man, how are you doing? I heard about the breakup between you and Ashlyn."

Marcus shoots him an extreme glare, "Louis, I really don't want to talk about it right now."
Moments go by without either of them saying a word.

The Chosen: Breaking Bonds

Louis taps Marcus on the shoulder and hesitantly says, "Hey, not to upset you even more, but I thought that you should know what the talk around school is right now." Marcus listens intently as Louis finishes his statement. "Apparently people were talking and now everyone is saying how that little brat Devonte, said he can beat you in a fight. There were some other things said, but nothing as consistent as the part about him beating you up."

Louis steps back to avoid getting wet as Marcus grips the can so tight the contents of the can erupt out in a volcanic like effect. A small adrenaline rush shoots all throughout Marcus as he grabs Louis by the collar and asks, "Where is he now?"

Moments later, Marcus shoves the doors to the cafeteria open. He scans the room for Devonte who he finds sitting by himself in the middle of the room. Marcus goes straight towards him ignoring all the people calling out to him. With each step he takes towards Devonte, Marcus gets increasingly upset. Once he reaches Devonte he immediately snatches him up out of his seat. A distorted look of confusion swept across Devonte's face as he says, "What are you doing... put me down!"

Marcus tightens his grip on Devonte and says, "So you can beat me up... let's put your theory to the test," he says as he cocks his head back and then throws it forward colliding with the bridge of Devonte's nose. He then throws him back into the table, at which point the crowded lunchroom erupts into a roar of confusion. Before Devonte was able to get to his feet, Marcus kneels on top of him and begins to punch him repeatedly in the face.

Devonte tries to fight back when out of nowhere Louis kicks him in the rib cage. The force of the kick makes Devonte fall flat on his back opening him up for more punishment from Marcus. Not far from the cafeteria, Xavier can hear the commotion of the crowd. He makes his way to the cafeteria doors where he sees everyone gathered around something.

Reluctantly Xavier pushes his way through the crowd to catch a glimpse of the action. He is shocked to see the two-on-one scuffle happening before his eyes. Xavier's eyes pan the length of the room; it appears that no one is going to step in and try to help Devonte. Giving it little thought, Xavier enters the fight; he starts by lifting Marcus off of Devonte and punches him directly in the jaw causing Marcus to fall backwards.

Louis tries to fight Xavier, but is punched in the mouth, kneed in the groin, and then kicked back into the crowd. Marcus stands up and wipes the blood from his lip. "You want some of me too, nerd," Marcus says as he becomes more enraged. Xavier seems unaffected at the sight of Marcus charging right for him.

Xavier throws a punch right at Marcus's face, which Marcus miraculously catches. While Xavier is in disbelief, Marcus takes the opening to kick him in the chest. Marcus then lands a series of punches to the gut of Xavier. After the onslaught Xavier spits up some blood and tries to recover his breath, but while he is bent over, he was kneed in the face. Xavier stands there in a daze but quickly shakes it off.

This time Marcus initiates the attack with a lunging punch. Having regained focus, Xavier is able to move out of the way in time to respond with a roundhouse kick to the ribs of Marcus.

He then kicks Marcus in the back of his knee, causing Marcus to stumble forward. Marcus is able to recover and turn around only to be hit in the face with punches from Xavier. Xavier follows them up with an uppercut. Just then, Louis tries to get back at Xavier, but is intercepted by Devonte who tackles him to the ground. They start to wrestle when some administrators and several guards rush in and break up the fight.

All four of the boys are escorted to the principal's office. They spend the remainder of the day in the office where they are kept separated. Devonte is the first one called in to speak with the principal.

"Ah Mr. Coleman, I see you are up to your same shenanigans. Wasn't it just last week you were in here for disorderly conduct? Well, because I know just how much young people hate to be here at school, I think it is only fitting to give you in school suspension. The same goes for all of you," he shouts! "And to help get my point across you all will have an assignment that is due directly to me. It will be a report on proper school house behavior and how we can improve on becoming one united body." Devonte leaves the room and the next one called in is Marcus.

Marcus sits down in the chair across from the principal. As the principal is about to speak, Marcus cuts him off saying, "Look I already heard what you said to the kid. Can I leave now?"

"If I were you, I would watch my tone, Mr. Daniels. Being that you are the one that started the fight, you should be expelled. To me that would be too easy, Also it would require too much paperwork, so I thought of something else that would have a greater impact on you. Not only do you have in school suspension and a report due directly to me, but also as of right now, you are permanently removed from all sports teams for the remainder of the year. You are a good guy Marcus, but you need to learn not to let your anger get the best of you."

The room gets eerily quiet as Marcus gets up and storms out of the office. Xavier enters the room next and just sits down in the chair. As the principal speaks, it appears Xavier is not listening to a word he says. "Mr. Evans... do we have a problem? Now you are one of my brightest students; you never gave me any problems before, why now?"

Xavier shakes his head and responds, "I don't

know Sir, I
was just doing what I thought was right."

"Yes, Xavier, but at what cost? Now you are in a lot of trouble for doing what you thought was the right thing. You are a very quiet and unassuming person, and I know talking isn't your thing, but next time you need to use better judgment and come get an adult. We are here to solve the problems that you can't."

Moments later, Xavier walks out of the office, and the school bell echoes through the entire building. Once outside, Xavier catches a glimpse of Jessica as she enters a car and it drives off.

Xavier slowly begins to walk home when his arms start to go numb. He stops and shakes his arms wildly trying to get the feeling back. As he shakes his arms, he is unsuspectingly tackled to the ground. Xavier is shocked to see that someone is still around; he thought everyone had already left. Xavier tries to get up but is forced down by Marcus who than begins to punch Xavier in his face. Marcus was able to get two hits on him and was preparing for the third when his fist burst into flames. Xavier panics at the sight of the flaming fist coming at his face. He throws his hands up to protect himself when electricity starts to dance around his hand. The electric energy then shoots off of Xavier's hand, right past Marcus's face and blows out a nearby streetlight.

Both boys get up and heavily stare at the other

before they both run away in separate directions. Marcus is sprinting down the street when a speeding car approach. There is almost no time to react, but Marcus finds himself jumping out of the way of the car at the very last second. While in the air, fire erupts from the soles of his feet and propels him through the air momentarily until he lands in a pile of garbage. Marcus slowly rises to his feet and examines his body. *Not again*, he thinks to himself. He looks around to see if anyone was watching him; then he proceeds to walk home.

Meanwhile, Xavier had made it home and was put on punishment for fighting in school. He locks himself in his room. After a couple of hours, Xavier finds himself extremely tired, so he tucks himself into bed. As he lies in bed images of what happened outside the school continuously play through his head. He finally drifts off to sleep unaware of the changes that he and his peers are going through. Their very DNA was being rewritten… a new chapter of their lives is about to begin.

Chapter 2

Acceptance

The next morning Devonte wakes up to the warm soothing aroma of freshly baked pancakes. He slowly makes his way downstairs to the kitchen. Upon arrival, he is surprised to see his grandfather standing in front of the microwave. Devonte sits down at the table and puts his head down.

"How are you feeling today?" were the words his grandfather said as he hands Devonte a plate of pancakes.

"I still feel a little sore, but it's nothing I won't heal from. Hey, listen, Grandpa, I'm not in the mood for pancakes; as a matter of fact, I am not all that hungry either," Devonte says while he pushes the plate of pancakes away from him. Devonte stands up and walks towards the door when he notices a picture of his sister on the wall.

His grandfather walks over to him and says, "I know it hurts you a lot not knowing what happened to your sister. You and Sarah were extremely close, and I know you blame yourself for her disappearance, but you shouldn't. Devonte, sometimes bad things happen to good people." Before he could finish, Devonte grabs his board and rushes out the front door.

At the bottom of the steps, Devonte stands wiping the tears from his eyes. As the tears fall, they collide with the grass causing that small portion of the grass to freeze. After noticing this, Devonte bends down to examine the grass. He grabs one blade of grass and pulls it. Instead of tearing like paper, it snapped like glass. He then drops the blade of grass when he notices frost wafting around his hands.

He panics and runs back toward the house. Once his hand touches the guardrail of the steps, it almost instantly freezes onto it. He struggles to pull himself free, as his hand finally separates from the railing. He trips and falls backwards down the steps. As he comes to rest face first on the concrete, the frost from his hands starts to freeze the ground around him.

Devonte panics and gets to his knees and crawls away from the ice as if it was chasing him. His back now rests on the bark of a tree and a thin layer of ice now covers his entire front lawn and the tree he sat underneath. Just then, the front door to the house next door opens, and out walks Xavier. He stops in his tracks after noticing Devonte curled up underneath the tree next door.

"Hey…Devonte are you ok over there?" There was no response, so Xavier walks over to his fence and climbs over to the other side and now stands in Devonte's yard. With each step he takes, the grass shatters beneath his feet.

He steps carefully not to walk on Devonte's abandoned skateboard left in the grass. He finally reaches Devonte and says, "Devonte, are you ok…and why is it so cold over here?" Out of terror and confusion, Devonte snaps at Xavier and makes him leave. Xavier slowly walks away towards the street.

He walks along the sidewalk until he reaches the school where he almost instantly makes his way to the principal's office. As he opens the door to the office, he pulls out a folder with some papers in it. When Xavier enters the principal's office, the lights flash off and on. Without saying a word, he places the folder on the desk and turns to walk away when he notices a man sitting in the chair he sat in just the day before. He was an African American male in a nice three-piece suit with subtle blue eyes.

The principal stands up and grabs the folder off the desk.

"Xavier Evans, nice to see someone did my assignment."

"No problem, Mr. Tavern, I had some time to think about my actions yesterday and I'm sorry. I shouldn't have gotten involved in the fight," Xavier responds calmly.

"Yes, but before you go, I would like to introduce you to Mr. David Graham. He is here on behalf of the local youth center to promote their fundraiser."

David stands up and extends his hand to Xavier saying, "Nice to meet you Xavier. I would like to give you our card, it has the address and a list of the activities we are offering on the back. Feel free to come in and check it out anytime."

Xavier takes the card and places it in his back pocket, "Thank you. I will definitely look into this," he says. He then leaves the office and casually walks through the halls. He peers into every door he walks past as if he is searching for someone. As he walks past the drama room, he comes to a halt. He smiles at the sight of Jessica walking up to him.

She smiles and says, "Hi! It was Xavier right; how are you doing today?"

"Me, I'm good, but what about you? How are you adjusting? I hope everything is going alright for you."

Jessica chuckles then says, "Yeah everyone here is so friendly, and I've already made some new friends. So far the teachers are nice; the food could be better though." She becomes momentarily distracted by the sound of her name being called from across the room.

Xavier backs away slowly and waves goodbye. "See you tomorrow in class." As he turns and starts to walk away, he catches a glimpse of Marcus walking down the stairs. Giving it little thought, Xavier walks up to Marcus who looks upset. "Marcus can we talk," Xavier says as Marcus pushes past him.

Marcus stops and take a pause before saying, "What is there to talk about? You stuck your nose where it didn't belong and embarrassed me in front of everyone."

"Listen. About that, I know it doesn't mean much, but I just wanted to-"

Xavier is abruptly interrupted, "Save it; if you want to make it up to me, then you'll meet me in the parking lot at the end of the day for a rematch. So, until then, I don't want to see your smug little face, or I might not be so cordial next time." Marcus walks off leaving Xavier behind; Xavier smirks and turns to go to class before the bell rings.

To Xavier, the day seemed to go by even slower than usual, but finally it comes to an end. As the rest of the students clear out Xavier takes his time getting to the parking lot. Upon his arrival, he glances at Marcus who starts to take off his backpack and drop it to the ground. As Xavier comes to rest mere feet from Marcus, he is greeted with the sight of Marcus cracking his knuckles.

"Despite what you might think, I did not come here to fight you. I came to make amends for my actions yesterday."

Rage consumes Marcus as he says; "Your stupid apology means nothing to me. Your little superhero act not only pissed me off, but you tarnished my reputation. I now have people coming up to me and trying to intimidate me just because they saw us in the lunchroom yesterday. Not to mention my friends won't even talk to me."

Xavier folds his arms and responds; "So you think by fighting me here and now with no one around to witness will help get your reputation back?"

Marcus calms down slightly. "I wouldn't expect a guy like you to understand what I'm going through. These people are all mindless tools and none of them really have a life to call their own, so they feel the need to be a part of yours. You must constantly be on your game or they will turn against you and make your life a living nightmare. I had a position in this place that very few people could say they had…and now it's all gone because of you!"

Xavier's expression went from calm to stern as he says; "Marcus, contrary to what you believe this world does not revolve around you. You are not the only person to have everything taken from them; you see I know your pain all too well. Some years ago, I was just like you, the friends, and the popularity. I thought I had it made until one day I met this girl for whom I shortly developed feelings.

Her name is not important, but she was the first girl that I ever cared that much about. One day she asked me to sit with her at lunch, so I can meet her 'friends'. So, I did, and knowing what I know now I shouldn't…but I am glad I did. When I get to the table, I am almost immediately surrounded by a group of guys. Seven… there were seven of them and they all began to beat me right there in front of the entire school."

A look of disgust swept across Xavier's face; "As I laid there and was unable to defend myself I see that same girl walk up and kiss one of the guys who got tired of beating me, so he sat down to catch his breath. Not a single person in that lunchroom went out of their way to help me. After that day, the social status that I thought I had seemed like a distant memory. I went from having it all to having nothing but my shame to wear as a constant reminder. I recall learning martial arts to ensure that this could never happen again. It is only then did I came to realize; I was blaming everyone else for not helping me when the blame is all mine. I lost everything that day because I wasn't strong enough to stop them from taking it away from me."

Xavier takes a deep breath; "It is that very

reason why I got involved yesterday. No one was helping him, and I couldn't let my fate be his as well."

Marcus snaps back saying; "That's all well and good drama queen, but do you even know what we were fighting for?" Marcus was interrupted by the sight of Devonte riding up towards them on his skateboard.

Devonte hesitates and says; "I heard everything...Marcus whatever I did to make you want to fight me I didn't mean it."

"I know this much, you better keep your mouth shut! It's because of that big mouth of yours that I stomped you out yesterday." Xavier gets in between them and forces Marcus to back up. "There you go again...Xavier to the rescue. You know maybe he should learn how to fight his own battles," Marcus says while tightly clenching his fist.

Xavier looks Marcus right in the eyes and says; "Trust me I am not going to fight you again I just wasn't done talking. I want to ask you about the episode that we had after school yesterday. Was that fire on your hands?"

Marcus turns away from him and responds; "Yeah thanks for bringing that up genius. Yes, it was fire on my hands...but I don't know where it comes from. It was the freakiest thing to ever happen to me...it didn't even burn. Although I am not the only one who should be explaining themselves; or were you not the one who blew up that light over there!"

Xavier looks away in uncertainty, "You know what, let's just forget about it"

"No, you brought it up so let's talk about it. This has been happening to me for the last two days now, and if you know what is going on, you need to tell me. Because the last thing I want is to become some sort of freak," Marcus states.

Devonte's eyes widen as he asks; "Well Xavier do you know what is happening to us?"

"Us?" Marcus says in disbelief.

Xavier looks at Marcus then to Devonte then begins to shake his head; "Unfortunately, I haven't the slightest clue what is happening to us." Silence filled the air for a few awkward moments. The sound of shoes stepping on concrete breaks the tension. The boys turn their attention to the noise. Xavier's eyes widen as he sees the man from the principal's office earlier walking right towards them.

"Please do not be alarmed. I do not mean to intrude, but I couldn't help overhearing your conversation and think I might have the answers to all your questions. For those of you who I haven't already met, my name is David Graham. I am almost one hundred percent certain I know what you boys are going through. I need you all to hear me out before you say anything…based on the untimely occurrences of these 'outbursts' it sounds like you three have awaken the untapped powers that have been lying dormant inside you since you were born. You have no control over them yet, that is why they seem to activate at random. I know this because I too have special gifts. We are what the world calls meta-humans." David extends one hand forward and almost instantaneously pure energy engulfs his hand.

"You see, I have the power to generate and bend light to my every whim. Over time I have learned to do some extraordinary things with this gift." David launches the mass of energy skyward into the air where it disperses leaving a small plume of smoke in its wake.

David takes a deep breath then says; "If you three are willing to give me a chance, I can give you three the knowledge to control your new gifts…but the choice is ultimately yours. If you decide to pursue my offer I will be at the youth center on Saturday morning…hopefully we will meet again." David turns and walks away towards a car and drives off towards the youth center.

The boys stand there motionless until Xavier looks at Marcus and says; "There you go, we got our answer."

Marcus gets in Xavier's face and says; "This doesn't change anything." Marcus brushes past him and starts to walk across the parking lot.

Xavier turns back around to Devonte who looked uneasy. "What's the matter with you?"

Devonte hesitates then finally says; "I can't

go…I can't go back there."

"You aren't making any sense Devonte, what are you talking about?"

Devonte looks away and says; "I can't go back to the youth center…not since she died. Sarah…my sister; Sarah was last seen at the youth center before she went missing and they gave up the search for her and declared her dead with no evidence to back it. That is why I can't, won't go back there; it holds too many sad memories."

Xavier looks uneasy as he says; "Listen, this is the only way we are going to get a handle on these 'powers'. But given the circumstance I understand if you don't show up Saturday. I never knew what happened to her."

"That's just it, no one knows what happened to her," Devonte says as he walks away.

Friday night at about ten o'clock P.M., Marcus sits on the edge of his bed. There was a blank expression on his face. The only thing that was able to jolt him back to reality was a knock at his door. As the knob turns, his father enters the room. "Marcus, Slim and I are going to the court tomorrow to shoot some hoops. Do you want to come along?"

Marcus takes a lengthy pause before he says, "No thanks, dad, I kind of already have plans for tomorrow." His father shrugs his shoulders and turns and walks out the door.

The next morning down at the youth center Xavier stands patiently in front of the doors. His attention is drawn behind him to the sound of wheels scrapping the hard surface of concrete. A gentle smile comes across his face as Devonte slowly steps off of his board. He launches it up into his hands as he walks pass Xavier and up towards the door.

As Devonte comes to rest, he looks right at Xavier and says, "This better be worth it, Xavier."

Moments later, Marcus comes running up behind them. Xavier says, "Nice to see you decided to show up." There is no response as Marcus brushes past him.

The door to the youth center slowly creeps open; on the other side David was standing in the doorway with a slight smile on his face. The dim light gives a slight shine to his ebony skin. "Hello there. I am truly happy that you boys decided to show up. Please come on in and we can begin as soon as possible."

The doors close swiftly behind them; they walk up to the information desk where they stand and listen to David as he reintroduces himself.

"Now that you all know who I am, it is time I found out who you are." One by one the boys introduce themselves. "It is very nice to formally meet you all, but I feel it is time to get straight to the point. You three are here to learn more about what is going on in your body…you are here to learn how to control these new gifts. So, if you will follow me into the gymnasium, I have set up an area where we are going to train."

David leads them into the gymnasium where he positions them right in the center of the room. He takes a deep breath then says, "Ok. So today I will be teaching you two things. The first being exactly what are your gifts. The second is how to control those gifts."

David paces the floor for a quick second. "Like I said before you boys are now classified as meta-human. Basically, it's a sub-group of humans with powers. So, for me to be able to help you, I need to first know what powers you boys have. What I am going to have you do is think back to that moment when you became aware that they were there. Once you remember, I need you to duplicate that emotion."

Marcus asks, "What do our emotions have to do with anything?"

David calmly states, "Often times when one lacks control of their powers, it usually reacts to the person's emotions. Although that is natural, it can also be very dangerous to the person or anyone else. But in a controlled situation such as this, it is not that harmful."

The room is filled with stillness as the boys each begin to recall their individual moments. Within minutes the boys are making progress; Marcus' hands burst into flames, lightning begins to dance around Xavier's palms, and Devonte's hands become frosty.

"Wow!" David shouts, "So we have a fire, lightning, and ice elementalist. What is an elementalist you ask? An elementalist is person who can control one of the eight elements. In your case it is fire, ice, and lightning. I want you to think of these powers as another part of your body that you have to become accustom to using."

The boys stand motionless in suspense, David continues, "Ok, so what I am going to need you to do is take a deep breath, then concentrate on turning your powers off. This is easier said than done; at first it will feel as though nothing is there but the more you work at it, the more comfortable it will become." The boys stand there for what seems like days but was only thirty minutes. One by one they shut off their powers starting with Marcus and ending with Devonte. David has them repeat the same process nine more times. By the tenth time, the boys were exhausted, and David decided that they have reached their limit. "That was outstanding. I never would have imagined you'd gain control that fast. You boys are naturals at this."

A light smile was the boys' reaction to the events that have just taken place. David looks at them in admiration; he is proud of the progress they have made. Just then the buzzing of a phone can be heard faintly in the area. David reaches into his pocket and pulls out his phone. At that moment, his tone changes; it went from proud to sorrowful.

"Listen up boys, I am extremely proud of all of you, but unfortunately I have to cut this meeting short. For you see, I have been away too long as it is and sadly have no more time to spend here."

"Away... away from where?" Xavier asks.

David reluctantly states, "Boys, what would you say if I told you that I am here on an assignment As well, I am a member of Atlas."

"Wait a minute, what is Atlas?" Xavier questions.

David says, "Xavier, Atlas is an organization that specializes in protecting the lives of those around the world who can't protect themselves. It is made up of meta-humans like you and I. Currently I am on an assignment and should have returned to HQ earlier this week, but fate led me to you three, so I decided to stay. I can see great potential in you and if it were possible, I would like to take you back with me to become a part of Atlas. But sadly, this is where I say goodbye."

"Now wait a minute you can't just up and leave like that, I still need help," Marcus proclaims.

"My deepest apologies, Marcus, but I am out of time...but I tell you what once I get another chance I will return to finish what I started. I will come back and finish training you boys, and who knows maybe next time you guys can go back with me."

David takes a brief pause; he takes a deep breath and exhales. "Boys before I let you go, there is one more thing I feel I have to mention. Now that you three have control over your powers you must promise me that you will be cautious as to how and where you use them. If you should ever feel the need to use them let it be a dire situation, or in someplace secluded. You may not be aware of this, but meta-humans are treated differently because of our gifts.

Humanity looks at us in fear, so they separate themselves from us. But please do not let this taint your view of humanity; I shared this information with you to make you aware. That is what we at Atlas truly fight for, that day when humans and meta-humans will live together in harmony as one body of people. So take heed my young friends. Always be mindful of your actions and how they can affect you and those around you."

The boys nod in agreement and turn and walk out the front door. Once they are out of sight, David pulls out that cell phone and dials. After a couple of seconds, the call goes through. "Hello... yes, I am ready, you can send the transport. I will be waiting at the rendezvous point."

Just outside the youth center the boys are just about to go their separate ways. "Well today was...different, but at least we got what we came for," Xavier says.

"Yeah, whatever," Marcus says as he walks

away.

Just before Devonte leaves, Xavier turns around to him and says, "Devonte, the other day at school…it was not my intention to make you look incapable. I was just trying to help."

Devonte looks right into Xavier's eyes; he sees that Xavier is truly sincere. "You know…you are too nice. I don't know whether that is a good thing or bad. You and I have been next-door neighbors for the better part of four years, and I don't know a single thing about you except that you are nice. It has been hard for me since she disappeared.

I haven't really been myself; outside of my grandparents, you are the only person to show the slightest sign of sincere kindness. I don't know what the future has in store for us. But if I never get the chance to, let me say that I am thankful you jumped in to help me. So, I guess I will see you around…Xavier." Devonte gets on his skateboard and rides off into the distance.

Xavier nods in compliance, "See you around…kid." He begins to walk home in silence. In his mind, he wrestles with thoughts of the things he could possibly accomplish with his new powers.

Later on, that day, a local taxi pulls up to an abandon airport just outside the city. When it stops, David exits the back with a suitcase in hand, and then heads onto the runway. He climbs aboard a very stylized aircraft. Moments later it takes flight and heads north at great speeds.

Chapter 3

Reconciliation

Several weeks have gone by since David's departure. As the last bell rings throughout the school, Xavier steadily makes his way outside. There was a slight look of relief on his face as he exits the school doors. *Yes, finally after twelve long years I am done with general education.*

While on his way home, he catches a glimpse of Jessica standing at the bus stop. Casually he makes his way over to her; he can see the disappointment on her face.

"What's the matter, Jessica, you look a little down? Is there anything I can do to help?"

She smiles and replies, "Oh hi, Xavier, no I'm okay, it's just that my mom was supposed to pick me up today, but she couldn't make it at the last minute. I am not a big fan of walking through the park by myself, so I decided to wait for the bus. The only problem with that is the bus does not go straight to my house."

Xavier takes a second to think then says, "Well if you want, I can walk with you through the park, so you won't be alone?"

Jessica blushes and says, "Wow, I couldn't ask you to do that."

"No, it's okay. I insist; and besides, I was going to just go home and go to sleep anyway."

"Okay, let's go," Jessica says gratefully.

Xavier follows Jessica as she leaves the bus stop and heads for the park. Xavier is silent for the beginning portion of their walk until Jessica breaks the ice. "Are you always this quiet? Even in class you didn't talk much."

"I'm sorry, I am not the best at starting conversations. To be honest I always have a lot on my mind and just zone out."

Jessica places her hands on her hips and proclaims, "You know what, I have known you for almost a full two months. I don't know anything about you except your name and that you don't talk much. So, tell me what you do?"

It takes him a moment to answer, but he finally says, "Well, I like to build things, you know like engineering."

"Okay, so you are an engineer; what are some things that you have built?"

He hesitates for a second before saying, "Well the most recent thing would have to be this robot I made about four years ago out of everyday household appliances. I even designed the operating system myself on my computer. It wasn't that impressive, but it was just my first try at robotics. Also, in my spare time, I practice Martial Arts; it's a great way to stay in shape."

Jessica sarcastically proclaims, "You don't look that tough; I bet I can beat you!"

"Really, okay, then we will have to see about that one day." They share a brief laugh together. They stop laughing when Xavier asks, "What about you, what do you like to do?"

Jessica answers, "I am a six-time Regional Gymnastic Champion. I have been in gymnastics since I was a little girl. It's funny because I have never had any injuries. I am a little upset that I missed the gymnastics season at school."

Xavier smiles and says, "Well there is always next year."

Jessica chuckles as she says, "That's right, you are a senior this year. It must be nice to not have to worry about the stress of school anymore. So, what are your plans for the summer?"

He takes a deep breath then says, "As of right now I really do not have any immediate plans. What about

you, Jessica, do you
have anything planned?"

"Well this weekend, I'll be leaving to go
spend some time with my dad. This will be the first
time I have seen him since he and my mother split up.
Boy I can't wait to see him and my little sister Sophia
again!"

After some time, they emerge out of the park
just a few blocks from Jessica's house. Xavier walks
her all the way to her front door. She unsuspectingly
gives Xavier a hug; his body tenses up from the
surprise. "Thank you again, Xavier, that was really
nice what you did for me and I really appreciate it."

"No problem. Enjoy your trip and stay safe.
Maybe I'll see you around sometimes, Jessica."

He starts to walk off but turns around and
waves back to her before she goes inside. He
continues to walk down the street until he veers off
back into the park.

At the end of the next week, Marcus was just
returning home from the graduation ceremony. He
takes off his cap and gown and casually throws them
onto the back of his chair. As he flops on the edge of
his bed, there is a knock at his door. "Come in,"
Marcus says as he removes his tie and throws it onto
the floor.

The door opens, and his mother enters his

room, "Marcus, what's the matter with you? You have been in one of your 'moods' all day."

"Mom, you do realize that today was my graduation, I was actually looking forward to having a good day. But instead of showing your support for me, you and dad just spent the whole day arguing."

His mother had a look of disappointment on her face as she said, "Marcus, despite what happens with me and your father I need you to know that both of us love you and are very proud of you. I am sorry that things didn't go the way you planned today. It was never my intention to ruin your day. It has been extremely tough for me going through this divorce with your father. But I know it has been the hardest on you."

"Mom, I am tired of being forced to choose sides! I can't wait to get out there and make a life for myself!"

"You are a very passionate person and you have a good heart. It was wrong of us to make you pick a side." His mother takes a lengthy pause. "There is more that needs to be said, but unfortunately I have to go for now. Call me tomorrow and we will finish talking about it."

She walks over to him and places a kiss on his forehead, then leaves and closes the door behind her.

Early the next morning, Marcus is up at the crack of dawn and is wearing sweatpants and a tank top. He grabs a towel and a bottle of water from the kitchen then rushes out the front door. He heads to the local park where he hangs the towel over a tree branch and begins to stretch. After a series of stretches, he starts to practice some form of martial arts.

After about thirty-five minutes Marcus takes a seat on the ground; in his right hand cupped tightly is the water bottle. He then raises it above his head and pours; water rushes through the narrow opening of the mouth of the bottle and falls onto his head. He lets out a sigh of relief when suddenly he hears a rustle in the bushes not too far out in front of him. Marcus takes in a deep breath then summons his fire to the surface of his hand. The fire fades away into the air as he calms down at the sight of Xavier walking out of the bushes.

"Sorry; I didn't mean to startle you. I was just watching you train. It has been a while since I have seen a good kickboxing demonstration," Xavier states.

"Yeah thanks, what do you know about kickboxing anyway?"

Xavier folds his arms across his chest, as he answers, "Well I don't know much, but that kind of stuff intrigues me. As I myself know karate, so to see another martial artist is a nice change of pace."

There was an awkward moment of silence; Xavier starts to walk away when the word "Wait," echoes through the trees. "Listen, it has been quite some time since that day in the lunchroom and I feel I should apologize. I was stressed out and had a lot of personal problems that I didn't want to deal with. I wasn't thinking clearly," Marcus says while closing the lid to his water bottle. "So, sorry."

Xavier lets out a sigh before saying, "Thanks but it was not all your fault. As a matter of fact, things probably wouldn't have been as bad if I hadn't gotten involved. So, I am also sorry."

He and Marcus have a brief stare down; Marcus says, "So you know karate huh… how about we have an unofficial rematch pitting your karate against my kickboxing?"

Xavier's eyes widen in shock as he asks, "Now?" Marcus nods his head in accordance to the question.

Not even fifteen minutes later Marcus hits Xavier with a final blow. Down to the ground he falls but is helped up by Marcus. "I must admit that was the most fun I have had in a while, and you are pretty good. Your karate matches my kickboxing blow for blow, you just need to work on your defense and you are golden," Marcus says as he helps Xavier up off the ground.

Xavier wipes some sweat from his brow, "Thanks, you are a good sparring partner, and we should definitely do this again sometime. If you don't mind me asking, how long have you been studying kickboxing?"

Marcus thinks for a second then responds, "I

would say for five years now." Marcus takes a deep breath then lets out a sigh of disbelief. "Xavier, tell me do you honestly think that David will keep his word and come back to finish training us? Do you also think he was telling the truth about that organization he supposedly works for?"

"I don't know. I hope he comes back; it would be great to learn more about these powers. I have gotten used to turning them on and off now. As far as that organization he spoke of, I have a strong feeling that it does exist."

Marcus hesitates then states, "Why do they fight for those that show no appreciation for the things they do?"

"Because when you are doing something good, you don't do it to get recognition. You do it because you know it's the right thing to do."

"I guess you are right; the right thing to fight for is peace and unity for all mankind. I believe I was given this gift to do something great. These powers are the start of my future, one that I make for myself. Just think about it Xavier, we could use our powers to save the world."

Xavier smiles and nods in agreement, "For most of my life I have been afraid to face my demons. I can't tell you what opportunities I missed hiding in the shadows. When I think about it, one thing I always wanted was to be a part of something great."

Moments later, Xavier takes a subtle glance at

his watch. He starts to walk away when he is tapped on the shoulder. He turns around to the sight of Marcus extending his hand out towards him. Xavier takes a firm grip of his hand and shakes it; they agree to leave their differences in the past and move forward as allies

The next two months come and go with little time to enjoy them. Summer break is winding down and there is now a week left before school starts back. Dusk approaches and Devonte casually rides through the neighborhood. He cuts through the backyard of two houses. Once he reaches the sidewalk he can hear a grunt like noise coming from a house nearby. As he gets closer, he can hear a basketball hitting the rim.

He comes to rest at the base of the fence surrounding the backyard from which the noise originated. He peers over the fence and to his surprise he sees Marcus dribbling the ball across the ground. Devonte slowly tries to back away but rattles the fence as he steps back. Marcus stops dribbling and turns around to see Devonte stepping away from his fence. "Can I help you," Marcus says as he slowly walks towards the fence. Devonte takes a few more steps back; his actions spark a bit of caution in Marcus. "What is your problem?"

"Oh nothing...I just didn't want you to attack me like you did back at school. You know since I haven't done anything to you...yet."

Marcus lets out a sigh and rubs the bridge of his nose before saying, "Look...about that day, I just want to apologize. I guess I went a little overboard; the problems in my life all came crashing down on me at that time. I guess I needed something to take my anger out on...although you are not all that innocent."

Devonte lets out a chuckle at the realization of his mistake; Marcus looks at him in disbelief of the obvious oblivious tone of his laughter. "Right. I guess I should apologize then too...um let's see it all started when I was chilling at my friend's house and some guys we skate with were there too. We were all talking and having a good time when the question was asked..."whether or not we could win in a fight against someone from the current basketball team" and your name was brought up. I was just playing when I said that I could beat you in a fight, I honestly didn't know that they would get a rumor started and make it such a big deal." Devonte waits for a reaction from Marcus; his palms start to sweat in anticipation.

Marcus looks unimpressed at the story Devonte just shared with him. He finally replies, "Look, however it got started doesn't matter anymore...it is in the past and I don't see the need in dealing with it anymore. My advice to you kid is just watch what you say and who you say it to; it could come back to bite you."

Marcus turns around and takes one step towards the goal when Devonte asks, "Hey…do you want to get a quick game…I mean if you don't mind." Marcus stops and turns around and throws the ball at Devonte who catches it at the last second. He hops the fence and heads over to the goal; the two engage in a quick one on one game. Only an hour later, Devonte was walking towards the door to the backyard.

"Not bad kid…with more practice you just might beat me. So, you and I…there are no hard feelings, right?"

"Yeah, we're cool," Devonte says as he exits the backyard. "Cool, I will see you around kid."

Many months later at the headquarters of Atlas, David is sitting at a round table. "Please, Commander, I am simply asking that you allow me to go back for a few days. I gave them my word that I would return to help them with their training."

The Commander replies, "David you are putting too much interest in these teenagers."

"Sir, with all due respect, you are not putting enough interest into them. They are different…they are special; never have I seen anyone gain control over their powers in that short amount of time. They just need a little more guidance, and then I will return."

The Commander sighs and responds, "Very well, I grant you one week, but not a minute longer. I can't afford to have one of my Elite Operatives gone for too long."

David gets up and leaves the room; he heads straight for his room in the Living Quarters. While in his room packing, David hears a knock at his door. Without hesitation he opens the door and was greeted by Hector. Due to his sheer size, Hector had to slightly duck to enter the room.

"Well…what's the final verdict; did Commander Maximus give you clearance to go back?"

David continues to pack his suitcase as he answers "Yeah he did, Hector, and I leave tomorrow. I should be gone a week."

"All right just don't get lost in the good old days. We wouldn't want to replace you with Dillan after all." They share a quick laugh at the comment made by Hector.

By this point it has now been over a year since David visited the town of Mercury North Carolina.

In his backyard, Marcus sits at a table with Xavier. They are just casually talking when Devonte walks up to the fence. "Hey, you guys are not going to believe it; David is back. I just saw him pull up to the youth center in a taxi. You can come see for yourself."

Marcus and Xavier follow Devonte to the youth center. Upon arrival, David immediately greets them. A warm smile consumes his face as he shakes each one of their hands. "It is good to see you three again. I hope everything has been all right since my last visit."

Marcus shakes his head in disbelief, "I honestly didn't think you would come back."

"Marcus, you all are very special, and I see great things for you in the future. I had to make sure you all were prepared for what is to come." David inquires as to the progress they have made since he left. Marcus and Xavier have practiced to the point where they can summon their powers at a moment's notice. Devonte still struggled a little.

After their brief demonstration, David has the boys go home and told them to return the next day to start their training. They leave in anticipation and before they knew it morning had come. They all arrive at the youth center almost simultaneously and make their way inside. David comes out of a room in the back and escorts them to the gymnasium where he has set up targets all around the room.

"Wow! What are these targets for? Are we going to be shooting at them?" Devonte asked.

As everyone comes to rest in the center of the room, David says," Now that I have come back, I figure we move onto the next step in your training.

Discharge…discharge is the act of releasing your power. Often in a projectile like attack." Energy began to form within the palm of David's hand.

The boys watch as David launches the energy at one of the targets. Upon contact, the target burst and what remains is a small plume of smoke and the stand the target was mounted on.

"That's all there is to it…now to start, I want you to bring your powers to the surface. Once you have done that, I want you to focus the energy to a single point. Might I suggest, start with the palm of your hand. After you have gathered the energy to that point, I want you to aim at the target. Take a deep breath then release the stored energy.

Very few minutes pass until Marcus and Xavier can focus their powers to their palms. Devonte follows shortly after them bringing his powers to its focal point.

Marcus takes aim at a target near the bleachers. He takes a deep breath; sweat runs down his forehead as he begins to exhale. Mere seconds later a large ball of fire shoots from his hand and hit the target completely engulfing it in flames. The flame was so forceful that a small section of the bleachers caught fire.

As David goes to put out the fire, Devonte takes aim at another target. Devonte takes a few deep breaths before he releases a flurry of ice at the target. David looks over at Xavier and says, "Ok, it is your turn Xavier." Xavier turns his attention to a group of targets. He takes aim at the target that sits in the middle. He inhales then releases his electrical energy. The attack is so untamed that it not only hit the target in the middle, but also the ones that surround it and everything in between.

David walks over to them and stands firmly in front of them. "Wow…very nice display, especially for your first attempt, although there is still much work to be done. Marcus, I will start with you; that was a great shot, but you seem to be exerting too much energy at once. Try to release in smaller bursts. Devonte… again great shot, but ironically your problem is the opposite. You need to exert more energy, but not too much. Now Xavier you are going to have to work on precision. You see the nature of lightning is that it wants to spread, so you will have to work on controlling where it goes. Overall boys, not bad for your first try…now let's do it again. This time take into consideration everything I have told you thus far."

About four hours later the boys are all exhausted and exit the youth center and return to their homes. For the next two days it was the same routine. At the end of the third day, David walks the boys to the door. He has a very proud expression on his face as he says, "Excellent job today boys, and keep up the good work. Tomorrow we are going to kick it up a notch so make sure you all get plenty of rest and be here bright and early, so we can start. They all start to walk their separate ways home.

Across the street, the lens of the traffic camera focuses its gaze on David standing in the doorway of the youth center.

Dim lights illuminate the screen of a computer. sadistic laughter erupts out of the man sitting in front of the computer. "Hey 'scar face' you might want to come and see this," he says with a slight northern accent. Shrouded by darkness was the indistinguishable silhouette of a man.

"What do you have to report, did you find him yet?" he asked sternly.

While chuckling the man at the computer says, "No not exactly, but I did find someone that might interest you a lot more." The shadowy man glances over the shoulder of his comrade and glares deep into the screen; his eyes begin to glow a deep red.

He stands up straight and says, "Excellent work Hardwyre…give me those coordinates and assemble Delta. I am going to eliminate Quazar while he is unsuspecting. And Hardwyre do not speak a word to anyone regarding my actions…not even to 'him'."

The next morning at the youth center, David sits at the front desk of the lobby. Moments later the boys walk into the building and David greets them by saying, "Great, you guys made it…let's get started."

Chapter 4

Trial One

Inside the youth center, David escorts the boys into the gymnasium. "Alright boys, go ahead and get set up. I have to finish some paperwork then I will join you all." David turns around and walks back out into the lobby and takes a seat at the front desk. He takes a firm grip of his pen and begins to sign some documents. Moments later, the roar of an engine catches David's attention. After a quick glance outside, he gets up and rushes to the back.

The door to the gymnasium swings open; the loud thud startles the boys. David slams the door behind him as he says, "Boys listen up…I need you to follow my next instructions to the letter. Some very dangerous people are pulling into the parking lot. Now for your safety, I want you all to escape out of the back door."

Marcus steps forward and says, "Wait, we can help you, I mean what have we been doing all of this training for?"

"Listen to me boys, this is not the time to discuss this, just know that these men are highly dangerous and will stop at nothing to make sure you are dead. Trust me, I recognize your potential and it is that very reason why I will not let you die here. Now please leave out the back; there isn't much time." David turns around and runs back out into the lobby. Not even ten seconds later the boys hear the roar of gunfire. Devonte gets startled and slowly backs away towards the exit.

Meanwhile out in the lobby, David is single handedly fighting back the intruders; swiftly and precisely David take them out. Just then, all the windows were blown out by a massive sonic eruption. The vibrations make David stumble to one knee. An eerie silence fills the room; David begins to launch energy projectiles at the swarm of oncoming troops.

Standing motionless in the back, the boys listen to the commotion in the lobby. Marcus grows increasingly frustrated and says, "We have to do something…we can't just sit here and let him do this alone. I mean what good are these powers if we can't use them?" Xavier stares hard at Marcus who had abandoned fear for courage. Then he looked at Devonte who was scared stiff.

In the lobby, bodies fly left and right from the intense sonic vibrations. Two armed men run full speed at David; one was wielding a sword and the other a staff. The man bearing the sword swings first; David swiftly dodges the attack and can subdue his foe. With almost perfect timing, he uses the sword while it remains in the grasp of the trooper to deflect the oncoming attack from the staff. David takes the swordsman and slams him into the other troop; he manages to pry the sword from the hands of his now unconscious foe. David extends his hand forward and releases an energy projectile taking out a half dozen men.

As David continues to fight back the intruders, a dark shadow slowly slithers its way towards him. At the very last moment, David becomes aware of the imminent attack. He jumps out of the way of a spike that lashes up out of the pursuing shadow. When David comes to rest he is met by the sound of sadistic laughter causing him to grip the handle of the sword tighter.

"It has been such a long time, Quazar," The shadowy spike starts to recede and form into the shape of a human being. The eyes of the shadowy figure slowly open to reveal the deep red irises fill with blood lust. Slowly the shadow begins to fall from his body to reveal a young Caucasian male with brown hair and piercing red eyes. "I have waited for the day when I can take my revenge on you. I have become stronger, many have fallen victim to my blade, all in preparation for this moment," he says while slowly rubbing the scar over his right eye. "Today will be the day you die...today the darkness consumes the light!"

The young man runs straight at David; unsheathing his sword and slashing at him. The two engage in a fierce sword fight.

Marcus peers his head out of the door; he is filled with both anger and apprehension at the sight of David being overrun. "You two can leave and get help. I am going to even the odds." Marcus bolts out of the gymnasium doors into the heat of battle.

Xavier makes his way towards the door, but suddenly stops. "Devonte...it's ok if you want to run, but nevertheless Marcus is right, so I am going to do whatever I can to help out. If you leave now there might still be a chance for you to get away." Xavier continues towards the door when he stops and looks up at an air duct.

Out in the lobby, Marcus has taken shelter behind an overturned table. He takes in a deep breath, then ignites his hands. Marcus jumps over the table attacking; he hurls fireballs at everyone that moved. As one person closed in on Marcus, their feet are frozen to the floor. Just then Devonte lunges out and punches the man right in the face. Marcus attacks two more guys with a series of kicks. Just then Marcus is sent flying across the room from a sonic blast. A tall male with wild unkempt green hair rushed over towards Marcus. His face was completely hidden by a mask. While he stands over Marcus, he continues to blast him with the sonic vibration.

Seemingly out of nowhere, Devonte jumps in between the sonic vibration and Marcus. In a state of panic, Devonte forms an ice dome over Marcus and him. The dome offered a moment of protection from the sonic vibrations.

"Kid, you showed up…thanks for the assist. Where is Xavier?" seconds later a loud pop could be heard outside the dome.

"Hey guys are you ok in there," Xavier says while tapping on the outer layer of ice. The ice slowly melts away leaving a puddle of water in its wake. The boys stand their ground against the remaining troops. They engage in battle with the villainous group, using every little bit of power they had left.

On the other side of the lobby, David is still locked in a deadly sword battle. Blow after blow, their swords clash. They use their respective powers to try and get the advantage. As the young man continues to battle, he becomes more enraged causing his eyes to glow that deep crimson color. He uses his dual bladed pitchfork like sword to catch an oncoming attack from David. With a flick of his wrist he throws the sword away. It flies and lands right in front of Xavier. He picks it up and glances over only to witness the young man slashing wildly at David.

Xavier takes off running towards them when he suddenly disappears into thin air leaving only static electricity. He then reappears in front of David and blocks the oncoming attack with the sword.

"Valiant effort, however I can see right into your eyes. You are weak. You do not have what it takes to defeat me," the young man shouts.

Xavier stares deep into his menacing red eyes and states, "He will not die today…I won't let him." The man begins to attack Xavier who manages to block all his attacks. As the young man twirls his sword through his fingers, signs of a light yet eerie smirk could be seen on his face. He begins to attack with more ferocity making it increasingly more difficult for Xavier to defend against his attacks. He manages to catch Xavier on the face with the hilt of his sword causing Xavier to lose his footing and fall to the ground.

Without hesitation, the young man thrusts his blade towards Xavier, but was instead hit with an energy projectile that sends him flying. Before he realizes it, the young man is hit in the face by an illuminated blade held by David. The cold steel cuts right through his right cheek causing him to stagger back in pain. David then finishes it off with a rushing right cross charged with his energy. The punch sends the young man falling to the ground.

Beaten and broken the young man lets out a chilling shriek. He follows it up by yelling, "This is not over Quazar…Screech, time for a tactical retreat!" He then begins to seep into his own shadow while the green haired man leads the rest of the troops out.

What was left in their wake was a demolished youth center, three battered teenagers, and an extremely tired adult. As the tension settles David walks over to Xavier just as Marcus and Devonte are helping him up off the ground.

"Are you boys ok? That was an extremely foolish thing you did putting yourself in harm's way. Thank you…you three demonstrated tremendous courage today and because of that I survive to fight another day."

Marcus looks left, then right at all the wreckage, then asks, "Who were those guys David?"

"Those men were members of a rouge group that calls itself Nova."

"Who was that guy with the demonic red eyes that was trying to kill you?" Xavier questions.

David sighs, then takes a short pause before he says, "That…that was Stargazer…believe it or not, he used to be considered to be the top Elite Operative of Atlas. He was good, but he was also his own worst enemy. Not much is known about his past, but when I first met him I was shocked at the fact that he had such little regard for life itself. He and I were somehow destined to cross paths. At first, I even questioned why my Commander allowed him to join Atlas. The Council fought hard to reverse the decision on a count that Stargazer managed to kill one of their high-ranking Operatives with relative ease and taking his weapon as some sort of trophy.

However, my Commander saw things differently; to him Stargazer needed help and he felt that he could provide it for him. To Stargazer, help wasn't enough…he wanted more. He was aware of his potential and thought he deserved better. Eventually, he gave in to his own twisted desires and tried to kill the Commander. I was there and did what I had to do. I fought Stargazer and won but not before he caused lasting damage to the Commander. Since then, Stargazer has been a member of Nova and has been set on seeking revenge on me for getting in his way."

David takes another pause before he says, "Marcus, Xavier, Devonte, today the three of you showed me that my coming back had not been in vain. You all went against Nova and survived. I am both proud and grateful that you boys decided not to retreat. If you recall the last time I was here, I told you that this time you would be able to go back with me to join Atlas. Well, the offer is still on the table. I think you three have tremendous potential and can-do great things for this world. So, what do you say?"

There was a momentary silence that ended

with everyone on one accord. "Excellent…we will leave the day after tomorrow. Now if you haven't already, you will need to inform you parents about your powers. They need to know the truth…that is the least we can do."

Marcus and Devonte inform David that their parents are already aware. Everyone turns and looks at Xavier who replies, "Ok I'll tell them tonight!"

After taking one more glance around what was left of the youth center David proclaims, "Listen I want you three to go on home now and spend time with your families. Get a good night's sleep and meet me here at ten in two days. Also, I want you to use the back door when you leave…see you then."

As the boys exit the building one by one, David pulls out an ear piece from within his pocket and places it in his right ear. He presses firmly on the center piece. "Hey, Gizmo, can you hear me? Listen, my trip has been cut a little short due to heavy interference from Nova. For now, I am going to lay low and get some rest. Tell Commander we might need Newman to handle the press. I will be ready to be picked up in two days at the abandon runway…and I am bringing them with me. Quazar out!"

Slowly, Xavier walks up the steps to the front door of his house. He turns and waves goodbye to Devonte as he enters the house next door. Xavier takes a deep breath and then turns the knob and goes inside. Immediately, his mother who was stretched out across the couch watching TV greets him. "My God, Xavier, what happened to you? Are you hurt?" she asks as she hastily gets up to check Xavier.

"Mom…mom I'm fine where is dad? I need to talk to you both." Xavier's mother takes a long hard look into his eyes before she runs into the kitchen and finds his father.

His parents come back and sit on the couch when his father asks, "Xavier! What happened to you?"

"Dad please give me a minute I will explain everything." Xavier hesitates for a couple of seconds then says, "Mom…Dad, what I am about to tell you might seem a bit ridiculous, but you must believe me and understand that it is all one hundred percent true. Last year about this time my life changed forever. I was blessed with the ability to control and even generate… electricity."

Before he could finish, his mother begins to chuckle under her breath while his father remains composed and watches as Xavier lifts his hand forward. Just then electricity begins to erupt from his palm causing his mother's laughter to stop. His father smiles and states, "I always knew I was wrong about you." His mother turns her head to the father in disbelief.

Xavier continues speaking, "Afterward, I met

a man who works for this organization called Atlas. He helped me, and a few others control our powers."

His father's face lit up with surprise, "Wow, Atlas huh…now there is a name I haven't heard in a long time."

Xavier's mother turns her head towards the father and says, "Robert, you know about these people?"

"Honey, it's ok…many years ago when Xavier was about three years old, these people came to the house looking for my father. They said they were from some organization called Atlas and that they wanted to speak to him with regards to joining their organization. You see they knew my father had powers, but he didn't even give the thought a chance. He openly refused their offer…so before they left, they came to me and asked if I too had powers. I told them the truth…that my son and I were just normal humans. There was always a part of me that knew I was wrong about you."

A very faint smile was on Xavier's face. His mother turns her attention back to him and states, "That is all well and good but why are you so filthy?"

"Right…so the guy from Atlas left and then came back earlier this week to help us finish our training. Which now brings us to today; when we showed up to the youth center for our training, everything seemed normal enough. That was until the gunfire started; as it would turned out a rival organization had somehow found David, the guy from Atlas. It was a relentless battle; we all were terrified. Then it hit us, it was for situations such as these that we were blessed with powers. So, we entered the fight and through our combined effort…we won! Afterwards David extended the invitation to go back to join Atlas with him. I chose to go…I just know that this is what's best for me and therefore I will not miss out on this opportunity. He said that we leave the day after tomorrow."

His mother rises to her feet and walks up to Xavier and wraps her arms around him tightly. "Xavier, I am so proud of you; you have come a long way, but you have finally found your place in this world. I want you to know that with or without powers you are still our son and we love you and nothing will ever change that."

"Son, your mother is right. You are our only child and no matter what choices you make, we will always love you. We can rest easy now knowing that you are out there making the world a safer place for humanity. Just promise me one thing, if you should happen to see my father out there somewhere, tell him we miss him," Robert says while joining the hug

Deep in the dark corridor of Nova HQ, Stargazer kneels in the doorway of a dimly lit room where a man, shrouded by darkness sits behind a

desk. "For...forgive me my Lord, I did not mean to betray your trust and leave without your consent. I merely..."

"You merely acted on a whim; you were giving into the hatred that dwells inside of you. You were foolish to think it would be easy to stop him. You haven't yet reached the level of power that he has. You are by far my greatest warrior, but at the same time you are my greatest burden. You still have much to learn, Stargazer. Do not make me regret the decision I made six years ago as to which of you I chose to be my disciple."

"My lord, for my foolish actions I am ready to take the punishment"

"Oh, but you already have...look at you Stargazer. Every time you two fight, he walks away the victor and leaves you scarred and looking like a fool!"

"But my lord, he was not alone there were these boys that interfered and cost me the fight."

"From my understanding, Stargazer you had the entire Delta unit as well as Screech...tell me again how teenagers over powered you. I have no time for your excuses Stargazer, and even less patience for failure. It seems as though after our last demonstration, Atlas is desperately trying to increase their man-power."

"Might I suggest we try to keep a more watchful eye on these troublesome teenagers they could prove to be annoying."

"Very well, now is the perfect time to put the next phase of my plan into action." There was a momentary silence; Stargazer gets up and turns to walk away when his name is called. He turns back around to face the desk only to see a strip of fabric gliding through the air towards him. "Make yourself decent…your disfigured face sickens me." Stargazer wraps the purple suede cloth around his head just enough to cover up his injured face.

Chapter 5

The Journey pt1: Introduction

The morning of their departure, the boys wait in the abandoned parking lot for David. A heavy fog smothers the open sky. Within minutes, David walks up to them, there was a distinct look of pride on his face.

"Are we already to go?" he says just as the taxi pulls up. The boys take turns putting their belongings in the trunk of the taxi. One by one they enter the taxi with Devonte being the last one. He takes one last glance at the remains of the youth center then takes his seat inside the taxi.

Not even an hour later, the taxi was letting them off at the entrance to the abandoned runway. After the cab is out of range, David walks the boys over to the runway towards a stylized VTOL aircraft. Their faces light up with excitement as they start to walk a little faster towards the craft.

"Boys, the vessel you see before you is the official Atlas Sonic Transport Cruiser or STC for short. This is our main vehicle for long distance travel. It uses an extremely long-lasting energy source designed by the lead scientists at AstroTec Industries. They are the biggest supporters of Atlas, providing us with the technology we need to protect humanity."

As they approach the rear of the STC, the back-paneling separates and forms an entrance ramp. Standing in the doorway was a Caucasian male, short in stature with light brown hair. "Wow David! You look tired; don't tell me you couldn't handle three teenagers."

"That is very funny, but if it had not been for these teenagers, I might not be here right now. This is Marcus, Xavier, and Devonte. Boys, this is Adam Baker. We call him Gizmo; he is our leading Technology Specialist."

Adam waves hello to the boys, then has everyone follow him onboard the STC. Everyone takes a seat and straps in tightly. "So, boys, David has told me great things about you all. I look forward to working with you. David tells me you boys are Elementalists…not bad we could use a few good Elementalists right now." Adam gives the pilot the signal to take off.

"Adam, exactly what can you do?" Xavier asked.

"Well, you see I am what they call a Technopath, I can interact with and control any matter of technology with a mere thought."

"Basically, you talk to machines."

"You catch on fast Xavier; in a nut shell I can talk to machines."

"Hey Adam, will we get cool names like yours?" Devonte asks enthusiastically.

"Well, that depends on the results of your training. If you become an Operative, then yes, you will be issued a codename to protect your identity. But to reach said status you will first be put through rigorous training that will test the very limitations of your soul!"

There was an eerie silence for a few seconds before Adam says, "Lighten up guys, I am just trying to scare you. Trust me it won't be that bad."

Adam turns his attention to David, "Where did you find these kids? Anyway, the other day you said you had some interference of the Nova variety. Any idea how they found you deep in the suburbs of Mercury, North Carolina?"

"I haven't the slightest clue but how they

found me no longer matters, what does matter is the fact that Stargazer was leading the charge."

"Stargazer huh…it's been a while since he defected to Nova. Six years, right? That is one twisted dude; I am just glad you are ok…I'm glad you all are ok."

It is not long before the STC is making its descent into the Hanger at Atlas HQ. As everyone exits the STC the boys stand speechless at the Modern Urban interior of the Hanger. David steps forward, "Welcome to Atlas, your new home away from home. I would like you to follow me to the Council Room."

Steadily, they walk the halls of Atlas until they reach the Council Room. David tightly grips the knob and enters the room; all conversations suddenly stop.

"Commander, I would like to introduce you to Marcus Daniels, Xavier Evans, and Devonte Coleman. These three teenagers are the ones that I have told you about." David turns his attention towards Marcus, Xavier, and Devonte. "Boys, this is the leader of the Atlas, Commander Maximus. He has superhuman strength and can lift up to ten times his body weight. Surrounding him are the other members of the Atlas High Council.

This is Neim Duffy; a young Irish hothead with the power to phase through solid objects. Over here we have his older brother, Arthur Quinn; he has the power to manipulate any metal substance on this planet. Then it's Rose Owens, she is one of the strongest telepaths of our generation. Victoria Richardson is our chief Medical Specialist, with the power to heal herself as well as others. Her husband Nolan is not here today. To my right you have Clarance Werner, a Mystic who is master of the light arts. Joyce Patel here is an empath, and Richard Hawkins can morph his limbs into various things."

The boys take a slight step back as Commander Maximus stands up, his right hand gripping his cane while he uses the left to fix his jacket. "David, it is good to have you back in one piece, and it's nice to finally meet you three. David speaks highly of you all. I am anxious to see what kind of results you can deliver. David, Gizmo informed me of your battle. I must say Nova's tactics are getting harder to read. First, the attack in Regal, Nevada, to now attacking you in a suburban youth center in broad daylight. Not to mention their numbers have increased significantly. We need to figure out what they are looking for, what is their goal?"

Directly to the right of Commander Maximus sits Richard, an older man with an eye patch over his right eye. "Sir, after that attack in Regal, Nevada, we lack the proper personnel to achieve such a task. I move for a more direct assault...catch them off guard."

"Richard, you make a valid point, but if we were to take the fight to them we would be at a huge disadvantage. Not only do they now outnumber us about four to one, they would have home advantage. So, for now what is best is to keep watch on the Grid and deter all Nova activity. Until we have time to prepare, I don't think fighting them head on is the best idea. David…are these boys as good as you say they are?"

"Sir, these boys saved my life from an unsuspecting attack from Nova. They put their very lives on the line and showed true valor. They showed me that they are ready…they are more than ready, sir. These boys showed me that they are willing to rise above themselves for the protection of others."

"David, I do hope your faith is not misplaced, but nevertheless we welcome you boys with open arms. David will show you around and on Monday when the rest of the new recruits get here, you will be given a proper orientation. David, if you can stop back by here so we can finish the meeting. In the meantime, take them on a little tour and let them get acclimated to their new surroundings."

They are dismissed as David begins his tour of the base. He starts at the Rec. Room; "Ok boys, this is the first stop on the tour. Here is our Recreational Room…or Rec. Room for short. In here is where we eat and socialize among other things. I do believe this is the largest room in the entire complex except for the Hanger of course."

The boys take a couple of seconds to examine the Rec. Room before David motions for them to follow him. He escorts them to the Gymnasium and then the Battle Arena.

As they approach the doors of the Battle Arena, Marcus asked, "Hey what did that guy mean when he said you all do not have the personnel? What happened in Regal, Nevada? Are you short-handed? I see a lot of people here. Why couldn't you just use them?"

"Not exactly Marcus, you see before I met you three in Mercury, we suffered a great loss at the hands of Nova. Nova managed to capture one of our Operatives and made him call what we have dubbed 'Code Red'. Now this can range from a lot of things, but while one is in the field this usually means they need immediate assistance. When the call is received, all available persons close in on the distress."

"Wait, how would Nova know to make that call?"

"There is a lot you will come to know about Nova. One thing is the fact that they broke away from us. But nevertheless, they lured us into a trap and killed a lot of our Operatives. Believe it or not, the only reason I was in Mercury, North Carolina was to meet with your Principal, Dennis Tavern. He owns The Liberation Charity, which specializes in building buildings for the community."

The Chosen: Breaking Bonds

The boys look to David in puzzlement. They were trying to process what was just said.

He continues, "We sought him out to help us in providing the families of those we lost a care-package; it was a way to extend our condolences. He, along with a couple of others like the CEO of AstroTec are big financial supporters of Atlas.

To answer your other question, the reason why we can't just use one of these other people is because the training they receive is not the same as that of an Operative or Soldier. These people are not field savvy, therefore would not be effective."

David pushes open the doors of the Battle Arena; a cool breeze rush from within. They walk inside and head to the main room; once inside, they stand in the middle of the floor.

"Welcome to the Atlas Battle Arena. In here is where all Operatives and Soldiers receive their training." Just then the sound of an electronic door closing draws everyone's attention. "Good, perfect timing. Boys allow me to introduce our leading Combat Specialist and my best friend, Hector Hernandez or Brick. He is an Elementslist like you; he controls earth."

The tall muscular Hispanic male towers over everyone; he pats David on the shoulder. "Wow what a lively group you got here, David. I'm kidding, nice to meet you. They call me Brick. It is my job to whip all of the New Recruits into shape."

"Hector, would you like the honor of going over the Battle Arena? I mean this technically is your office," David states.

"Gladly…let's get the boring stuff out of the way first. There is the door, behind you are the bleachers, up there are the lights, and below you is the floor. Now we can move into the fun stuff," he says while walking towards a large closet in the corner. When he opens it, he met by a plethora of weapons and tools.

"This is where we keep the weapons that are used during training. I usually have you go through and find one you are comfortable with rather than assign you a weapon." He turns to his left and points to a room nuzzled in the corner. "Over here is the Control Room; in there we can control every aspect of your training. It utilizes one of the most advanced AstroTec simulators to ever be manufactured."

Hector walks inside of the Control Room and flips a switch on the console activating the Battle Arena. "The inside of the Battle Arena is made from AstroTec's toughest and most durable substance. Working simultaneously with the main computer we can recreate almost any environment; giving us the most effective results."

Motionless they stand as Hector demonstrates one of the programs in the Battle Arena. Moments later, David insists on wrapping up their tour as he has business to conduct. He and the boys say goodbye to Hector as they exit the Battle Arena.

David takes the boys back to the Council Room with him where he has them sit outside on a bench. He goes inside and stands before the Council again. Commander Maximus stands to his feet followed by the rest of the Council.

"Quazar, we have been talking and would like to know if you truly believe you were wise in your judgment of bringing those boys here? For the last few months your mind has been set on fulfilling a promise you made to a couple of misguided teenagers who you felt pity for."

"Richard sir, with all due respect it was not pity that influenced me...it was hope. It was fate that I was in Mercury, North Carolina. I overheard their cry for help; they needed guidance, and they needed answers. So, I took it upon myself to help them. It was only after the training started that I realized their true potential. Besides we needed help, so I brought you help. I don't get it, is all of this a lack of faith in me?"

"David, please understand it is not a lack of faith in you as much as it is a lack of faith in them," Joyce says from across the table.

"Joyce, I appreciate the concern, but you don't need to worry. Those three out there, if given the chance, can do extraordinary things. Please give them the same chance that you gave to me and...Kyle."

"That is a mistake we cannot afford to make

again. You turned out great, but Kyle…I mean Stargazer turned on us, and look where he is at now! Look we are not trying to offend you, but what if they don't work out so great? What if they get themselves killed? All we are asking is for you to give it some thought," Joyce says.

"I have, and my decision remains the same. The point is that we need new Operatives and I brought you three great candidates."

Commander Maximus raises his hand, and everyone gets quiet. "David, I see a lot of myself in you. I admire your determination and for that I want you to personally oversee their training. Normally this is a task more suited for Hector, but something tells me you will do just fine. I have no doubt they will do fine…as a matter of fact there will be no further discussion regarding those boys. They are now one of us and will be treated like such."

David smiles and turns and walks out of the Council Room. Outside in the hallway the boys sit patiently on the bench. "Sorry that took so long, but if you are ready, I will take you to your rooms in the Living Quarters." They make their way to the Living Quarters where they head to the second floor. As they stand in the middle of the hallway they are surrounded by rooms 20J, 20K, and 20U.

"Alright here we are, and here are your keys. Marcus you will be in Room 20J, Xavier you are in Room 20K, and Devonte you will be right across the hall in Room 20U. Listen, while I was in the Council Room I was informed that I will be personally overseeing all your training. So, after orientation on Monday, we will get started Tuesday with your next lesson."

The boys enter their rooms and close their doors behind them. David slowly nods his head as he walks away from their rooms.

Monday comes without warning; standing in front of his mirror, Xavier takes a hard look at himself. Moments later there was a knock at his door, "Xavier, open up its Marcus," said the voice from behind the door. Xavier opens the door to see both Marcus and Devonte standing there.

They head to the Rec. Room where a presentation is being set up. At first glance, they notice Adam up on the stage. "Dillan bring it this way," Adam says as he motions towards himself.

A man with a slight tan and sandy blonde hair extends his hand forward and glides it through the air. Telekinetically, he places a speaker next to Adam.

It takes very little time for Adam to realize the boys were in the room. He steps off of the stage and walks over to them. "I see you boys are up bright and early, that's good. Look I just got word that the rest of the recruits have just arrived. So, if you want, you guys can take a seat anywhere you would like; we will begin momentarily."

As they take their seats, they can hear footsteps clattering through the hallway. Soon a group of people poured into the room and filled in the seats around Xavier, Marcus, and Devonte. The boys watch as David, Hector, Commander Maximus, as well as a few others gather on the stage in front of the group.

Joyce steps forward; her short skirt and full breasts instantly catch the attention of the audience. "Good morning to you all and welcome to Atlas," she says with a slight British accent. "My name is Joyce Patel and I am here to welcome you all to the start of the next chapter in your life. You all have made a big decision and have chosen to use your gifts for the safety of this world."

Joyce motions to Adam to turn on the projection screen. The first slide was a picture of an African American man with an all-black suit on. "Ladies and Gentlemen allow me to introduce you to our founding father, Amir Robinson. He was the man responsible for the birth of Atlas after the First World War. It was his dream that meta-humans would stop being used as weapons and treated more like humans.

He formed this organization to fight the evil in the world and unite the meta-human and human groups into one body. He rallied a small group of meta-humans to his cause, and over time they grew from tens to hundreds even thousands in numbers. He spread his followers out across the world; each continent having its own branch of Atlas. To this day each branch of Atlas still operates by Mr. Robinson's instructions."

Joyce gives Adam the signal to proceed; he slides his hand to the left. The slide changed to a blank page with a picture of a speaker on it.

"Here we have the speech Amir Robinson gave to his followers just days after the war ended."

"My brothers...and sisters, today we do not focus on what makes us different. Instead let us focus on how we can live in prosperity and harmony even though we are different. Apart we are weak, but together we are strong. The world was at war, and we were merely pawns in an otherwise hopeless situation. No longer... no longer will we have to hide who we are. No longer will we be weapons of destruction. Instead we shall be tools for justice, peace, and unity. Humanity fears us and for that we are treated unfairly.

What humanity fails to realize is that you and I are just as much human as they are. Gone are the days of hiding in plain sight; from now on we shall embrace our gifts whatever they might be. Together we shall fight; however, we shall not fight to kill. Instead we shall fight to unify. Humans are motivated by three things: love, hate, and fear. We will fight for the love of humanity. In return we will use our love for humanity to combat the hate that plagues this world. Finally, we must eliminate the veil of fear from the eyes of man and live together as one united body of people. My brothers and sisters, to achieve this goal, we must first rise above ourselves. Being blessed with gifts such as ours does not give us the right to misuse them. We have been chosen to make a difference; therefore we must rise above ourselves and put the future and safety of those who fear us before our own.

Nothing is gained without a little effort, or pain. Sacrifice is a necessary aspect of unity. The day will come my friends when they will tell stories of the world's finest hour, that in which meta-humans and humans alike live together in true harmony. If you agree to stand with me, brothers and sisters, you will embark on a journey of unimaginable proportions. Stand with me now and in the days to come the world will see that you and I are more than just meta-humans. They will see that we are their equals."

Once the recording ends, Adam slides his hand to the left again. As such the slide changed to a group of people in various outfits. "Here we have a breakdown of the classes at Atlas. This person in everyday urban attire...well that's you, or what we call recruits. Recruits are trained in a variety of skills and techniques. Based upon your overall performance we will determine what you become next.

Soldiers, this is the rank of our assault squad. As a Soldier, you will be working with a unit to assist in combat and deter any opposition. Within the

Soldier class there are sub-classes; you have Captains, Grunts, Enforcers, and Heavies. Each Soldier unit is made up of one Captain and an assortment of other sub-classes. Their uniform ranges from lightweight body armor to heavy armor.

Operatives are like Soldiers except they work in much smaller units. Operatives get assigned to teams of three based upon your compatibility during training. You will also receive a code name for your protection and the protection of those you love. Operatives are assigned the more challenging tasks because they have special training to deal with it.

The draw back to this is that you are working with less people therefore each teammate will have to contribute to succeed. Operatives can be promoted to the status of Elite Operative in which they can go on missions alone. As an Operative you wear a light weight form fitting armor that can resist most substance as well as small arms fire.

Specialist have an entirely different role. You see a Specialist is an expert in one of ten fields. There are P.R. Specialist, Combat Specialist, Technology Specialist, Medical Specialist, Intelligence Specialist, Infiltration Specialist, Engineering Specialist, Transportation Specialist, Communication Specialist, and finally Weapon Specialist. Each Specialist is an expert in their field making sure things around the base are running efficiently.

A select few have been chosen to sit at the

table of the Atlas High Council. The Council advises
the Commander and helps come to decisions for the
better of the organization. Speaking of Commander,
allow me to introduce Commander Maximus."

Joyce steps back as Commander Maximus
steps forward. He takes a long look into the crowd
before he says, "Thank you Joyce for that wonderful
speech. I am the Commander and as Commander it is
my job to oversee everything that goes on here. But
like any group we are most effective when we work
together.

This big guy you see here to my left is our
Leading Combat Specialist and one of our top Elite
Operatives...we call him Brick. Now don't let his
size scare you; he is a nice guy. But like the rest of us,
he takes his job serious. Not only that, but Brick came
to us straight out of the U.S. Military and has vast
knowledge on various combat strategies. Brick will
oversee training most of you.

To my right is a young man that came to us
six years ago and has risen through the ranks and
become one of the top Elite Operatives. He has
showed true strength time and time again. He has
wisdom well beyond his years, as well as a love for
this world. Not to mention...he has saved my life. He
is unlike anyone I have ever met before and at times it
even seems as though he is from another world.

He is like a son to me. We call him Quazar,
and the reason he stands here, and I bother to tell you

that little story is because it is a perfect depiction of what I think every one of you that sits in the audience has the potential to be. Over time you will come to know him as I have; he is humble, passionate, and trustworthy. All of which are qualities that would make a great Commander someday.

Quazar, Brick, myself and everyone else here look forward to working with you all. Before we take the tour, I will give you time to meet and greet with your new peers."

Commander Maximus along with the other members step off the stage and begin to talk to the new recruits. Xavier, Marcus, and Devonte slowly stand to their feet and listen as the room erupts into a roar of conversation. Before they knew it, Commander Maximus was standing behind them; they turn around to greet him.

"Nice to formally meet you boys, I hear you are very talented and will be of great use. But in the meantime, I want you to get to know your new teammates, as we will have plenty of time for us to talk."

They all turn around and head into the crowd; unknowingly Marcus bumps into a girl and knocks her to the floor. Her blonde bangs flail wildly as she hits the ground. He realizes his mistake and helps her up off the floor. "Oh my God, I am so sorry I honestly didn't see you there."

"It's ok, accidents happen…I'm Trish by the

way."

"Nice to meet you Trish, my name is Marcus, I do apologize; I am usually more observant than that. So…I guess I should start by asking where you are from?"

Trish smiles and replies, "I came here from Trybech, Maryland, but I have lived in over a dozen places before that. Because of my father's job we were always relocated wherever his job would send him. I only recently had a place to call home. I would say that I have attended more schools then the average person would in two lifetimes."

"Wow, now I have moved around myself but nothing like that. You know you look really good for a person who has gone through so much."

Trish chuckles, "What do you mean by that?"

"I mean you don't seem stressed out, as a matter of fact you appear to be very…girly."

"Is that a good girly…or a bad girly," she asks while blushing.

Marcus looks slightly confused as he states, "Good girly."

Meanwhile Xavier and Devonte are walking through the crowd when out of nowhere a blue haired young man jumps out in front of them. "Hey" he shouts at Devonte, who flinched from the spontaneous gesture.

"Hi there, my name is Kenneth Scott, but everyone just calls me Kenny. This is my friend, Charlie Miller."

"Kenny, for the last time call me Charles," says a young man with dark crimson hair.

"Nice to meet you Kenny and Charles; my name is Xavier Evans, and this is my friend, Devonte Coleman." Devonte casually waves at Kenny and Charles.

Kenny starts to fidget as he says, "So what can you do Xavier...oh I got it, I bet you can fly...no wait, you turn invisible...wait I got it, you can talk to animals!"

"Actually, I am a Lightning Elementalist," Xavier responds.

"Wow! That is so awesome...I wish I was a Lightning Elementalist."

Charles places his hand over his face in frustration while saying, "Kenny...you are a Lightning Elementalist. Please excuse my friend; you see he suffers from short term memory loss."

Devonte shakes his head, "Wow, that's sad."

Realizing what he said Xavier elbows Devonte in the arm. "Don't mind him he has issues of his own. Anyway, Charles, what are your powers?"

"Finally...I thought you'd never ask. You see my good man, I control the most powerful force ever to be witnessed by natural eyes...fire! With my hands burning bright, with my heart burning brighter, with skills unmatched, and looks unparalleled to anyone; I, Charles Miller, will rise above the rest and become the best Operative this place has ever seen...or ever will see."

Xavier leans over to Devonte and whispers, "Ok I don't remember asking him all of that." Just then, Xavier peers past Devonte's shoulder. His eyes light up with excitement and without a single word, he walks away from the conversation.

He walks up to Jessica who he had spotted through the crowd. He taps her on the shoulder and says, "Hey there, do you remember me?"

She turns around and takes one look then realizes whom it was that was speaking to her. "Oh my God, Xavier, what are you doing here? It's been about a year since the last time I saw you."

"Believe it or not I am still in shock myself." Xavier goes on to explain the story of how he came to be at Atlas.

"That's crazy. I never would have guessed back then that you had powers too, Xavier. I also had my powers by then; at first, they would only activate a small percentage of the time. That was until I went to visit my father this most recent time and they became unbearable. Lucky for me, my father is old childhood friends with the Commander, and I was able to get in here."

"Ok, so what can you do?"

"Well, I am not exactly sure, it's glowing green energy that tends to form on around my hands and feet. My father seems to think it is plasma energy, but I am not all that sure."

The Chosen: Breaking Bonds

While the crowd continues to talk, Commander Maximus takes the stage one more time. He calls out to the crowd one time, then another. Finally, after three tries, he can get their attention. He informs them that the tour of the facility is about to begin. Before they could say anything Xavier and Jessica were separated by the crowd.

Eventually he meets back up with both Marcus and Devonte. "Man, oh man, there are some nice-looking women in this place. A man could really get used to this," Devonte says as he throws his arms around the necks of Xavier and Marcus.

They are the last of the recruits to leave the Rec. Room. As they exit, Xavier taps Marcus on the shoulder, "So is it safe to say we made the right choice?" he asks.

"One would say this is a lot better than sitting at home waiting for some overpriced college to tell you how happy they are to take your money," Marcus says enthusiastically.

Chapter 6

The Journey pt2: Training

About a day has gone by, and all the recruits have now settled in to their rooms in the Living Quarters. Marcus and Xavier wait for Devonte to show up for their first day of training. They both stand there almost motionless as if in anticipation. After twenty minutes, the door to the Battle Arena swings open. Devonte comes shuffling in on his skateboard. "Sorry I am late...I kind of forgot how to get here."

Marcus looks over to Xavier who just shakes

his head in disbelief. He looks back at Devonte and says, "You brought your skateboard with you? For what?"

"What else, to ride it. I mean I'm not very good with it, but it still gets me from point A to point B faster than walking."

"Whatever," Marcus states nonchalantly.

Moments later David comes from within the Control Room. He walks up the boys who seem excited. "Good to see you boys. I hope you are settling in just fine?" David's eyes pan the length of the Battle Arena. "As I already told you, I have been given the go-ahead to personally train you three. So, as to not interfere with Hector's class, I decided to schedule our lessons earlier in the day."

Marcus raises his hand, "So exactly what kind of training will we have to do?"

"First off, we will structure your team. After that, we will work on some team-based exercises. Once all of that is out of the way, we will move on to combat training, both hand-to-hand and with weapons. Because I trained you three at the youth center, there are a few less things we must do now. After all your physical training is done, you will be given a series of lessons on the finer points of being an Atlas Operative. Then, once that is done, you will be given an evaluation. This coupled with the results from your physical training will give us an understanding of how to utilize you. You are going to learn a lot in a short amount of time, but I believe you three can handle it."

David has them do a series of warm up exercises before he called them back to the center of the Arena. "Ok, I think we have wasted enough time. Let's get started with your first lesson." David pulls out a remote-like device from his back pocket and proceeds to press a series of buttons. Panel by panel the arrangement of the Battle Arena shifts, until finally it resembles a vibrant forest.

From the soil to the smell of the oaky bark, the Arena had perfectly mimicked the forest. "You boys look as if you've seen a ghost. The Battle Arena uses a prototype Nano molecular environmental replication system. This system can recreate almost any environment down to the texture and smell. The Nano-machines secrete pheromones that help make the experience more authentic.

Operatives work in three-man units. The reason being is that they are trained to handle any type of situation, whereas the Soldier class is trained for certain situations. Every Operative has the skill equivalent of three or four Soldiers. Each team of Operatives has a team leader." David takes a brief pause, he points to Marcus, "Based on what I know about the three of you, Marcus will be your team leader." Marcus stares at David with uncertainty in his eyes.

David throws the remote into the air and

catches it. This continues while he tells them about their task. "So here is what you three need to do. I have the controller and it is your job to take it from me and hit the red button to shut off the system. Being that this is a simulation, you are more than welcome to use your powers. Good luck boys…begin!"

David steps backward, disappearing in the darkness of the trees. Marcus looks to Xavier then to Devonte. They wait anxiously for his plan. Marcus' hands burst into flames, "We take away his cover giving him nowhere to hide." He then starts to light the trees on fire one by one. As Marcus sets the trees ablaze, Devonte catches a glimpse of David moving through the trees. Devonte takes off running, but inevitably loses sight of him. Xavier scans the trees searching for David.

"Xavier, whenever you are ready to help us, we could really use the-" Marcus loses his train of thought as Xavier runs off into the opposite direction. Marcus shakes his head then turns his attention over to Devonte, who was punching at shadows. Ignoring Devonte, Marcus continues to press forward. He hears the word "Hey" come from over his right shoulder. When he turns around to look, he is hit in the chest with an energy blast that sends him flying backwards into a tree.

Feeling extremely frustrated, Marcus slams his hands on the ground then flings a massive fireball at David. As David waits for the oncoming fireball, Xavier jumps him. David reverses his attack and throws him into the path of the oncoming fireball. The force from the blast sent Xavier hurling through the air. David takes flight and zooms straight towards Marcus. He accelerates past Devonte with such force, that it propels him backwards into the trees.

With David closing in, Marcus tenses up. Just then, the Arena starts to revert to its original state. Both David and Marcus look down at Xavier who acquired the remote and shut off the system.

David slowly descends while clapping his hands. "Not bad, unfortunately you guys did not pass. This was a team-based exercise in which I witnessed very little teamwork." David takes the remote from Xavier then turns around and walks to the control room.

While inside the control room, David can clearly hear the three boys bickering amongst themselves. He calmly walks back out onto the Arena floor and stands behind Marcus. "Listen up, this is not the way a team is supposed to behave. What just happened was not the fault of one person, there is no use trying to place the blame. Marcus, you are probably wondering why I chose you to be the team leader? I thought you would be able to handle it given your athletic history and experience. You were used to leading a team."

"True, but the teams usually followed my

orders."

"As a leader, you need to be able to rally your allies to stand with you. Also, work on your temper; you get too emotional. When that happens, you start to make unnecessary mistakes."

Marcus looks away in frustration, his arms folded tightly across his chest. David looks at Xavier and Devonte, "As for the rest of you, following orders is a crucial aspect to be an Operative. If you can't follow the orders of your team leader, how do you expect to carry out orders from anyone else? Working as one is how we will achieve our goal of unifying the people of the world. Now all of you catch your breath, we are going to run the drill again. And will continue to do so until you succeed. Keep in mind that the environment will be different each time; this will eliminate the trap of repetition.

Within minutes, the second drill begins; after that the third, and soon the fourth. After doing the drill five times, the boys finally emerge victorious. With everyone tired and beaten, David congratulates them on passing their first drill. "Impressive. I want to commend you boys on a job well done. Your teamwork has improved tremendously. I knew there was something special about the three of you. You have made such gains in such a short time… unfortunately it only gets harder from here on out.

The next phase of their training begins just one week later.

David gathers the boys in the Battle Arena to explain the next step.

"Welcome back, you guys have been doing tremendously well so far. That's great. Then I guess it is time to move on to the next phase. Ok, having powers is one thing, but what if you are in a position where you can't use them. This next lesson will teach you all how to properly defend yourself in close quarters hand-to-hand combat."

Excitement consumes all the boys and their faces light up in response to David's statement. Xavier takes in a deep breath before he finally raises his hand. "David, you are aware that I already know karate. However, over the last few weeks I have been reading up on the history of…ninjas. My question is how hard would it be for me to learn Ninjutsu."

"Really Xavier, a ninja. Why do you want to be a ninja?" Marcus questions.

"Well, my Grandfather learned the style while he lived in Japan. My Grandfather was my hero and my dad told me right before I left that my Grandfather had powers just like me. So, I figured if he could do it, then why not me."

David smirks and responds, "You are the first person to ever make a request like that. Very well. We will just have to modify your routine." David pulls out the control device to the Battle Arena. "Here is what will happen next. What I am going to do is set up a BOT for you boys to spar with. Now the BOT is specially made to record your performance. Based on the recording, we will come up with a personalized training routine for each of you."

With the click of a button a structure resembling that of a metallic skeleton raises up from the floor. David walks over to it and unlatched a panel from its back. He pushes a series of buttons before informing Marcus that he would go first. The eyes of the BOT illuminate, and it gets into a fighting stance. David, Xavier, and Devonte clear the floor as Marcus faces off against the machine.

After each boy had their turn to face the BOT, David pulls up their results in the Control Room. Based on their results, David compiles a training routine each tailored to fit their specific needs.

After an intense two days of training, Xavier decided to stay after their session. He sits Indian-style on the floor deep in thought. Moments later he springs to his feet; he performs a combination of kicks and palm strikes into the air. He propels himself into the air completely flipping upside down with his foot extended forward. Once his feet touch the ground he immediately repeated the flip kick two more times. On his third flip, he is unable to stick the landing and falls to floor.

Xavier rests for a while on his knees when he hears the creaking of the door's hinges. He looks up, his eyes fixed on a female standing in the doorway.

"Oh…I'm sorry I didn't mean to startle you," she says in a hushed tone.

"No, it's no problem, I was finished anyway. I'm Xavier, what's your name?"

The girl walks a little bit closer, she moves very timidly. "Kimberly…my name is Kimberly Young…um nice to meet you Xavier."

As he stands up, Xavier puts a smile on his face. "So, Kimberly if you don't mind me asking, how did you get here?"

"Well originally my parents are from Korea but moved to the states. They were here for two years before they had me. I grew up in a very sheltered environment, my parents were always cautious of the outside world."

"Believe me, they are right for feeling that way. I had to learn the hard way that the world is a very dangerous place."

"I got so tired of being scared for no reason…so I came to this place. I am hoping I can overcome my fears and help rid the world of those that prey on fear."

"So, your parents actually let you come all the way out here?"

"I told them this was some sort of exchange program for school. So, I am ok on that front."

Xavier stands to his feet; his sweat stained shirt clenched his chest tightly. "You said your parents were from Korea. I have heard some interesting stories about that place from my grandfather. He was a bit of a drifter in his heyday, traveling the world for reasons unknown. On a different topic, how is it being a student of Brick?"

Kimberly lets out a faint sigh, "It's hard…I mean he is a good teacher, but I just have a hard time memorizing all of the techniques. Then I look at you and you make it look so easy."

Xavier takes a second to think before replying, "Tell you what, if you can meet me here about this time every day, I can help you with your training. I will also show you some cool techniques I have been working on myself."

Her face lights up with happiness as she nods repeatedly. "Thank you, Xavier, you are a lot nicer than some of the other guys I have met here. I really appreciate-" She looks past Xavier's shoulder; her heart begins to race and without saying a word she flees from the Battle Arena.

Marcus places a hand firmly on Xavier's shoulder. He has a towel draped over his left shoulder. "Who was that," he asks.

Xavier stands there in shock and disorder, "That was Kimberly, I offered to help her with her training. I think you scared her off, but I am not entirely sure yet."

"Ok…sounds wonderful. So, you got yourself a girlfriend and she has pink hair. That is rare to see."

"Marcus, she is not my girlfriend I just offered to help her train…that's it."

"Calm down; it was just a joke. Now let's get out of here before the next group shows up."

The next morning, Marcus and Devonte were walking to the Rec. Room when Marcus spots someone in the distance heading into the small structure nestled in the corner of the field. He lets Devonte go on ahead to the Rec. Room. Once Devonte was out of sight, Marcus slowly creeps towards the tiny building. Now just outside the door, Marcus takes a deep breath before rushing inside.

Once inside the feeling of tension suddenly leaves him as he gazes upon Trish. "Oh, my bad I didn't realize it was you. I saw someone rush in here. What are you doing?"

Trish takes a slight step to the side revealing a small blooming plant. "I planted this flower, I thought this place needed something special. I approached the Council about letting me turn this building into a Green House." Trish says as she smiles from ear to ear.

"Wow it's growing really fast, how is that?"

"I have the power to control earth as well as produce it."

"So, you are an Elementalist."

I just love flowers, it's kind of funny because

most people do not even realize the fact that flowers and humans have things in common. You see flowers have a lifespan; they need nourishment to grow big and strong. Like us, they feel pain, grow old, and eventually die."

Marcus becomes relaxed and sits on a shelf beside Trish. "You know, you have a point. Most people are unaware of the fact that plants are living organisms too. Why not make your garden outside, because your flowers aren't going to get much sunlight in here?"

"Don't worry, my flowers are special. They do not need as much sunlight to grow as other plants would. I figured out quite some time ago that my body could absorb and store sunlight. Therefore, when I produce a plant, it can grow ten times that of a normal plant."

"It must be nice to have such a docile power. To be honest with you, I use to fear my powers. I have since grown out of that fear; I am learning to embrace my fire." Marcus states softly.

"Fire is another victim of common misconception. To most people, fire is a tool of destruction, when fire is natural and has a lot of good qualities. Fire helps us in our everyday lives; some see fire as a beacon of hope. Personally, I find the heat from fire to be very soothing, like cuddling up with the one you love. It's for that reason that I don't fear fire."

Marcus stares deep into her eyes for a few seconds. Trish begins to blush as she stares back into his. "Listen Trish, I was on my way to the Rec. Room. I was wondering if you'd like to join me for a quick bite to eat?"

She gently places her soft hand into his, "I would love to." Marcus escorts her out of the Green House and into the Rec. Room.

The following morning inside the Battle Arena, the boys gather around the weapons closet. Marcus opens the double doors to the closet, weapon after weapon plummet to the floor. Slowly, Marcus starts to rummage through the weapons, he shakes his head in irritation. "Uh…there are so many weapons here, but not one of them catches my eye," he says as he walks away.

Xavier is next to step up to the pile of weapons. He glances through them until he sees the handle of a sword. He wraps his hand around the handle and lifts it from within the pile.

"What is that?" Devonte asks.

"This is a shinobigatana or Katana for short. It is the signature weapon of the ninja. My grandfather used to bring me back a toy replica every time he went to Japan. Growing up, it has been a dream of mine to hold the real thing…it feels amazing."

Xavier grips the sword tightly as he takes a

few steps back, allowing Devonte to look through the pile. Devonte grabs two identical pistols; a slight smile creeps across his face. "I think I am going to rock with these. My Dad use to be a police officer. As a result, he taught my sister and me how to handle a gun when we were old enough to learn. He was my hero growing up; double guns was his trademark. I vowed one day I would be just like him."

"Well, what happened to him?" Xavier asked.

"He got hurt pretty bad...it cost him his job. Then times got tough you know. Living where we were was becoming too expensive, and my parents didn't want to put Sarah and I through that problem. So, they sent us to live with my father's parents in Mercury, North Carolina.

At first, I didn't understand why we had to leave, but Sarah helped me get through it and from what I can tell, mom and pop are doing better now that it's just the two of them. I am going to be like my father and use these guns to protect the innocent."

"Do you still think you will find her somewhere out there?" Xavier questions with care.

"I have to or else me being here is a huge waste of time. I won't abandon my sister because I know she would never abandon me."

Xavier nods in acknowledgement, then takes a quick glance over his shoulder and sees Marcus walk into the control room.

As David stands at the control terminal,

Marcus stands in the doorway. "Is there something wrong Marcus?"

"Nothing…I just can't seem to find a weapon that catches my…" Marcus abruptly stops talking as he walks up to the back wall. Hanging on a plaque mounted to the wall was a double-ended blade. Marcus could tell the blade had been there for quite some time by the thick coverage of dust. "David, what is that?"

David hesitates to answer; he takes a deep breath before he states, "That is what's known as the Roaring Twin Dragons. It used to belong to Nova himself."

Confusion consumes Marcus, "Wait, there was an actual Nova?" he asks.

"Yes, there was, he is long since dead. The story goes like this; many years ago, there was an Operative among Atlas unlike any other. Nova, he was an Elite Operative and said to be one of the most powerful fire elementalists to ever exist. Nova seemed to have an overabundance of energy and could go for literally hours before he needed to rest. Knowing this, the previous Council exploited this and kept him out in the field as much as possible.

Nova began to rebel against Atlas; he questioned our ideals as well as the way we operate. As you know we believe killing to be a last resort, to Nova killing was the only answer that made sense. He felt we needed to be more aggressive in our fight for unification. Instead of imprisoning our enemies, he felt we should slaughter them and anyone else who should get in our way.

For Nova, unification wasn't enough. He felt that there needed to be one power, a symbol, something the people could look up to, but also fear. The Commander at that time deemed Nova unfit to operate in the field, so he had him imprisoned in a holding cell. It was said that Nova spent so much time in that cell that he had time to plan a revolt. The day came when Nova broke free, he and his followers were planning to seize control of Atlas and turn it into a symbol of fear.

During the battle, Nova made his way to the Council Room where he assassinated the Commander. While trying to escape, he ran into a young Operative; you know him as Commander Maximus. Maximus fought with everything he had and managed to successfully drive Nova away from Atlas. Thus, for single handedly saving Atlas, he was awarded the title "Commander".

As for Nova, he and his followers started their own group and grew to be as powerful as Atlas. When Nova died, the leadership of their group fell to Quake at which time he started calling their group Nova in honor of the real Nova. As you can imagine, Quake is not Nova; therefore, their ideals are not the same. Little is known about their goal. That is why we must maintain a watchful eye on the Grid."

"So, basically you all created your own worst enemy." Xavier says as he stands in the doorway.

David peers past Marcus to Xavier and Devonte who were standing in the doorway. "Yes, we did create our worst enemy. And it was us who planted the seeds for their hatred. Unfortunately, fixing the mistake we made is going to remain a pipedream as long as we remain in the dark of Nova's true intentions."

David brushes the dust from on top the blade; he carefully lifts it up off the plaque. "This blade holds too much value to be used for full on combat. I am giving you permission to use it as a trial, and if you find that you are satisfied, we will have you one custom made," he says as he hands the double-ended blade to Marcus. "Now, can you boys follow me out onto the floor? We will begin our lesson."

Everyone gathers in the center of the massive arena; David has a BOT already prepared and ready to begin. "Alright, for this portion of your training, we are going to revisit the methods of training laid out for you in your hand-to-hand session. Only this time you will be using your weapons. Now I am pretty efficient with every weapon we have here on hand, so I will have more of a hands-on role this time around. You will need to follow my instructions as I go over the proper way to handle these weapons.

After instructions, you will have an opportunity to practice on the BOT, and like before it will record your data and we will go from there. I feel I should tell you that starting tomorrow we will also be preparing for your mental evaluation, so just be prepared."

From then on, every day they came to training, they were tested on both physical and mental readiness.

It has now been three months since their first day of training. All the recruits gather in the Rec. Room, where they wait in anticipation of Hector who was on his way to speak to them. One by one the recruits take their seats as Hector enters the room and walks onto the stage.

He stands poised and straight; his arms tucked away behind his back. He takes one long glance over the crowd of recruits. "I am going to get started," he says. "Three months ago, you all were brought here to us at Atlas. You made the decision you wanted to do something positive with your powers. However, a good handful of you seemed apprehensive when you first started training. But, having watched you all grow over these last three months, you make me proud as an instructor, and happy as your friend to know that you are ready to become official Atlas members!

In these three long months, you have gained new skills and abilities, new allies and friends, but more importantly, a new foundation, one that you will use to stand on in our fight for unification between humans and meta-humans. In a couple of moments, you all will be called into the Council Room based on the groups that were formed during your training."

As Hector steps off stage, the room immediately erupts into a roar of conversation. After about forty-five minutes, Xavier looks over at Devonte who had a look of sadness on his face. "What's the matter Devonte? Today is the day we're promoted, you should be excited!"

"She won't laugh at my jokes!"

"I'm not following, what are you talking about?" Xavier questions in uncertainty.

Devonte points across the room, "Do you see that girl over there?"

"Are you sure we are looking at the same person?"

"She's not a boy, Xavier, it's just her hair cut. Her name is Janet; she hangs out with Kimberly a lot. I always hang out with them with Jessica, Kenny, and Charles. We all have a lot of fun except her; at times it can be weird. She is always wearing black too. Charles calls her gothic. But, it's like no matter how hard I try, I can't get her to laugh let alone crack a smile. Come on Xavier, I have even managed to make Charles laugh, and that guy's a jerk!"

"So, that's what you are upset about…you can't make a girl laugh! Something seems wrong with that logic," Xavier says sarcastically.

"I wouldn't expect you to understand, it goes deeper than that. I am trying to get her to notice me, but she is the first person to completely ignore me."

Marcus interjects by saying, "Cut the crap guys, it's our turn!"

At the door to the Council Room the boys stand in anticipation of what will be their foreseeable future. Slowly, they walk into the Council Room. All eyes locked on them as they stop in front of the circular table. One after the other, the council stands up.

Commander Maximus walks out from behind the table and stands directly in front of the boys. In his right hand, he clenches the top of his cane firmly while his left hand remains tucked away in his coat pocket.

"Welcome! Today is the day you three worked so hard for three long months to reach. Momentarily, you will hear from some of the other council members." Maximus pulls his hand out of his pocket. "I hold here your official Atlas Identification Cards. These cards are always to remain with you while you are at base. With these cards you are granted access to all of the facilities hear at Atlas. On each of these cards are your personal information--- things like name, class, code name, security code, and more."

Commander Maximus pulls the first card,

"My fellow council members let us give a warm welcome to DaRock...an Operative of Atlas!" Maximus says as he hands that card to Devonte. "Please join me in welcoming Atlas Operative...River!" he says while giving that card to Marcus. "Last but not least let us welcome Atlas Operative... ShaXdow," Maximus hands the last card to Xavier.

A round of applause was presented to the three boys, as they are now recognized operatives of Atlas. Commander Maximus directs their attention over to David who steps out from the table.

"Thank you, Commander Maximus, and congratulations to you guys on your success," David states as Commander Maximus walks back to his seat.

"Words cannot describe how proud I am of you boys. Last year I was on a special assignment in Mercury, North Carolina; fate led me to you boys and I knew from the moment I met you three that you were destined for big things. You all come from different walks of life, but when faced with a common goal you managed to rise above yourselves and work together to achieve that goal. I see in the three of you a bond that cannot be broken, a resolve that cannot be undone, and a ray of hope that will shine brighter than all else in the time of darkness.

I am honored to have taken this journey with you up till this point. You have grown to be more than just my students, but I now see you as my brothers and my equals.

With that aside, this is the beginning of the next chapter of your lives. The dangers you will face and the situations that you will be forced to deal with are all very real. I am not going to lie to you and tell you that everything will go the way you want because it won't. Just remember everything I taught you and remember to trust in yourselves as well as your teammates because the only way we are going to succeed is together."

Joyce walks out towards the boys with a sheet of paper in her hands. "Thank you, David, for that heartfelt speech. I will make this as short as possible then. For three months you three trained both your mind and body all in preparation for your evaluation. Two days ago, you all were given this evaluation and having just finished scoring them last night, we have the results.

Marcus, if you would be so kind as to step forward please. During your training you were named team leader... after reviewing your scores, it is safe to say that you will remain team leader. You scored the highest overall out of any of the new recruits, putting you in the top twenty highest scores ever. The BOT recorded you at a 94% physical efficiency and your evaluation has you at an 86% mental efficiency, for a combined score of 90%."

Everyone in the room applauds Marcus as he

steps back in line.

"Xavier, you are next, would you please step forward. Xavier you performed admirably on your evaluation, scoring an 86% physical efficiency and a 92% mental efficiency giving you a combined total of 89%. You received the second highest mental evaluation score right behind that of Gizmo. Congratulations."

As Xavier steps back in line Devonte takes two deep breaths.

"Devonte, please step up out of the line. You received a 78% physical efficiency and a 76% mental efficiency, giving you a combined score of 77%. Devonte, if I may, I want to say don't feel bad about your score. They do not define you, I have been told that you have something a lot of people don't, and that's resilience. No matter what obstacle came your way, you never gave up and for that you should be commended."

Joyce returns to her seat as Richard walks up. He stands at the corner of the table, "Boys, now that you have become Operatives, you will now be issued the official uniform for our operatives. You will be given a tactical, formfitting, non-stretch shirt. Regulation pants and boots, as well as the standard lightweight tactical vest. Your uniforms are light but armored so that you can take a hit yet move around comfortably.

As operatives, you must be ready to adapt to

any situation and find a solution. And remember, we do not believe in killing unless presented with no other alternative. With that said, you all are given weapons as a last resort." Richard steps back to his seat.

Commander Maximus takes the floor once again. "Thank you all for your contribution in today's ceremony. Boys, after you leave the council room you will be escorted to the Armory where you will receive your uniforms and weapons. Be ready, as you could be called for a mission at any time. Congratulations again and welcome aboard!"

The council gives them one last round of applause, as they leave the room.

Chapter 7

The Journey pt3: Mission 1

As they walk the halls of Atlas, Marcus lets out a giant sigh of relief at what has just transpired. He meticulously examines his newly acquired ID card, "River…I like the sound of that," he says, "Its official, we are now Atlas Operatives!"

"I know it's so cool. I can't wait to get out there and rough up some bad guys! DaRock saving the world one broken jaw at a time!" Devonte wraps his arm around Xavier's neck, "DaRock, sounds really powerful doesn't it?"

Xavier takes a few moments longer to study his ID card. "ShaXdow…that's an interesting way to spell that word. But nevertheless, I like it."

Having finally reached the Armory, Marcus tries to open the door. Noticing that the door will not open, Xavier points to a security panel plastered to the wall next to the door. He insists that Marcus try to input his four-digit security code. Marcus types his code into the panel; there was a feint buzzing as the door unlocks.

Upon entry, they are mesmerized at the interior and the armaments that decorate it. Hector stands behind a table with three cases stacked neatly at his feet.

"Well, look who it is! You boys look happy; it feels great to be promoted. Well, congratulations again, but since I am not here to give you yet another speech, I say we cut right to it."

Hector lifts the cases from the floor and places them onto the table. One by one he hands the cases out to the boys. "Ok, inside each of your cases are your uniforms. You each have a pair of boots, pants, and gloves. You also have your tactical shirt; Xavier, yours has been slightly modified. We managed to incorporate the traditional half-mask worn by ninjas into your tactical shirt. Lastly, you all have your armored vest.

Those devices in the bags are your communicators. The receiver clips onto your belt and the earpiece goes into your right ear. This little thing has the capability of receiving a signal even if you are clear across the ocean. Along with your uniform and communicator, you each have a personalized weapon."

Hector turns his attention to Devonte, "Devonte, these guns took some time to develop, but our good friends down at AstroTec figured out how to make it work. Inside each one of these pistols is a power core. Now to use them, you need to channel your powers through the gun itself. The reaction from your ice will cool down the core at which point the core will try to heat up once again and it expels the ice in the form of a bullet. Pulling back on the trigger causes friction, which helps the core heat up faster. So, basically it is a normal gun, but instead of lead, it shoots ice.

Because this gun uses your own natural power, it has no need for extra ammo. This however does not mean you have unlimited shots. Be mindful of how much you cool down the core, because you could cause the gun to freeze up and from that point you will have to wait for the core to heat up again."

Devonte grins from ear to ear as he takes out his guns and holds them in his hands.

Hector looks at Xavier, "You are an interesting character, kid. You wanted to become a ninja, although slightly unorthodox, it's unique. This Katana was forged by Arthur himself, lightweight, yet extremely durable. The metal that was used in its design conducts electricity better than any other metal. Therefore, if you were to focus your power and send a current through the blade, you could essentially cut through anything. Just be careful how you use it, because though it is highly durable, it can still break."

Xavier nods in acknowledgement.

"Ok Marcus, David told me you took a liking to the Roaring Twin Dragons. He gave you permission to train with it and you seem satisfied. So, we made good on our word and had a custom made, battle ready Roaring Twin Dragons built. It is stored in two halves; a feature the original did not poses. When the two halves are joined together, then you get the complete weapon. It took a while to get this right; if I am correct, you are the first person to use this weapon since Nova defected all those long years ago. Therefore, crafting this weapon was a process, let me tell you."

Just as Hector is about to finish he gets a call on his communicator. Moments later, Hector informs them that there has been a change in plans. "Boys, I got good news and bad news. The bad news is that you will not have an opportunity to celebrate. The good news however is that you have just received your first mission."

There was an eerie silence in the room. The boys stand there conflicted as Hector looks on. "Don't worry the first mission is always the hardest. You guys will do fine; now go to your rooms and get suited up. Then report to the briefing room when you are ready. Good luck."

The boys meet back up at the Briefing Room. Inside, Dillan waits for them at the control table in the middle of the room.

"Good, you all are finally here. My name is Dillan Snyder, but you can call me Shift. I will be briefing you on your mission for today. We have lost contact with a squad of our troops. Now before communications went out, we were informed that they had apprehended Twister. Twister is not the smartest guy in the world, but never underestimate him or you will regret it. He is one of Nova's most destructive members."

Dillan clicks a series of buttons on the table. A holographic globe appeared and Dillan homed in on North America. "They picked him up just outside of New Haven, Connecticut," Dillan states as the holo-globe focuses in on New Haven, Connecticut.

"There is something you should know about Twister. He is a criminal in every sense of the word. He was once a part of a very notorious crime syndicate that terrorized Helix City, Kentucky.

But due to untimely circumstances, he wound up destroying the whole syndicate as well as most of Helix City. He is not to be taken lightly, but things should go smooth. Our troops should have him in custody. What we need you to do is rendezvous with them and pick up Twister to transport him to the Baldwin Correctional Institute. They will hold him there for the time being." Dillan salutes them and sends them onto the Hanger.

They climb aboard an STC and within seconds it was airborne soaring through the sky. It wasn't too long before the STC reached the last known coordinates of the missing troops.

Marcus takes a lengthy inhale only to slowly exhale. "Ok guys, Shift said to secure Twister. ShaXdow, I want you and DaRock to make sure Twister gets back to the STC. I will rendezvous with whoever is in charge and inform them of the change in plans."

Upon arrival, the pilot informs them that he sees something wrong. As the STC lands and the hatch opens, the boys could see the problem right away. The terrain was littered with large sharp jagged pieces of broken metal. Suddenly, the wind begins to howl and stir up dust making it harder to see.

"Pilot, when we get off, I need you to get airborne; we need some eyes in the sky. If things get too crazy you need to get away, you are our only means of escape," Marcus states.

One by one, the boys exit the STC, they walk cautiously towards a nearby broken structure. Within moments, the STC has ascended skyward.

"This is bad; there is too much dust in the air. I can't even see what's directly in front of me, let alone any survivors," Xavier proclaims.

"Hey, do you guys hear that? It sounds like…talking," Devonte interjects.

"I hear it now, but where is it coming from?"

Marcus takes a deep breath and moments later his eyes burst into flames. He leans out from behind cover enough to scan the field. "Guys I see him. He is about a kilometer north out by the pier." Marcus states. "We need to move now but watch your step."

They move single file behind Marcus avoiding large debris. Now just feet from the pier, they watch as Twister diligently rummages through a large pile of debris. Dust falls to the ground from his armored Nova uniform as he rose to his feet. The wind course swiftly through his long flowing golden locks, as the sun illuminates his otherwise pale skin.

"You can come out now, there is no use in trying to hide. I can hear even the faintest whisper in the wind. I heard you when you landed in that little birdie. Word of advice, I would just hand it over, negotiating didn't really work out well for your friends," he says sarcastically!

Devonte steps out with his guns drawn. They were pointed directly at Twister. "Don't move," Devonte states firmly.

"Really…this is too much. Kid, do yourself a favor and put the toys away and tell me where you put the case!"

Marcus and Xavier slowly make their way

towards Twister, Xavier grabs the handle of his sword while it rests on his back. Marcus stops Xavier from being too hasty.

"Wait, what case?" Marcus inquired.

Twister clenches his fist tightly as he said; "I don't take kindly when folks try to insult my intelligence. The briefcase... the one from AstroTec, containing their new self-sustaining energy compound! Your friends were transporting it when we picked up the chatter." He starts to chuckle to himself. "Boy, you have to love these nifty little beacons. They let you listen in on communications...as well as disrupt them. I guess since it won't make a difference, I will go ahead and tell you. As you probably guessed by now, I let myself be captured to get closer to the case. But I reckon I got a little carried away and wound up crashing the dang thing. I got thrown from it, everyone else died, and now I can't find the case!"

Devonte's hands start to shake in fear. Marcus and Xavier stand stunned in silence. Marcus shakes off his fear and states; "We don't know anything about a briefcase. But you will pay for those you've killed. Let's get him ShaXdow!"

Twister grins from ear to ear as they approach him. The wind begins to howl; Xavier tackles Marcus's to the ground. Having just narrowly avoided being smashed by giant debris, the two attempted to crawl back towards Devonte. Twister uses the wind to lift them into the air and swing them around wildly as if playing with a ragdoll. Devonte takes two shots at Twister who rolls out of the way. The brief loss of concentration results in Marcus and Xavier plummeting back to the ground.

Dizzied and bruised, Xavier and Marcus get to their feet. "We need to get in close," Marcus says as he rests his arm on Devonte's shoulder. In the midst of conversation an intense gust of wind pushes them all into a broken wall. Then came another gust, which blows them back towards Twister.
"That was fun, but now you-"

Twister is hit in the face with a burst of fire. He loses concentration as he frantically puts out the flame. The boys take this opportunity to retreat behind cover.

"Huh...huh...like I thought we have to get in close," Marcus states as he catches his breath.

"But how do we get close, he keeps pushing us back," Devonte interjects.

"Listen guys, I think I see a potential weakness that we can exploit. I noticed that he could concentrate only on a few things at a time. If we were to divide our efforts, we might be able to subdue him."

"ShaXdow is right, we need to make him play our game! DaRock you have the best range, you stay back here and give us some cover. I will draw his attention long enough for ShaXdow to sneak around him unnoticed. Once you get close enough,ShaXdow you put him down.

As they are talking, a jagged slab of rock comes hurling at them. To avoid it, they jump in three separate directions. Marcus gives the signal and Devonte stands up and starts firing at Twister's feet. Marcus takes off running full steam at Twister at which point he is lifted by the wind and slammed back onto the ground. As Marcus lies there, Twister moves another piece of debris in place to smash him.

Devonte then fires a shot that grazes Twister across the arm. The frozen bullet travels so fast that it leaves a burning sensation causing Twister to lose concentration yet again. The hovering debris falls from the air and plummets to the earth. At the last second, Marcus summons enough strength to roll out of the way of the falling debris. Twister then turns his attention to Devonte but is hit in the back by an electrical discharge.

Xavier goes to grab Twister; having grown increasingly upset, Twister lets out a violent roar followed by a powerful gust of wind. The intense gust sends Xavier flying backward; he uses his static adhesion technique to cling to a rooted piece of debris. Twister uses the wind to propel himself vertically skyward. Having reached about fifty feet in the air, Twister pans the ground below. "Now I see it," he says as he began to interlock the wind currents forming a funnel cloud around him.

Debris from the ground begins to ascend skyward. Devonte forms a knife out of ice and plunged it deep into the surface. He catches Marcus, and the two struggle to keep themselves on the ground. Meanwhile Xavier fights to stay perched on the broken wall; he watches in horror, as the funnel cloud becomes a raging tornado.

Twister starts to hurl debris down at them at great speeds.

"We can't keep this up," Marcus says over the communicator. "We need another plan!"

Devonte chimes in; "Why don't we blow him out of the sky…look!" Devonte points up at floating propane tanks rotating around the tornado.

Marcus pats him on the back and says, "Good thinking, kid!" Marcus reaches for his communicator again. "ShaXdow, do you think you could hit those propane tanks with a lightning bolt?"
"No problem, but I am going to need a minute."

Debris falls just feet from Marcus and Devonte. "ShaXdow we don't have a minute! Whatever we are going to do we have to do it now!"

As the tornado gets closer, it opens, revealing Twister hovering in the center. "Sorry, I can't stick around and play, but I found what I am looking for, meaning there is no more use for you; it's a shame really you three are so young. Ah, what the heck, that's life!"

The debris disperses as the tornado widens.

"ShaXdow, now!" Marcus yells as he and Devonte are lifted into the air. Xavier concentrates and extends his hand forward. The clouds darken and a bolt of lightning jolts from within. It collides with the brim of one of the propane tanks. The collision results in an explosion which caused a chain reaction that sends everyone flying away.

As Twister is sent flying to the ground, the tornado slowly disappears. He lands hard on an unknown object and bounces off. When he regains his composure, he examines the object he landed on, and much to his surprise it was the briefcase. Without giving it another thought, he grabs the case and staggers off into the distance.

After a couple of minutes, Marcus wakes up due to the buzzing of his communicator. "Can you guys hear me down there? What was that explosion…come on somebody answer me!"

"This is River. I am a little dazed, but alive and in one piece. ShaXdow, DaRock are you guys ok?"

"Cough…cough, yeah I'm ok. It's a good thing I am not afraid of heights," Devonte states sarcastically while suspended from a pole.

"I'm ok, sorry about that. I guess I didn't account for a chain reaction. Did we at least-" Xavier abruptly stops and stares in horror at the water. "Guys…I found them. I found the missing troops, I can't tell if they were drowned or put here after the fact. I don't get it, weren't they trained to handle situations like this?"

An unsettling feeling consumes Marcus as he listens to Xavier. He takes one big gulp then says, "None of that matters now; just regroup at my location so we can get the heck out of here."

"But River, what about Twister?"

"From the looks of it, he got away. As for the case, unfortunately it was not priority, so it is not our problem," Marcus says undecidedly.

Having now regrouped the boys wait for the STC to land. As they walk aboard the pilot says, "Wow, you three look terrible. Not bad for your first mission, nevertheless it's good you are ok." None of the boys bothered to respond to his comment, their eyes filled with shock, anger, and disbelief.

"I will send a cruiser to take care of clean up." The pilot takes a long pause, "Listen I understand how you all are feeling right now. Death is an overbearing burden, one that you can't escape. We tend not to think about it you know, until it happens, or we see it. Most of the time we are unprepared, but when you have seen it as much as I have you start to become numb to it.

My advice to you guys, is to not be like me. For the job I've been given I try not get too attached to people; this way you don't have much to miss. Don't be naïve like me, always remember death is not something you should become comfortable with."

Before long, the STC was landing in the Hanger. The boys stand up to exit the STC when the pilot calls out to them.

"For fifteen years I have been a pilot here for Atlas. I have made just as many friends as I have lost. I have seen new recruits come and go. You know I heard about you three, how you fought back Nova while you were just civilians. That is not an easy feat; I guess what I am trying to say is, don't beat yourself up about what happened today.

You must remember that the outcome of a mission is strongly based on those involved. From what I hear, Twister is not an easy one to beat. He alone has dealt a lot of damage to Atlas. What I am telling you is although you were not able to secure him, the simple fact that you live to fight another day is reason enough to be happy. Tell you what from here on out you have my support; whenever you need transport, I'm your man. The name is Scott McMillan. I look forward to helping you guys save the world!"

Inside the four walls of the Briefing Room, Dillan, Richard, and David stand huddled around the Grid. Seconds later the boys enter the door behind them.

"What happened?" Richard says while neglecting to turn and face them.

Marcus stands up straight, "I beg your pardon, sir!"

Richard turns around and focuses his gaze right at Marcus.

"I asked what happened out there, why were we not informed as to your status? Did you all secure Twister, and what about our troops?"

"Sir, we were unable to secure Twister; he proved to be too strong for us. And the troops…well they were dead before we got there, sir."

"So that is why we lost contact!"

"Not exactly sir, Twister told us how he got captured in the first place. He says that Nova has placed these beacons all over that allows them to tap into various frequencies. It also allows them to send out jamming signals."

"So, he allowed himself to be captured so he could get close to the case. Which by the way where is it?"

"It's not here. Why were we not told about the case, we could have made it a priority!"

"You were given the information that you needed to know. Inside that case was a new self-sustaining energy compound developed by AstroTec"

"Sir that much we know. My question to you again is why weren't we told about the case before hand?"

"You would be wise to watch your tone! We have our reasons for not telling you and I do not have to sit here and explain them to you-"

David steps forward and places his hand on Richard's shoulder. "That's enough Richard. Listen boys, you weren't told about the case because we were counting on our troops to finish the delivery. We did not want you to be overwhelmed on your first mission. Unfortunately, we neglected to plan for the worst. It is not your fault we lost the case; it's ours. Next time we will make sure we do not make the same mistake."

Dillan folds his arms against his chest and states; "So what do we do about those jamming beacons?"

"If you would like, I could try and isolate them on the Grid. Then we can have Adam work up something to counter act them," Xavier says while stepping forward.

"You know how to work the Grid," Dillan questioned?

"Yes. I studied on it while I was training not to mention Adam taught me a lot."

"That's right, you and Trish were like his interns for a while. Ok, then meet me here tomorrow and we will begin the isolation."

Richard turns his attention back towards the Grid and says; "We are done here. You three are dismissed. Go enjoy what's left of your day!"

Chapter 8

Allies

About a week later, Devonte finds himself hanging out in the Rec. Room with his friends. He sits in between Kenneth and Janet, directly across from Charles and Kimberly.

"Devonte, I heard about what happened last week. So, where are the other two losers, off saving the world…I hope not," Charles says sarcastically.

Devonte looks upset and snaps, "Shut up Charles! You have no idea what we had to go through last week. We busted our butts and almost got killed. And for your information, they are in the Battle Arena training right now."

"Training, how appropriate. You should probably be in there with them, because you three can use all the training you can get. You guys will never be as strong as me; I come from a long line of heroes. My older brother Simon aka Hotstreak, my uncle Mark aka Burner, my father, and his father before him-"

Kenneth interjects, "Hey Charlie, didn't they all die in a hail of gunfire?"

Embarrassment and shame consume Charles. His face turns as red as his hair as Devonte chuckles under his breath.

Charles shoots Devonte a menacing glare, "It is not funny. They all died fighting for what they believe in."

Janet moves the long strands of hair from in front of her eye, it fell right back into place. "You are very ugly when you get mad."

Apart from Kimberly, everyone stares in shock at Janet. Charles slams his fist on the table and storms out of the Rec. Room. Devonte takes the opportunity to stare at Janet before she turns back around to face him.

"So, Kenny, how did you even meet Charlie anyway?" Kimberly asks.

"Well I can't remember much because of my memory loss, but I will never forget the day I met Charlie. It was about five years ago at school. Back then my memory loss was much more severe. I would forget almost instantly. I remember being at school and this big guy was picking on me. So, I took his nice new watch and hid it. The only problem was that I forgot where I put it.

I found Charlie skipping class out back behind the library. I saw he had the box that the watch came in. then it came back to me that I needed to find that watch. I asked him for it and he tried to charge me sixty bucks. So, I told him what happened, and he laughed at me. Usually, I would feel bad or upset, but this time I didn't. In fact, I was very happy. Anyway, I then tried to take the box away from him. We wrestled for a minute until I was able to get the box. I opened it, but it was empty. Charlie was just as shocked as I was. He got so mad that his face turned red and his hands caught fire.

At first, I was scared, but then I forgot everything that just happened. I asked him who he was, and he reluctantly told me his name. He walked away, and I literally followed him the entire day. Most people would have been mean to me, but he was surprisingly receptive of my company.

I was finally able to remember what I was doing with an empty box. Charlie was looking for the guy who gave him the box in the first place. He never found him, but the owner of the watch found me. He was just about to beat me up when Charlie tackles him to the ground and beat him up for me.

I know this is going to sound weird, but the only reason Charlie doesn't like your friends is because he sees them as his equals. Charlie is very overprotective of those he deems less fortunate than himself. That is how we became friends, and are still friends, and will forever be friends. He even helped me with my memory loss; that's why I am a lot better now. At the end of every day I make a recording of myself via my computer. It was Charlie's idea. He said it's so that if I should ever forget, then the memories won't be lost forever."

Kimberly sits there motionless before saying, "Wow, I never would have guessed he was so…so noble."

"Yeah, he gives your friends grief because he wants to become the strongest and protect those weaker than him. As for me, I want to make a world where no one is treated badly just because they are a little different."

Kenneth gets up from the table and left to go check on Charles. Devonte looks over to Janet and says, "What about you Janet. Why did you join Atlas?"

"I joined to ensure that this world would one day be safe enough for everything to live in harmony. Both man and beast are precious to me, so I fight those who would threaten them." Janet summons a little pigmy creature; it was fury and purple.

"What is that, and why is it purple?"

"This is one of my pigmies, her name is Zoe. She is the youngest of her litter."

"Litter?" Devonte questions.

"Pigmies are born into a liter usually a really big litter. Females are short and furry while the males are taller and hairless."

"So, where do they come from?"

"They are from the Echo."

"Where is that?"

"It is here on earth, only it's not here. It is a different plane of reality that most people are unaware of. Summons like myself can interact with both planes. But in order to summon a beast you must first tame it. Once it becomes yours you can than transport it between planes."

"Wait, so there are two planes of existence. Then how do they survive on our side?"

"The Echo is earth. Think of it like a reflection. The creatures' breath is like the animals on this side, only they are more unique. Essentially every creature that are considered fake or mythological exists in the Echo."

"I don't believe this. That is mind blowing!"

Janet starts to pet her pigmy on the head, and then she wraps her arms around it tightly and gets up and left the table. Kimberly smiles at Devonte as she gets up and follows Janet out of the Rec. Room. Devonte shrugs his shoulders and gets up and leaves as well.

Inside the Battle Arena, Marcus and Xavier

are in the middle of a training session with Trish. After about forty-five minutes of training, the three decide to take a break. Xavier stands at the corner of the bleachers with a sweat soaked towel draped over his shoulders. Marcus sits next to him with Trish placed firmly on his lap. She wraps her arms around his neck and gives him a soft kiss.

"So…exactly how long have the two of you been dating?" Xavier inquires.

"About two months now," Marcus says as Trish lays her head on his shoulder. "Xavier, I don't know about you, but I am still upset that they didn't tell us about the case. And then Richard is treating it like it was our fault…the nerve of that guy!"

"Adam was telling Trish and I a little about AstroTec. I never really knew this, but they have almost every aspect of science and technology sown up. They are the proprietors of most of the world's known technology. That being said, I take it that the new compound that was in the case was their latest project. Unfortunately, Nova is in possession of the compound. I just hope this won't bring too many problems for us in the future."

Trish leans her head up off Marcus' shoulder and says, "Xavier, I had a chance to read the file on the mysterious case. Scientists at AstroTec found a way to harness this unknown substance that they found while on an expedition in Southeast Asia. When damaged, the substance will replicate cells to restore the damaged area. They were able to isolate the cells and produce this self-replenishing energy compound."

"Ok, I get it. So, when the energy is nearly depleted, it will recharge itself. Tech like that in the wrong hands would amount to incalculable casualties. We have to find some way to neutralize the effects of that compound."

Marcus clears his throat and shakes his head before saying, "Unfortunately, there is nothing we can do about it now."

At Nova HQ, Stargazer walks the hall with a hooded man. They are deep in conversation. As they slowly stalk the halls of Nova HQ, the hooded figure comes to an abrupt stop.

"Are you ready, Cordell?" Stargazer inquired.

Cordell drops his hood; his dark reddish hair was slicked back into a ponytail. He hoists the cane he kept clenched securely in his right hand. His eyes as well as the eyes on the serpent that adorned the head of the cane begin to glow. Slowly, he and Stargazer fade away only to appear in the main chamber.

"What is it?" a voice from within the shadows squawked.

"My lord, we wish to speak with you regarding our latest acquisition. Stargazer and I feel that it would benefit us greatly to turn the case over to more…capable hands."

"Speak clearly, Cordell. Who is more capable to understand this compound if not Hardwyre?"

"You misunderstand me Lord Quake. I am not speaking in a lack of faith of our illustrious, free spirited, and somewhat outspoken scientist. I merely mean to provide you with an advantage over Atlas."

"What did you have in mind my old friend?"

"Why not turn the case and its contents over to the highest bidder? Stargazer has found a suitable candidate. And in exchange they will weaponize its contents and provide us with weapons for your 'accelerated' meta-human armada. With the responsibility of the case belonging to an outside source, this will ensure everyone here is available to help you reach your goal."

"Like always Cordell, you seemed to have planned this out. I am sure you have thought of a contingency just in case our 'allies' try to double cross us?"

"Many times over Lord Quake. Stargazer has personally agreed to oversee the exchange."

"Very well, do as you wish. What are the latest results from Project Acceleration?"

Stargazer steps forward; "My lord, groups A and B have just begun phase 5. Likewise, groups C and D have just begun phase 4."

"Excellent, inform Hardwyre to increase his

efforts in his search. It shouldn't be this hard to find one man!"

"It shall be done my lord," Cordell states as he and Stargazer vanish into thin air.

Two days later, Marcus, Devonte, and Xavier wait out in the field behind Atlas HQ. Kimberly, Jessica, and Janet join them. After a few moments, David walks up behind them, in his hands were three folded maps.

"Alright ladies and gentlemen, I have been given orders to oversee this training op as Brick is away on an assignment." David says. "In this routine you will experience what it is like working with another team while in the field. I would like Team Leaders River and Starbolt to step forward please."

Marcus and Kimberly step up and walk towards David. He hands them both a map, the last one he places in his back pocket. On the map are directions to a building.

"Ok, Starbolt, you Plasma and Chaos will work alongside River, ShaXdow, and DaRock to find your way to the building indicated on your maps. This exercise is likening to a race; you six must beat me to this building. To make things fair, I will travel on foot same as you. Figure out how you wish to handle this and good luck," David says as he runs off into the trees.

Marcus takes point by saying, "Alright, we have lost a couple of seconds as it is. Starbolt, any suggestions on how we should handle this?"

"Um…uh I don't know," Kimberly says shyly.

"It's fine I will think of something. Ok quick introductions…go," Marcus, says while pointing to Jessica.

"I'm Plasma and they call Janet, Chaos."

"Ok, I'm River, this is ShaXdow and DaRock. Now for my plan, I say we split into three teams of two. Chaos and I, ShaXdow and Starbolt, and that leaves DaRock and Plasma. If we split up, we can increase the chances of us passing this exercise. We have wasted enough time, so the target is east of us, so everyone should head in that direction."

Marcus and Janet head into the field, while Xavier and Kimberly run into the trees. Devonte and Jessica head down towards the riverbed.

While they run through the field, Marcus takes a glance at Janet. "Do you think we will make it there before Quazar does?"

There was a long awkward silence before Marcus said, "Not much for conversation. You have a point though. We need to keep focus on our task-"

"Given the amount of time we wasted with that 'meet and greet' back there, I say our chances are slim to none." She looks around briefly; "Starbolt and your friend ShaXdow are about a half a mile ahead of us already. Plasma and DaRock are bringing up the rear."

"Wait, how can you tell?"

"I can sense energy…having worked with Plasma and Starbolt for so long I am used to their energy signatures and can pick them up almost instantly."

"Wow, that's a very useful ability. Something like that will come in handy on a mission. So, you are Janet right… Devonte talks about you a lot."

"Interesting, because he doesn't talk about you at all."

Over in the forest, Kimberly and Xavier run through the dense trees.

"ShaXdow, I am worried that we won't make it in time."

"Don't be, River is a pretty good strategist, splitting up is a very logical alternative to traveling in one large group."

"He…he is pretty amazing."

"What, oh yeah." Xavier looks at Kimberly with uncertainty. "I notice the way you act around him. Behavior like that usually stems from a romantic attraction."

"I don't know what it is. I just get so shy around him. He probably thinks I am weird."

"He doesn't., He is a nice guy. You only get the 'jerk' if you piss him off."

"Please Xavier, you got to promise me that

you won't tell anyone about this."

"Don't worry. I won't say anything. But right now, we should probably speed up so that we can make up some time."

"Fair enough, Quazar has more than likely done this a dozen of times. There is no doubt that even though we have him out numbered, we are the ones at a disadvantage."

Xavier and Kimberly increase their speed, while down by the river Devonte and Jessica scurry along. Jessica walks a couple of feet in front of Devonte. Small clouds of dust rise from the ground as he drags his feet along the soil.

"Adios Mios, we will never make it in time. What's the matter with you?"

"I can't believe I lost it!"

"What are you talking about? Lost what?"

"Look, I don't care about this training exercise. I am more worried about where it went."

"Where what went? You are not making sense!"

"Look, I had this really awesome prank I wanted to pull on River. I rigged this old toy I found to explode and cover a person with ice. I had a great plan and everything. Now I can't find the toy."

"Wow! you really need to grow up. You are too old to be pulling pranks."

"You are never too old to have fun, and besides, everyone is so uptight, I was just trying to lighten the mood. You know and have a laugh or two while I do it." Devonte crouches down and gets ready to run. "Hey Plasma…let's have a race…ready-"

Devonte takes off running past Jessica. "What is wrong with him?" she says to herself.

Some time has passed and Xavier and Kimberly emerge from within the trees. They stand riddled with confusion until Marcus and Janet show up behind them. Moments later, Devonte and Jessica walk up behind Xavier. Devonte was soaking wet and was fighting his hardest to avoid eye contact with his teammates.

Marcus motions for everyone to advance towards the structure. Their advance was halted at the sound of a loud thud! Thud after thud the sound gets closer. They all turn around; motionless they stand at the sight of a giant mechanical titan. Everyone prepares to fight when an energy blast collides with the hull of the titan.

It lets out a shriek and then falls over. One by one they turn their heads to see David sitting on top of the building.

"Nice to see you all made it. Due to an unexpected distraction I was delayed. Someone pulled a little practical joke that didn't sit well with Clarence." David turns his attention to Devonte, "You wouldn't know anything about this…would you?"

Devonte looks away in guilt, "Sorry," he says somberly.

David shakes his head then proceeds to point at the mechanical titan. "You all are probably wondering what that was. It is a refurbished titan that we salvaged after a battle with Nova a long time ago. We have since reprogrammed it for this training exercise. The titan is set to deploy unless the necessary codes are put in to shut it down. Only instructors have the shutdown codes."

"So, wait, it only comes out if we win the race," Marcus asks.

"Precisely, it has been set to appear as a signal that you completed the exercise. However, I put it down before you all could attack it because it is easier to replace a circuit board than it is a full twenty-five-foot machine. Due to circumstances, you all were not able to do the exercise as it was designed."

"So how was the exercise supposed to happen?"

"The exercise is at its core a race; however, it is a race that was designed to test your teamwork. Along the way you were supposed to encounter traps, BOTs, and hazards. Each placed strategically in key locations. The exercise would end one of two ways; either you make it to the structure first and trigger the titan, or you lose and get swarmed by a dozen BOTs set to level 6 intensity."

"Ok, I get it now. The exercise was designed

for us to work together as a collective group and overcome all the obstacles. So, can we take another crack at it?" Marcus looks around to the other teammates. "We want to give it another shot, but for real this time."

"Very well, it will have to wait until tomorrow though as the titan needs its repairs. I have to make sure the traps are set and ready to go." David sends everyone back to base to rest up.

Having almost completely dried off Devonte hurries past everyone else in the halls. Devonte constantly peers over his shoulder, paying little attention to where he is going. As he turns around to observe his surroundings he collides with Clarence who stands motionless in the middle of the hallway.

"Where I come from, the village fool was often beaten and tortured. Getting a laugh at another's expense is exceedingly childish. However, I know a thing or two about comedy myself." Clarence taps the tip of his cane on the floor as his eyes begin to glow. "Have you ever heard the one about the boy who couldn't find his way out of a paper bag?" Clarence makes Devonte shrink then places him in a paper bag that he conjures from thin air. Devonte scurries from corner to corner trying his hardest to escape his papery prison.

Three days later, Devonte is bent down on his

knees washing the floor outside of the Council Room. He mumbles to himself as he lathers the floor with soap. Suddenly, he notices a pair of nice designer shoes standing on the wet floor. Devonte's eyes travel up the length of the body until he reaches the man's bright orange sunglasses.

"I see they are putting you to work. Word of advice--- never pull a prank on Clarence. He's a mystic, and they are not known for their sense of humor."

The man opens the door and walks inside making sure to wipe his feet on the way in. He walks around the round table to his seat, three chairs left of the middle seat. Commander Maximus turns his attention to the man who just took his seat.

"Nolan, it's good to have you back."

"It feels good to be back, sir. Unfortunately, I come bearing very distressing news. At my meeting with the Mayor of Chicago, I was informed about their Sadist epidemic."

"The Sadist. I have heard stories about them. None very pleasant," Joyce said from across the table.

"The Sadist has become a regional problem. With the worst of it coming from California," said Rose whose dull pink hair bounced as she speaks.

"Rose has a point, California seems to be heavily Sadist driven." Neim interjects.

Nolan speaks up saying, "Neim you and Rose are correct in your observations; however, the threat in California is contained for the time being, while Chicago is reaching its breaking point. The Mayor is calling for war on the Sadist. Only problem is that the police of Chicago fear the Sadist and don't want to have anything to do with the matter. I suggested a deterrent, we send some operatives to take care of this threat. By doing so we just might be able to save Chicago from destroying itself."

"But what about Nova? We can't afford to let our guard down," Rose interjects.

As he sits back in his chair, Richard says, "Right now our hands are tied, but if we do not act now there might not be a later for Chicago. Lucky for us the Sadist are barbaric and lack one key thing…tact. I think our new operatives are ready to handle a mission like this. This way we keep our elite operative free incase Nova does try anything."

"Richard makes a good point. It's best we use our assets to their full potential. Commander, the mayor requests an answer by tomorrow." Nolan says in accordance to Richard's statement.

Commander Maximus responded by saying, "Very well, inform him that we will personally handle this Sadist threat. David, I want you to-"

He is interrupted by a loud thud that rang out from the other side of the door. David gets up from his seat and slowly walks to the door. Upon opening the door, Devonte falls into the room. He hastily gets to his knees and looks on as the council gives him an uneasy glare.

"Devonte, please tell me you were not eaves dropping on confidential council business?"

"Sorry about that David. I just wanted to know what was going on."

"Fair enough Devonte, but this is a private matter. The point of the council is to discuss the issues and problems going on in our region. Once we have deliberated and delegated the matters at hand then we share it with the rest of you.

"Wait, what do you mean by 'delegated'?"

"Once we understand a situation, we come to an agreement on who would be best suited to handle the task. Whether that be an Operative or Solider unit."

"So, have you guys picked a team for this mission yet?"

"Not at the moment Devonte-"

"Why not us!" Devonte abruptly states. "We can handle it…we can take those chumps down no problem."

"Really, because I seem to remember you all having trouble with just one man," Richard said from across the room.

"Well that time was different. Besides, we weren't ready for that fight. But we are ready for this one. David please, we won't let you down this time."

"You boys have yet to let me down, but unfortunately this is not my decision to make. But you three definitely get my vote… anyone else?" David asks as he turns his attention back to the rest of the council.

Everyone's hands raise up toward the ceiling. All except Richard who sits there with his arms folded across his chest.

"Know this, we need this situation handled correctly. There is very little room for error-"

"Sir just make sure we have all of the details before we go into the mission," Devonte says with arrogance. "We will take care of it…I promise there is nothing to worry about."

"Watch it boy, that mouth of yours will get you into a lot of trouble. Nevertheless, the decision is unanimous. However, I like to move toward the notion of sending a second unit. A situation as dire as this is much too important for one unit of rookie operatives."

Commander Maximus stands up, "Very well, the Sadist threat in Chicago will be handled by unit 407, led by River as well as unit 718 lead by Solara. Inform the rest of your teammates and we will contact unit 718. Report to the briefing room in the morning. Next time Devonte, you need to use better judgment in the way you voice your opinion. Like Richard said watch what you say as there could be repercussions. This time we will excuse it… now go on and get your rest, you have a big day tomorrow."

"Will do, Commander!"

Chapter 9

Blood Feud

The following morning, Marcus and Trish are walking together down the hall towards the briefing room. They meet up with Xavier, Devonte, Charles, and Kenny, who were waiting outside the briefing room.

Marcus addresses the group, "Are we ready to go?" he asks.

"I'm sorry, are we ready? I seem to remember standing here for almost a full five minutes waiting for the two of you. So, I guess a better question would be are you ready to go?" Charles states arrogantly.

"My apologies, Charlie, tell you what, save some of that fiery spirit for the mission. And hey, if you make it back in one piece maybe you can help me work on being more punctual."

"Bite me, Marcus!"

Marcus steps forward and gets in Charles's face. The tension between them becomes high when Trish steps in between them. Using all of her might, she forces them apart.

"Enough, Marcus don't get yourself upset. You need to keep a level head if we are going to succeed today. And Charlie, just this once could you try not being an obnoxious prick. Now let's go. We have wasted enough time already!" She puts in her code and opens the door to the briefing room. They gather around the computer as David accesses the Grid. He sets coordinates to Chicago, Illinois. He magnifies enough to where everyone now sees a digital recreation of the entire city.

"Nolan was informed by the Mayor of Chicago that the Sadist have grown to be a very serious threat. Your mission is to stop all the major Sadist activity within the city. I can assure you that this will not be easy. Unlike Nova, the Sadist seem to court chaos in a manner that is reckless and untamed. They will not hesitate to involve the innocent if it means getting what they want."

"David, where did these guys come from?" Marcus asked. "I have never heard about a group called Sadist."

"It surprises me to hear you say that, the

Sadist have been around for quite a few decades now. It is a wide spread problem throughout North America."

"Really?"

"Yes, the Sadist is a gang, one that like us contains only meta-humans. They have been spreading violence and madness for a long time now. They show no compassion to anyone, and if given the chance will kill you."

"So, we won't give them a chance then," Marcus states.

"Not that they had a chance to begin with," Charles says. "I don't care how scary they claim to be. I'll beat them all without breaking a sweat."

"Such confidence. You need to watch your ego, Charlie," David responds.

"Come-on, you are the great Quazar! According to your reputation, you are virtually unbeatable. Well, I am here to relieve you of such a heavy burden. Sadist is nothing more than dust under my boot!"

"God, would you shut up, Charlie!" Marcus proclaims.

"Alright that's enough, back to the matter at hand. Nolan says that Chicago is on the verge of destabilization. You six are the only thing standing between Chicago's future and its destruction! With that being said, get to the Hanger, and good luck."

Inside the Hanger, Nolan stands patiently on the ramp of an STC. Scott walks up to him and the two gentlemen exchange greetings. Nolan gestures with his head, Scott turns his attention behind him. Teams 407 and 718 walk up to the STC.

"Good to see you again, Scott," Marcus states.

"Boys, it's good to see you as well."

Everyone climbs aboard the STC and Scott starts the engine as everyone takes their seats. Once the STC is airborne, Nolan pulls out a tablet and places it on his lap. For minutes, he scrolls through log after log on his tablet. Finally, he comes to his log on the Sadist. He taps the touch screen twice to open the file.

"I have no doubt Quazar has already informed you all about the Sadist," Nolan says as he scrolls the page on his tablet. "Well, it seems they aren't wasting any time. There were just reports of Sadist activity in Lincoln Park, as well as the court house."

Marcus looks over to Trish, "Well Solara, do you have any suggestions?"

"My team and I are at your disposal, River. We will do whatever needs to be done to help complete this mission."

"Right," Marcus says without conviction. "I want you and your team to make sure Nolan gets to City Hall safely. I am going to send ShaXdow and DaRock to deal with the situation at the courthouse while I handle the problem in Lincoln Park. Solara, when you and your team finish, I want you all to rendezvous with us."

Marcus sits there in his chair, his body as stiff as a board. Nolan calls out to him to get his attention. "You seem nervous."

"I am trying to reassure myself that my plan is going to work."

"This is only your second mission, if I am correct. Being put in charge of a group is not as easy as some make it seem. Your judgment affects those around you, especially those that follow you. Anxiety is natural, but you must not doubt yourself. If this is how you decide to deal with the problem, then trust in your allies. Trust that they can successfully carry out your orders, and they will in turn trust you."

"But Nolan, the fate of an entire city rests on the shoulders of my plan. If it doesn't work, then the city is lost!"

"Don't worry, I have the upmost faith in you. You will do just fine."

The STC steadily hovers above Chicago. Marcus gets up and walks to the back hatch. The STC floats above a building exactly two blocks from Lincoln Park. The rear of the STC opens, Marcus gets nudged from side to side by the wind. "Good luck, guys. Radio in when you have completed your mission. Scott, I am going to need some eyes in the sky."

"Roger that. Watch your back out there."

Marcus chuckles to himself before jumping out onto the roof of the building. Once he is settled, he signals for Scott to pull off. When the STC is out of range, Marcus turns his attention to the park. He kneels at the edge of the building to survey the area.

He rises to his feet; he takes in a deep breath, then exhales slowly. As he breathes out, there was an explosion amidst the trees down at the park. The sudden combustion makes his body jump. *No time to waste*, he thinks as he cracks his knuckles.

Back on the STC, Trish is looking over the info on Nolan's tablet. She looks over to Xavier who had his eyes closed deep in thought. She calls out to him, his eyes abruptly open.

"Ok ShaXdow, you and DaRock are next so get ready. It says here that the police have sent in a SWAT unit to attempt to control the situation at the courthouse. You two need to lend them a hand however possible."

"No problem. About how many Sadist are we talking about?"

"There has only been reports of two…likewise there is just one back in Lincoln Park."

"Something about this doesn't seem right."

"I agree. You two better stay alert. Once Blaze, Storm, and I have escorted Nolan to the meeting with the Mayor at City Hall we will give you guys some assistance."

The STC is lowered to just above street level. Xavier nods his head towards Nolan and Trish as he stands up and heads for the exit. As Devonte stands up, he grabs his board and cups it loosely to his side. Charles blurts out, "Good luck DaRock, time to see what you boys are really made of!"

Devonte keeps walking as he replies, "Shut up Blaze!"

They exit the STC, it wastes no time taking off. Xavier and Devonte run towards an overturned SWAT trucks; they rest their backs on its cold frame. The padding of their armor makes a slight thud as it contacts the truck. Xavier peers his head out from around the truck. He steps from behind the truck; Devonte follows closely. Xavier notices an injured officer who was crawling towards them.

Cautiously, Xavier walks up to the man and lifts him up. Immediately, Xavier notices the wound to the officer's side. Xavier helps him over to the truck and sits him next to Devonte. Xavier pulls off the officer's vest to alleviate some of the pressure.

"Sir...sir stay with me," Xavier shouts as he holds onto the officer's shoulder.

The officer coughs twice; he raises his hand and takes hold to Xavier's arm. "Who are you guys?"

"It's ok sir, we are here to help."

"My...my men, inside the courthouse...they took my men into the courthouse." The officer tries to stand but collapses back down to the ground. Xavier sits the officer upright and lays him up against the truck. "You guys are kids…it's too dangerous for you to be here!"

"Believe me sir, we are not kids-"

"DaRock, that's enough. Just sit tight sir we will handle the rest from here."

Xavier and Devonte head towards the courthouse entrance. As Xavier goes to open the door, something catches his attention. He turns his head around and peers out into the street.

"What's up?" Devonte questions.

Xavier cautiously walks towards the street. "Just wait there, I thought I heard something." Once in the street, Xavier glances left then right. His mind is riddled with confusion. "Maybe it was nothing-"

Xavier hastily turns his attention to across the street. Two men emerge from the shadows of a nearby alley.

The one in front was about six foot with defined cuts and a chiseled chin. His skin, tan in color was glistening from slight perspiration. His clothes tattered and stained with blood. He slowly starts to massage his knuckles, his gaze locked on Xavier.

"Well what do we have here? You two must be lost. This city belongs to me, and I don't take kindly to unwelcomed guests. So why don't you kids run along home."

"As if you were really going to let us just walk out of here," Xavier proclaims firmly.

"Wow, so you must be the smart one. I like you kid... what's your name?"

"We are here to take back this city!"

"First, you show up unannounced, then you rudely ignore my question, and now you want to take what belongs to me. I was wrong; I don't like you that much anymore. Brad, can you please school these two young bloods on how we the Sadist deal with things we don't like."

Brad removes the sledgehammer from off his shoulder; he hoists it into the air and slams it down onto the roof of a nearby car. "We hit it until it bleeds." His large husky body was enough to cast a shadow on his friend. "Hayden has extended you an offer, yet you spit on his generosity. By the look of your clothes, I can see that you work for Atlas. Seems as though they are recruiting them younger every year.

Xavier and Devonte become tense. Hayden snaps his finger, sending Brad stampeding right at them. Xavier waits for the right moment to roll out of the way of Brad's sledgehammer. He rolls right into Hayden, who looked extremely displeased. Hayden swipes at Xavier, who rolls left out of harm's way.

As Brad approaches him, Devonte hops on his skateboard and moves out of the way. He rides a few meters down the street with his guns now held firmly in his hands. At the last minute, Devonte turns around to face Brad, but is knocked from off his board. The hit from the sledgehammer sends him flying and into a car door.

During the commotion, Devonte manages to drop his guns. Brad steps on Devonte's skateboard snapping it in half under his foot. With his hands wrapped tightly around the sledgehammer, Brad takes a giant swing. The attack comes with such force that Devonte narrowly avoided it. He takes another swing landing a hit right on Devonte's chest. The force lifts him up off his feet and into the air.

Hayden transforms his right arm into a blade and stabs at Xavier. Xavier rolls backwards, and when he comes to a stop, he unsheathes his sword. The two-clash steel again and again. Hayden comes down hard with a forceful swing.

Xavier falls to one knee as he blocks the attack. He struggles to stand upright as Hayden begins to apply more pressure. Finally, Xavier pushes Hayden off and then hits him with a roundhouse kick to the chin.

Devonte runs down the street with Brad hot on his trail. With one swing of his sledgehammer, Brad catches Devonte in the side and launches him into the door of a taxi. Brad stalks Devonte before taking another swing. Devonte freezes the water vapor around his hands and forms boxing gloves. He crosses his arms and blocks Brad's sledgehammer. As Brad goes for another attack, Devonte rolls out of the way. When he gets to his feet, he starts to punch Brad repeatedly in the chest.

After five hits, Brad stands motionless as his body starts to absorb the blows. "My body absorbs all forms of energy." A shimmer of light danced atop Brad's body. "You and I are the next stage of evolution. It is us who should rule this world. It's a shame you chose to fight for the weak rather than against it." Brad lunges forward and punches Devonte in the face.

Xavier continues to clash steel with Hayden. While they fight, Hayden transforms his other arm into a chain and wraps it around Xavier's leg. With one well-placed tug, Hayden causes Xavier to fall. Hayden takes advantage of the opportunity and tries to stab Xavier. At the last minute, Xavier clasps his hands together catching the blade between his palms.

"Not bad. You have a lot of fight in you...I like that. You know you boys have it all wrong. We are not doing anything bad, we are simply getting rid of the real problem. Humans...those weak sacks of flesh we call 'brothers'. Humans run the world because we stand by and do nothing. Well not anymore, meta-humans were meant to rule this world."

"You can't honestly believe that. There is meant to be a balance...harmony between them and us. Just because we have powers doesn't give us the right to rule!"

"You are so naive boy, humanity doesn't see

us as equals. To them we are nothing more than animals. Do you know what happens to an animal when it is threatened?"

"No, but I know what happens when you send an electrical charge through metal," Xavier says as he electrocutes Hayden.

As Hayden falls to the ground, Xavier gets to his feet and sees Devonte and Brad fighting across the street. Xavier picks up his sword and rushes across the street. As he gets closer, he throws a series of lightning kunai at Brad. They collide with his back and explode on contact. Brad then turns his attention to Xavier.

"And what was that supposed to be?"

"A distraction," Devonte shouts as he lands a giant right hook on Brad. The impact was so forceful that the ice shatters on contact.

As Brad stumbles backward, Xavier vaults over him and lands next to Devonte. Brad shuffles over to Hayden who just recovered from his shock.

"Screw this! No use blowing the whole plan in a fight with them. Get to the L and secure us a train." Brad nods to Hayden in compliance. They take off running back into the alley where they disappear into the darkness.

Xavier hands Devonte his guns from off the ground.

"That's right you better run! That freak broke my skateboard! It was my favorite one too. What do we do now?"

Xavier pulls out a small cubed shaped device. He stares hard into the screen, "We divide and conquer," he says while pressing a button on the device. "Great I can see the STC, backup will be here shortly."

Meanwhile back in Lincoln Park, Marcus has approached the perimeter of the park. He watches as fire engulfs a portion of the trees, and the sound of people screaming rings out through the air. With hesitation, Marcus puts his hand up to the flame.

Realizing that the fire has no ill effect on him, Marcus jumps through to the other side. He lands next to a bus. Cautiously, he walks out from behind the bus into the opening. He jumps back behind the bus to avoid an oncoming fire blast. The heat was so intense that it melts a portion of the bus.

Marcus takes a deep breath, then jumps back out into the open. Much to his surprise there was no one in sight apart from a group of people trapped on the bus. Marcus tries to force open the doors of the bus when another fire blast went off and slams his body into the bus.

"Tell me something, how does it feel to know that you never stood a chance?" A voice echoes through the trees. "How do you intend to fight what you can't see?"

With mere seconds to spare, Marcus rolls out of the way of another fire blast. *Where is this fire coming from? It's as if it appears out of thin air*, Marcus thinks to himself as he runs away from an oncoming fire blast.

"Pyro-kinesis is my weapon of choice. With this I can play sniper and take people out without having to get my hands dirty. I use the echo from the trees to make it harder to pinpoint my location. So, you might as well just lie down and die, because there is no one who can stop the Sadist!"

Another fire blast ignites and lifts Marcus up off the ground and propels him through the air. *This would be easier to handle if I could tell when the fire was going to start. Wait a minute, that's it*! Marcus concentrates and activates his inferred vision. The air in front of him rapidly heats up until a fire ignites.

Having seen it coming Marcus has enough time to avoid the blast. *Just like I thought, I can see the blast with my inferred vision. Now time to find our mystery pyromaniac*. Marcus scans the park for his attacker while at the same time dodging more fire blast.

In the distance, he can see a shimmer of heat condensed in the bushes. As Marcus runs towards the bushes he pulls out one half of his blade and flings it through the air. Propelled by fire the blade cuts through the air at immense speeds.

The blade gets lodged in a tree directly behind

the young man in the bushes. He turns his attention to the blade in astonishment. When he turns back around Marcus is standing over him. The young man attempts to summon another fire blast, but Marcus tightly grips his face. With his strength, Marcus lifts the boy off the ground and to his feet. Just as Marcus releases his face, the boy tries to attack Marcus. In mid-swing the boy's fist is caught, and he is thrown from the bushes.

While on one knee, the boy ignites one last fire blast. Marcus aided by his powers, rushes forward. Having jumped through the center of the fire blast, Marcus slams his knee into the boy's chin, followed by a hard elbow to the top of the skull.

As the boy lay unconscious on the dirt, Marcus retrieves his blade from within the tree. He makes his way back to the bus, where with all his might he tries to open the doors. He yells for the people to head to the back of the bus. Marcus places his hand firmly against the glass at which point he super heats the glass causing it to shatter.

With the glass removed, he can pry the doors open.

One by one, the passengers cautiously exit the bus.

By this point the ring of fire that surrounded the park had almost completely vanished. The passengers console one another as Marcus starts to walk away. There was a tug at his pants leg; Marcus turns to see what it is. A little child stands there with a handful of Marcus' pants.

"Hey mister, are you a superhero?" he asks as he releases the pants.

Marcus turns around and kneels until he is face to face with the child. "No buddy, I am not a superhero. I am a regular person like you, I just stand up to bullies like him."

"But you have powers, and my mommy says that I should stay away from people with powers."

Just then, the boy's mother frantically snatches him away from Marcus. "Stay away from this man, Corey. He is very dangerous."

"Ma'am with all due respect I just saved your life...I'm the good guy!"

"More like you were trying to save yourself. I know a cover up when I see one. How do we know that you two weren't working together and this is all a part of your plan!"

"Ma'am, do you hear yourself?"

"You meta-humans are all the same. You think just because you have powers you can do whatever you want. Why don't you all go back to wherever it is that you came from!"

"Go back where! I am as much a human as you are. I was just born different. Cut me, I bleed just like everyone else."

"Someone should bring back the M.R.A. because this is ridiculous. You're all just a bunch of barbaric, narcissistic, simple-minded people, and most of you are just a threat to our society!"

Marcus starts to grow increasingly upset, "What the heck is your problem, lady? I've had teammates put their lives on the line, and step blindly in the face of danger. All so that people like you can sleep soundly at night. Now I can't excuse the actions of others but let me make this real clear for you! I am not like him!

I use my powers to protect and defend. I fight so that kids like Corey won't have to live in fear of meta-humans. So, can you please do me a favor; help me help you. Keep your negative comments where they belong, locked up tight in that pretty little head of yours. While I continue to do the one thing you are unable to do...fight!"

Without saying a word, the woman turns and storms off with Corey in hand. The boy tries to wave goodbye to Marcus but is unsuccessful due to parental interference.

Marcus shakes off his frustration and turns his attention back to his foe when he realizes that he has escaped. Marcus frantically pans the park; there was a rustle in the bushes. He ignites his hand when out walks Trish; relieved, Marcus turns off his fire.

"Solara, did you deliver Nolan to City Hall?"

"Everything went just as planned. I sent Blaze and Storm to help ShaXdow. What happened here?"

"Some punk kid was holding that bus of

people hostage… seemingly for no reason."

"No, there was a reason. It was a trap. They were trying to lure in anyone foolish enough to make a rescue attempt. Then they would kill them and the civilians. I guess they weren't expecting you to foil their plans."

"Yeah well, he got away."

Trish places her hand on Marcus' cheek. "What's the matter, you seem upset?"

"It's nothing."

Just then, Marcus gets a call on his communicator.

"Roger…ok we will meet you down there." He takes his hand off the receiver. "That was ShaXdow. He managed to slip a tracer onto one of the Sadist. The signal is coming from down in the subway. Blaze, Storm, and DaRock are securing the civilians and ShaXdow wants us to meet him down in the subway."

Down in the subway, Marcus and Trish run down the steps onto the platform. "Where is ShaXdow?" Marcus asks.

"Up here," Xavier says as he drops from the darkness of the ceiling.

"How long have you been down here?"

"Long enough. You guys made it just in time. The signal is approaching fast. My guess it's probably on a train."

"So, how do you suppose we get onto a speeding train?"

"Simple. We make it stop," Xavier says as he points down to the third rail.

As the train approaches the platform, Xavier bends down and extends his hands towards the rail. Electricity from the rail ascended and into Xavier's palms. After about ten seconds, the rail was completely drained. Xavier, Marcus, and Trish hide in the corner of the platform.

Moments later, the train comes to a screeching halt parallel to the platform. As one of the doors open, Xavier, Marcus, and Trish sneak unto the last car. Out of the door storms Brad. He looks left, then right. He motions for his followers to check the surrounding area. Just as they exit the train, the doors close. Brad manages to get back onboard before they close. Within seconds, the train starts to move.

On the last car, the three manage to get inside. The otherwise unoccupied car was dimly lit and full of crates, most of which were blocking the exit doors.

"Nicely done, ShaXdow. We need to get up to the conductor's car, so we can stop this train," Marcus states.

"We should be coming up to the surface any minute now," Trish interjects.

"How do you know that?"

"I told you I moved around a lot as a kid. My

family lived here for three brief months."

"Right, ShaXdow, do you think you can get on top of the train and sneak up to the first car? Solara and I will hold off the Sadist in the meantime."

Xavier nods in agreement. Once they reach the surface, the bright rays of sunshine illuminate the entire car. Marcus nods to Xavier to make his advance, at which time Xavier opens the door and climbs up to top of the roof.

Marcus and Trish move steadily to the next car. Through the window in the door, Marcus can see that this car was full of people.

"Ok, I see about two dozen civilians as well as two Sadists, one of which being that punk from Lincoln Park."

"There are too many innocent people onboard to try and fight Sadist. What do we do then?" Trish questions.

Marcus looks out into the distance, "Instead of trying to move all two-dozen people, we should isolate them. We will have to cut these last cars off from the rest of the train."

"What about ShaXdow?"

"He will be fine. If anyone can stop this train it's him. Now, I am going to head to the other side. While I do that, I need you to get in there and keep their attention." Marcus can see that Trish is nervous. "Don't worry, I will be just on the other side of those doors." Marcus leans in and places a warm kiss on Trish's forehead before he climbs to the top of that car.

Trish opens the door and proceeds into the car without any hesitation. Brad turns around towards her. As he steps forward, Trish catches a glimpse of the second Sadist member tucked away behind Brad's heftiness.

"Thomas!" Her eyes open wide in disbelief.

Outside, Marcus reaches the end of the car. He slowly gets down; once he reaches the bottom, he starts to heat up the connection rig. In a matter of seconds, the heat melts right through the metal. As the cars separate, Marcus looks up ahead to Xavier who was knelt on the top of the one of the cars. Xavier turns back to look when he sees Marcus fading into the distance. Both men nod their heads in acknowledgement of what must be done.

Back inside, Trish stands motionless as Thomas pushes his way past Brad. Clasped tightly in each hand, Thomas holds onto a set of katars. He lifts one up to the throat of an extremely frightened civilian.

"I don't believe it. They let you out of that crazy house. That's assuming you even went in the first place!" Thomas snaps whimsically.

"Thomas, how did you end up back in Chicago? We were all worried sick!"

"Obviously not all that much that no one ever

found me!"

"What are you talking about? Mom and dad were heartbroken. I was heartbroken. Thomas, why would you run away like that?"

"I left because I got tired of the constant moving. I never had any real friends for longer than a couple of months. Mom and Dad were selfish; they were so caught up in work that they were neglecting us, their own kids! And don't you dare say that's not the truth!"

"But why come here and join Sadist?"

"Hayden took me in and gave me a stable home. I have friends, purpose, and power! Being with Sadist I can do whatever I want."

Just then Marcus enters from the other side causing Thomas and Brad to turn their heads towards him. "You," Thomas says in rage!

Brad takes a glance past Marcus and becomes furious at the realization that they had now been separated from the rest of the train set in.

"Hey, tough guy, let me ask you a question. Is severe depression a prerequisite to joining Atlas?" Thomas sadistically questions.

"Wait, how do you know about that? You had already runaway by then," Trish says emotionally.

"Trust me, Trish, I am well informed as to everything that happed after I left. It's sad really…I actually liked Kat-"

Before he could finish Trish turns her arm into

a vine and wraps it tightly around his neck. With little thought, Thomas cuts the vine and stares hard at Trish. Realizing what was about to happen, Marcus charges forward pushing Brad into Thomas. Suddenly, a fire blast went off on the ceiling, causing mass panic among the civilians.

Having fallen to the floor, Trish pans around the car at the civilians as they shriek in fear. A man cries out, "I don't want to die," as the fire spreads. Marcus gets to his feet; he directs his attention to the fire above him.

Brad and Thomas get up, Brad rushes Marcus, lifting him into the air and running to the end of the car at which time he slams him down hard on the edge. Brad attempts to push Marcus' head down onto the third rail. Marcus manages to let off one fire blast that struck Brad in the chest.

"My body can absorb all matter of energy," Brad chuckles. Marcus sees a platform approaching fast. He throws his arms up and locks his grip on Brad's collar. "Your body can absorb all kinds of energy. Thanks for the tip," Marcus says as he uses all of his might to throw Brad out of the car and onto the tracks.

As Brad's body bounces along the metal rods it absorbs all the electrical energy from the railing, causing the train to slowly lose speed, as it got closer to the platform.

Thomas gets ready to attack one of the

civilians when Trish tackles him to the ground. She places her hands firmly on the floor of the train. Moments later, a human-like structure started to ascend from the floor. She commands the husk to open the doors for the civilians. Forcefully it pries the doors open, and one by one the passengers run out onto the platform. Trish could no longer hold Thomas down as he pushes her from on top of him. By this point, Marcus was out on the platform directing the civilians down the stairs.

As Thomas rises to his feet, he sets off a fire blast that sends Trish flying backward. Her back collides with the door; she sits there dazed.

Thomas stares hard at her, his heart filled confliction. He turns around to leave when he runs face first into the husk. It grabs Thomas firmly by the shoulders before he could lift his arms. Without hesitation, it lands a head butt knocking Thomas unconscious.

As Thomas' body goes limp, the husk crumbles to the floor. Trish wakes up to the sight of Marcus standing over her. He helps her up; she looks above his head at the ceiling, which was no longer on fire.

"It's ok, I took care of it. Now come on we need to get you out of here." There was no response from Trish.

Meanwhile, Xavier sits perched on the speeding train car. He opens the door and immediately ducks. His attacker was a dark-skinned female. She swings a chain wildly, causing Xavier to back away. With his back resting on the wall, Xavier notices two wires coming from the main control terminal.

"What are you guys after," Xavier asks as he catches the steel chain.

"The people of this city are becoming too complacent. They need a reminder as to who really holds all of the cards."

"The city doesn't belong to the Sadist, it belongs to the people. Our powers are a gift not a weapon to be used to destroy the foundation of man. You should be using them to help people rather than terrorizing them."

"Sadist will bring back prestige to the title meta-human. All who stand in our way will die, and that goes double for you clowns!"

The girl screams at Xavier. The supersonic vibration left Xavier in a momentary state of paralysis.

"See what happens when you try to save everybody! When this train reaches its last stop, I will leave it, and when the time is right I will blow it up, blowing you up and each and every one of those weaklings as well!"

"I see, you all mean to go all the way. It's a

shame; with such determination you would have made a great member of Atlas. However, this is where you get off."

Xavier shakes off the paralysis and rushes at her. She swings the chain one last time. With precision, Xavier catches it while in motion, wraps it around her arm, and then pulls her arm around her face. With her mouth cupped in her arm, the girl is unable to use her sonic scream. Xavier peers outside and sees that they are over water. He escorts her closer to the door.

"I understand that you and I do not share the same view on humanity. I am fighting to change that. I hope someday you will see the light and realize that there are other ways to get what you desire."

Xavier pushes her out of the train into the water below. He walks up to the controls, taking a long look at the wires that ran from the terminal to a crate on the floor. Xavier removes the lid to the crate. *Man, she wasn't playing around. There are a lot of explosives here, and I don't know how to defuse a bomb. Not to mention, I am running out of time. I guess I must overload the circuit and ignite the bomb before it reaches the station.*

Xavier sees the station approaching in the distance. He takes a deep breath when the roar of an engine interrupts him. Outside flying right above the train was the STC. Scott descends and proceeds to turn the rear of the STC towards the train. Xavier watches as the hatch opens.

"What are you waiting for, we got to go!" Marcus yells as he hangs his upper body out of the STC.

"I have to stop this train before it reaches the station, or a lot of people are going to get hurt!"

"What are you talking about?"

"This train is rigged to blow once it reaches the station. I must blow it prematurely. It is our only shot."

"How are you going to get off the train?"

"Trust me River, I have been working on a new ability. It seems as good a time to test it as ever."

"Are you nuts. Don't risk it. We will find another way to stop the train!"

Xavier doesn't respond, and instead he gives Marcus a thumbs-up. He turns his attention to the control panel. Bolt after bolt, Xavier strike the panel with lightning. Sensing he only has seconds to spare, Xavier turns around and breaks into a run towards the door. On his last step his body disperses into electrical energy then reforms on the hatch in front of Marcus.

The sudden appearance startles Marcus, who grabs Xavier before he falls out of the STC.

"Scott, take us home," Marcus shouts!

As the STC ascends skyward the train explodes, the shockwave nearly flips the STC upside down.

"That was too close," Marcus says as he helps Xavier off the floor.

"Well, how did we do?" Xavier asks.

From the other side of the STC Nolan interjects, "We managed to save Chicago from more unnecessary bloodshed. The mayor plans to make some modifications to the city's law enforcement. We also managed to locate and apprehend a good number of the Sadist. Enough to ensure Chicago won't have any severe problems from them any time soon. The Sadist are currently being transferred to the Baldwin Correctional Institute."

"Wait, Shift mentioned that before. What is the Baldwin Correctional Institute?" Xavier asks.

Before Nolan had a chance to answer, Trish speaks out and says, "It's a holding facility for meta-humans. It's where they put you if you commit a crime or have a mental illness."

"That's right, the BCI was first opened about forty-five years ago and has housed over five thousand meta-humans in just the last decade alone. Atlas are responsible for over two thirds of their inmates. Although it spawned from rough beginnings, the BCI has come to be one of the greatest assets to Atlas."

After a while, the STC was landing in the hanger. Scott pulls the lever and releases the back hatch. Nolan is the first person to exit, followed by Trish, Charles, and Kenny. Devonte leans back in his chair and lets out a sigh of relief.

"That was awesome! We kicked so many butts today. Those guys didn't know what hit them. When they looked left we went right! Ahh…I love this team!"

"Someone seems excited," Scott says in humor.

"It's more than excitement, Scott, it's ammunition! They said we couldn't handle this mission. I said we could! I'm right. They're wrong and I can't wait to rub it in their face!"

"I wouldn't recommend that. You guys did a good job, but always remember to be humble. Never forget that things could have just as easily gone horribly wrong."

"Wow, Scott, you are better at killing my vibe than Xavier is," Devonte says as he gets up and leaves the STC.

Scott looks at Marcus and Xavier as they shake their head in uncertainty. They head inside to their rooms while Nolan goes over the results of the mission with the Council.

Chapter 10

Redemption

Early the next morning, Marcus is up before dawn. He spends some time sitting at the edge of his bed reminiscing on his confrontation in Lincoln Park the previous afternoon. After about thirty minutes, he gets cleaned up and heads to Trish's room.

After a series of knocks at her door, he realizes she is not there. Immediately, he heads out to the garden where he finds her lying in pile of daises. He calmly walks over to her and sits down next to her. Moments later, she wakes up and sits upright next to him.

"I guess I am not the only one who had trouble sleeping," Marcus says softly. "I had a pretty rough time on the mission yesterday. There are two things that keep eating away at me. The first is the conversation I had with that obnoxious lady back in Lincoln Park. The second was whether or not you were ok."

"I'm still a little shaky, I guess it hasn't set in yet. You know…daises used to make him smile when he was little. Believe it or not I have had my powers for a long time now. Whenever he would get sad, I would sprout him a daisy. It seems like our family's constant uprooting affected him the most."

"There is not much I can say here, but what I can say is that it's not your fault. Sometimes certain things need to happen for you to be who you were destined to be."

"Like, Kat?"

"Who's Kat?"

"She was my best friend in the whole world. We met in high school and were inseparable. Kat was always the voice of reason between the two of us. She had a knack for getting me out of trouble."

"Well, what happened to her?"

Trish takes a long pause. Her eyes become watery as she fights back tears. "After high school, Kat and I were supposed to move into an apartment together. But…she died in a car accident. It was hard you know…it took me a long time to get over it. I guess you can say I am still not fully over it."

"I am sorry to hear that. At least your family was there to help you get through it, right?"

"Help me through it...no they treated me like some freak. They tried to have me institutionalized at the BCI, but I ran away before they could. Do you know the BCI literally hunted me like a dog?"

"I guess that explains how you knew about them already-"

"I just barely got away from them. Then after that I heard about this place, so I guess the rest is history."

Marcus cradles Trish in his arms. He sits there with her for hours. It was about noon when he finally leaves the garden. On his way to the Battle Arena, Richard stops him. Richard escorts Marcus to the Briefing Room where Xavier and Devonte were already waiting for him.

Richard takes a seat in the corner and gives David the signal to proceed. David pulls up a small town on the Grid. Mercy Gardens was a small town that sits just south of Chicago. David plays back a short audio feed of some transmissions received from Mercy Gardens. The sound of citizens in terror made the boys cringe.

"This was recorded late last night at around eleven. It was recorded via cell phone as Sadist was attacking people. I would say you boys made quite the statement yesterday. This attack was meant to get our attention. There were some photos taken from the scene, but none matters as much as this one."

David shows them a picture that was taken of

the side of a building. There was writing plastered on top of the cement. 'You took what was ours, now we will take what's theirs.'

"We are sending you in to finish what you started yesterday in Chicago. Find them and stop them at all cost. This time we will have a unit of troops on stand-by just in case you need them." Richard stands to his feet and walks over to the Grid. He leans his head over the table avoiding eye contact with everyone.

"Despite my apprehensions, you boys are proving to be very valuable assets. Survive this mission and you will have won my full trust. Now let's not waste any more time, get to the hanger on the double."

As they approach Mercy Gardens, they are met by thick black smoke. Buildings were on fire, vandalized, the streets littered with broken glass and debris. The STC slowly descends onto the street. Before Scott opens the hatch, he reassures them that he would keep a watchful eye from the sky.

Moments later, the hatch opens, and the boys exit the STC. They wait next to an overturned car as the STC pulls off. Cautiously, they trek through the streets looking for any sign of life. Much to their dismay, it would appear that no one was around.

"The more we do this, the worst the world

looks to me," Marcus states as he stares into what used to be a barbershop. "We need some kind of clue, but there is nothing here!"

Without warning, a streetlight behind them explodes and the pole topples over. Devonte steps out of the way of the pole as it collides with the sidewalk.

"What was that!" he shouts at Marcus.

"I don't know kid, maybe we-"

"Watch out!" Xavier yells as he tackles Marcus to the ground. A blade like energy projectile cuts through the air at great speeds. Xavier peers up into the distance where he can see the feint shimmer of a person standing behind a blazing fire.

"Sadist?" Marcus asks.

"I'm assuming, come on we have to catch him," Xavier proclaims as he takes off running toward the fire.

Two more energy blades flew from within the fire. Xavier avoids them and responds with two lightning kunai of his own. This retaliation causes their mystery attacker to take off into a full sprint down the alley. With Team 407 hot on his trail, the assailant expertly vaults over everything in his path without losing any momentum.

Devonte uses his ice to propel himself forward up over everything in the alley in the direction of their target. He lands right behind him and attempts to garb the man before he could scale a nearby fire escape. Devonte misses and lands on the ground where he tucks and rolls to protect himself from harm.

Marcus forces fire from the soles of his feet and launches skyward towards the fire escape. He also tries to grab ahold of the man but misses and grabs the railing. He watches as the man reaches the roof and takes off running with Xavier in pursuit.

The man rapidly approaches the edge of the building, and without slowing up, he leaps from one rooftop to another. Xavier stops at the edge of the roof and watches the man in the distance. He takes two steps back and breaks into a run toward the edge. Once his feet leave the roof, he disperses himself into electrical energy. He reforms right above the man while in mid-air. Xavier wraps his arms around him, and they plummet through a skylight, landing hard on the floor below.

As they lie there in pain, the man pulls out a short sword and takes a swipe at Xavier. Xavier deflects the attack with his arm guard, then lands a right hook that makes the man lose his grip and drops the sword.

"Is that all you got? You guys will pay for what you did here!"

"Hold on, you think I am one of them? I was sent here to stop them," Xavier proclaims. "I am going to go out on a limb and say that you are not Sadist either."

"What, are you kidding? NO, I'm not!"

Xavier stands to his feet, "Well then, I am

going to need you to tell me what happened here yesterday."

"No way man, I am not saying anything until I get some answers of my own! Who are you?"

"My call sign is ShaXdow. I am an operative of Atlas. Yesterday, my teammates and I were sent to Chicago to clear out Sadist."

"So, I guess it was your attention they were trying to get with all of this. Well, great job, it worked. What took you guys so long to get here anyway? Do you know what the people had to go through that could have been avoided if you had been here to stop Sadist!"

"My team and I were not informed of this attack until this morning. Had we known about it, we would have been here; but nevertheless, we are here now. So, I need to know what happened; maybe it could give me a clue to where I can find Sadist."

"I don't know the whole story; I just know that late last night Sadist stormed the streets. When everything went down, I was going to try and fight back, but people needed my help. So, I waited until I heard some commotion in the streets. It was my plan to take them out one by one, but because of the fire, I couldn't even really tell what or whom I was aiming at. I panicked and ran."

"You did the right thing getting the people to safety. You wouldn't have stood a chance against them by yourself even if you do have powers."

The young man picks up his sword and walks over to a nearby chair and takes a seat. He lays his head in his hands. "It just keeps happening. It's like a never-ending cycle or a nightmare you don't wake up from. No matter how hard I try to fight back I...I just end up running away like a frightened little kid!"

"I am sensing that this is somewhat personal to you."

"Yeah, you could say it is. Sadist and I have a history together; more importantly Hayden and I. In case you are wondering, he is their leader."

"We've met, what happened between you two?"

"That bastard killed my brother and the rest of my friends! Now I am all that remains from Redemption."

"Redemption? Is that another gang or something?"

"Kind of. I mean, we never did anything bad. We were just sick of living in fear of Sadist. My brother and his best friend started Redemption after they split from Hayden and Sadist. He was a good guy, my brother. We just had it rough growing up. He joined Sadist to find the one thing we never had...a family. He got out though and wanted to turn his life around. He let me join the group two years ago when I turned fifteen."

"So, Redemption and Sadist battled over turf I

take it?"

"It goes deeper than that. Last year Hayden and his boys cornered us out in the open. I…I got scared and I ran. I abandoned my friends, but worst of all I abandoned my brother! Now he is gone. I vowed that day that Hayden would die by my hands. But you know that whole fear of dying always seems to get the best of me. I guess-"

Just then Marcus burst through the door followed by Devonte. "There you are ShaXdow. We lost you for a minute there. Lucky for us, Scott saw what building you fell into. Who is this?" Marcus inquires.

"The name's Tristen Reynolds…are these friends of yours?"

Xavier walks over towards Marcus and Devonte. "Yes, these are my teammates."

"Wow, only three of you. You guys are going to need a lot more guys if you hope to stop Sadist."

Marcus steps forward and stands firmly in front of Tristen. "Well, there aren't any more guys, we are all you get. Is there any information you can tell us about what happened here?"

Xavier pulls Marcus aside and explains the situation to he and Devonte. After a few minutes of deliberation, Marcus walks back towards Tristen who has now gotten up and is standing by a window.

"ShaXdow tells me you have a personal stake in all of this."

"You could say that."

"Well, I respect the fact you want to get your revenge, but this has now become bigger than a vendetta."

"What are you saying?"

"I'm saying this is too much for you, so stay out of our way!"

"Are you serious? You three are going to need my help. I know the Sadist better than anyone!"

"Listen, standing here and debating this is only wasting our time. There are others out there who could use your help now. We will handle Sadist from here…that's it, no more discussion!"

"Everyone is safe. I got a large group held up in the local high school. Now I want to help stop Sadist. I can take care of myself, and not to mention you need me," Tristen says firmly! "ShaXdow help me out."

"Alright enough, you can come. Should things get too intense you need to get out of there," Marcus proclaims sternly.

"I will be fine…and thank you." Tristen tells Marcus where he has hidden the civilians. This prompts Marcus to contact base and have them send the troops to secure the civilians. As Marcus relays the information, Xavier walks over to Tristen who sits back down in the chair, his body motionless from anxiety.

"You don't have to do this," Xavier says. "I

doubt your brother would want you to throw your life away for revenge." "It's ok, everything makes sense now. I see now why he wanted to join you guys' team. To him it wasn't about revenge, but about correcting a mistake. It took me until just now to figure out that I shouldn't be fighting for revenge. If anything, I should be fighting for…redemption."

Suddenly an explosion can be heard about two miles in the distance. The force from the explosion made everyone fall to the ground. Marcus and Devonte rush to the door where they could see the dark cloud of smoke in the distance.

It wasn't long before Scott radioed in from the STC.
Marcus looks back at Xavier who had made it to his feet and was assisting Tristen up off the floor.

"It looks like Hayden is giving us another clue," Xavier states.

Devonte forms ice around his tightly clenched fist; "Well, what are we waiting for? Let's go give him an answer!" Devonte snaps as he slams his fists together.

"I agree with DaRock. The severity of the situation just escalated. We have no choice; we have to make a move now, River."

"Fine! There is no time to waste. Let's get over there." Marcus says.

With assistance from Scott, Team 407 makes their way through the city. They are forced to stick to tight corridors and alleyways due to debris in the streets.

Upon arrival, they inspect the surrounding area of which no clues were found. Only the feint sound of coughing echoes in the wind. Its place of origin was a rundown distribution warehouse about a block south of their location.

They walk with caution towards the warehouse. The coughing had stopped; what was left was the sound of heavy breathing. Devonte points to a man kneeling attempting to stand to his feet.

"Hey...what happened here?" Marcus questions as he inches closer to the man. "You're coming with us...we will get you to a safer place."

"How do you intend to save me when you yourselves are already dead?" the man asks.

Tristen hastily jumps forward in front of Marcus, his sword pointed directly into the injured man's face. "STOP! It's a trap; he is one of the Sadists! Aren't you Niko?"

"I'm sorry. Have we met?" Niko says in confusion.

"You guys have to be more careful. Do you see that skull tattoo under his left eye? Every person who joins Sadist has a skull like that tattooed somewhere on their body." Tristen informs them.

Unease and suspicion consumed the group as the sound of clapping rang out from within the shadows of the dimly lit warehouse. Out walk

Hayden, and a dozen Sadist members.

"I must say, kid, you know your stuff; it's a shame you had to side with these criminals."

Tristen tries to lunge at Hayden, but is foiled by Marcus, who quickly grabs his shoulder.

"Oh, I am sensing some bad blood between you and me. Have we met before?"

"You killed my brother, you bastard!"

"Come on now. "You are going to have to be more specific than that. Heck, I've killed so many 'brothers' it's hard to keep track of them!"

"My brother, Sean! He used to run with you and your boys before he started Redemption! Then you ambushed us and killed him and the rest of my friends!"

"Sean...now I remember! I mean I don't know how I forgot. It was your brother that got us a lot of respect in Chicago. But, you know what they say, all good things come to an end...a very slow and painful end!"

Hayden smiles sadistically at Tristen who fights with all his might to get free from Marcus.

"Tell you what, since you miss him so much I am going to do you the favor of personally sending you to see him. Hey while you are at it, take your new friends with you!"

"You kill people for fun and you have the nerve to call us criminals!" Marcus snaps!

"I kill for the benefit of our kind. Think of it

as having an infestation of rodents… and I'm the exterminator. I call you criminals because you and your friends robbed me of my home, my domain, and my territory! Chicago was mine!"

"Chicago belongs to the people." Marcus responds.

"The people… the people are nothing more than a bothersome itch that I can't seem to get rid of!" Hayden shouts as he raises his hands up. "Ok, so it seems we have reached the point of no return. The one in which you four will not be returning home. Sadist… tear them apart."

As the mob of men charge at them, Marcus releases Tristen as he, Xavier and Devonte brace themselves. Tristen quickly ducks under an incoming attack, at which point he sprints straight towards Hayden. Marcus instructs Devonte to go after Tristen.

Marcus and Xavier stand back to back and take down everyone that ran at them. Two Sadist run at Marcus, one of which takes a swing with a pipe. Marcus dodges the swing from the pipe and counters by forcing the man's arm behind his back. Marcus then uses him as a human shield to defend against an attack from the second Sadist. Marcus drops the unconscious man to the floor and performs a three-hit combo, followed by a roundhouse kick to the face of the Sadist.

Xavier forces electricity to the palm of his hands as he faces off against three Sadists. As the first two Sadists come rushing towards him, Xavier uses his arm guards to absorb the blow from the first attacker. He retaliates by discharging electricity from his palms. The flash was enough to momentarily blind his opponent. The second Sadist begins to throw punches at Xavier, who manages to evade all of them.

Xavier hits the man with a palm strike to the chest. The electric fueled blow causes the man's body to go limp. As he falls, Xavier throws him into the first attacker. The third Sadist throws one straight punch at Xavier. Xavier catches the man's hand mid punch and tasers him as well. He follows it up with a series of palm strikes.

In the meantime, Devonte has formed two-ice fist and began fighting his way to Tristen. Hayden has morphed his arm into a blade and clashes steel with Tristen. Hayden constantly taunts Tristen, causing him to swing furiously out of anger. Capitalizing on Tristen's lack of self-control, Hayden disarms him and forces him to his knees. Just as Hayden is about to take his final swing, Devonte blocks it with his ice fist. He takes the other one and punches Hayden right in the bridge of his nose, causing him to stagger backwards. "My patience has run out. Now you all die! "Hayden shouts as he charges at Devonte.

Sparks fly as Hayden drags his bladed arm across the ground. He takes one giant swing at Devonte, who puts up his hands in defense. Upon contact, Hayden shatters Devonte's ice fists.

Skillfully Devonte ducks underneath the next attack, Tristen then rolls over Devonte's back and kicks Hayden in his chest.

Meanwhile Marcus and Xavier have engaged Brad in a two on one confrontation. As Brad swings his sledge hammer, the boys duck. The metal stub instead hits the faces of unsuspecting Sadist members. Marcus propels himself forward, landing a sharp elbow right at Brad's gut. Shortly after that, Xavier launched into the air for a jump kick.

Brad stands there seemingly unaffected by their attacks. "You still insist on trying even after I told you that my body absorbs all forms of energy."

Everyone halts their attacks after receiving an earful of Niko's brash shriek! His body tenses up as he falls to the floor. They notice a stab womb to his back as his body begins to convulse violently. Just then the shadow behind him started to move. Once the commotion settled down, Stargazer was left in its wake. His eyes glowing a bright red!

The fear of Stargazer causes Hayden to revert his limb to it normal form. "Screw this," he says! "Sadist we're out of here. Let's let our friends fight this demon guy for us!" Hayden, Brad, and the remaining Sadist ran to their nearest exits and disappears into the distance.

"So, the rumors are true. Atlas has been recruiting new Operatives. It's too bad for you that Quazar is not here to save you this time," Stargazer rants as he hoists his sword into the air. "No matter what, you will never be able to stop Lord Quake's plan!"

Marcus and Xavier pull their blades and move closer to Stargazer.

"So eager to die are we. Why rush it? Why not have some fun first. Let's make this interesting," he says while pointing his sword down towards Niko who was slowly dying. "Once he takes his last breath he will let off an explosion powerful enough to level this entire place and some of the surrounding area. I estimate that you have about three minutes to show me how much you have grown."

Marcus rushes at Stargazer and starts to attack him. Marcus takes four swipes at him, which Stargazer easily deflects. Stargazer takes a swipe at Marcus, but Xavier blocks it.

"You might wear a mask, but I know those eyes. Those are the same eyes I saw that day!" Stargazer proclaims stoically.

In Xavier's mind, visions of that day at the Youth Center flashed by.

"Now, much like then, you are only delaying the inevitable." Stargazer begins to swing his sword at Xavier who manages to repel every strike. Expertly, the two began to swing continuously at one-another. While attacking Xavier, Stargazer launches scythe shaped darkness projectiles at Marcus. He responds by twirling his blade and shielding himself against the volley.

Across the room Devonte fires a barrage of shots at Stargazer, whom conjures a dark void that swallowed up the frozen bullets. Stargazer uses his darkness to form a giant hand that snatches up Xavier. Surprisingly, the hand slams Xavier into a nearby wall with great velocity. It followed that up with a hard slam to the floor. The blow left Xavier unconscious.

Marcus launches fireball after fireball destroying the phantom hand. However, this left him open for an attack. Stargazer stabs at Marcus, who turns his body in enough time to only get impaled in his left shoulder. Seeing this, Devonte and Tristen rush at Stargazer as Tristen proceeds to attempt a jumping slash but is knocked to the ground instead.

Devonte continues to fire at Stargazer only for Stargazer to seep down into the darkness then reemerges right behind Devonte. Stargazer lifts his sword high into the air to cut Devonte down. As luck would have it, he stops, his gaze locked firmly on Niko. He lets out a demented and boisterous chuckle as he seeps back down into the darkness and retreats.

Devonte stands frozen in fear, his hands still outstretched in front of him. His body starts to shake as Marcus calls out to him. Finally acknowledging him Devonte walks over to Marcus. He instructs Devonte to grab Xavier and head to the exit. Tristen helps Marcus to his feet, paying close attention not to touch his injured shoulder.

With almost perfect timing, Scott lands the STC out front of the complex. Scott calls out to them to hurry. Once everyone is onboard, the STC takes off, missing the explosion by seconds. Scott manages to close the hatch just as Tristen was about to fall out of the STC. His back makes a thud as it collides with the metal hatch. Soon after, Scott lands in a field outside the city. Once the STC lands firmly on the grassy plain, the hatch opens.

"I guess this is my stop," Tristen says.

"Yeah, thanks for the help today. I doubt you will have too much trouble out of the Sadist after today," Marcus interjects whilst he takes off his armor.

"Are you ok? Who was that guy anyway?"

"I'm alive...and it's complicated."

"Fine. You might want to take this. I saw it fall off him when 'trigger happy' opened up on him." Tristen hands Marcus a small bag.

"Thank...ah. Thank you," Marcus says as the pain starts to set in. "We have to go, maybe someday we will see you again."

"Right...is he going to be alright?"

"ShaXdow...yeah he'll be fine."

Tristen slowly backs away from the STC and takes one more look at Marcus before he turns away and heads into the city.

Having finally regained consciousness, Xavier sits outside the Briefing Room with Devonte. Marcus is inside going over the mission details with David and Richard.

"Stargazer, huh." David says with understanding.

"Yeah, he came out of nowhere. Lucky for us he managed to drive Sadist from the city. But during all the commotion, he dropped this."

"What is that?" Richard questioned.

"It's some kind of rock or crystal."

"There were news reports of a break in at the Mercy Gardens Museum. This might be why he was there in the first place." Richard says. "We will keep this for Gizmo to analyze and figure out what it is. We'll have to contact Newman about checking on the civilians left in the city."

Marcus holds his arm in pain; sweat from his head ran down the length of his cheek.

"Alright, you can go now…head to the Infirmary. Go let Victoria look at that shoulder," Richard states.

Marcus exits the briefing Room where he finds Devonte and Xavier waiting for him. They escort him to the Infirmary where they receive treatment for their wounds as well.

Chapter 11

Mentors

Five days following the Sadist attack in Mercy Gardens, Marcus finds himself alone in the Battle Arena. His left arm in a sling, in his right hand he grasps tightly to the handle of his blade. He sits on the edge of the bleachers, in his mind feelings of conflict and disappointment cloud his thoughts. His focus is broken when David walks into the Battle Arena.

"Marcus, it's good to see you up and about."

There was no response, Marcus remains silent. David walks into the control room where he did not emerge for another ten minutes. David casually makes his way for the exit when he suddenly stops. He turns his attention to Marcus and walks over to him.

"Is something bothering you, Marcus?"

"Yes, I want you to tell me why you decided to make me team leader?"

"Ok, but why the sudden interest in my decision?"

"You said you chose me because of my athletic background, but I don't buy that! You and I both know that leading a team in a game is completely different then leading a team into battle."

"Actually, when you think about it, it's really not that different. You see every team has players, and every player has their strengths and weaknesses. A team has different positions so that people with different talents can work together and achieve a common goal. And every team has a leader, not to boss them around, but instead guide them.

I chose you because of your passion. I know that it was you that made the decision to fight back at the youth center. Marcus, you inspired your friends with your passion, and that is why they followed you into battle!"

"It seems like every time we go on a mission, I find myself questioning whether or not my plans are good enough."

"And this is natural. You are still very new to this, having just finished your third mission five days ago. As time goes on, you will become more comfortable with making the tough decisions."

Marcus takes a few seconds to think. The room grows quiet and still again. After a moment Marcus finally breaks his silence.

"David, can I ask you a question? What is the M.R.A? I got into an argument with an obnoxious lady while I was in Chicago. She mentioned how they should bring back the M.R.A."

"M.R.A. or Meta-human Relocation Act, was put in place by the U.S. Government about fifty years ago. From what I hear the purpose of the M.R.A. was to gather up all meta-humans and separate them from the humans. It was a very bad time in our history and is often thought to be where most of the animosity between humans and meta-humans stem from."

"So, tell me again why we are fighting to unify our kind and theirs?"

"We fight because there is no our kind, their kind. There is only mankind. We are just as much humans as a regular person is. Only we have different gifts, but it's no different than someone who can whistle to someone that can't."

"Well I'm not going to be much good to anyone using only one arm."

"Marcus, you have to stop beating yourself up. You let your anger and emotions consume you and that is going to do nothing but hurt you in the end. Yes, you only have the use of one arm now but it's what you do with that one arm that makes the difference."

"David, I just don't want to fail, and being injured is not going to help anyone!"

"On the contrary, it is helping someone. It's helping you! I like to believe that things such as these happen to us to make us stronger as individuals. Victoria used her healing power to speed up the healing process, but for this to heal properly, it has to happen naturally. I promise you that when that arm heals completely, it will be stronger than before. In the meantime, you just have to be patient."

Marcus cracks a slight smirk as he speaks, "Patient, now you are starting to sound like Xavier."

"He is a very bright individual."

"He's an even better friend. I remember when I first met him I couldn't stand him. I just wanted to deck him in that smart mouth of his. But overtime he grew to be like my brother. He has saved my life on multiple occasions and I don't know how to repay him," Marcus states in disappointment.

"Marcus, I doubt Xavier looks for you to repay him. I have known you boys for quite a while now, and I am one-hundred percent certain that Xavier would want you to rest up, so he could stand at your side on your next mission."

Marcus' face lights up, it was as if a weight had been lifted from his shoulders. "I guess…thanks David, you helped me put a lot of things into perspective. Is there anything you need me to do?"

"Indeed, there is. I want you to relax and get

your rest. There will be plenty to do when you get better." David walks out of the Battle Arena leaving a reinvigorated Marcus behind.

Outside the Rec. Room, Devonte hides behind a wall. He waits for an unsuspecting victim to walk into his prank. Person after person and no one manages to spring the trap. Devonte begins to get frustrated when his concentration is broken. Much to his surprise, Scott was standing directly behind him and had called out to him.

"Kid, what are you doing behind the wall?"

"Oh, you know, waiting." Devonte says innocently.

"Waiting for what?"

"Instant gratification!"

"What are you talking-" Scott was interrupted by the sound of Devonte's prank being triggered!

Devonte leans back onto the wall as he lets out a giant burst of laughter! Scott however looks on in disappointment.

"We really need to find you a better outlet, Devonte."

"Calm down, Scott, it's just a joke," Devonte rants.

"Really, then why are you the only one who is laughing?"

"Because apparently no one else understands

comedy like I do! I like to catch people in the moment; you know to get their real reaction. I prefer pranks that have been proven to work. To me, the older the prank, the better. Look I don't see the big deal, it's not like anyone got hurt.

"Don't you have something more constructive to do with your time? Why aren't you with the other two?"

"Xavier is meditating. That's extremely boring. Marcus is sulking in the Battle Arena and that's depressing!"

Scott folds his arms tightly across his chest as he says, "I know you just recently got promoted to operative, but have you ever thought about taking it a step further?"

"What do you mean?" Devonte questions as he slowly peers around the wall.

"I mean becoming a Specialist of some kind."

"I don't see the use in that, I am not good at any of that stuff."

"That's why we learn, kid. Now you have been here for over three months. There has to be something that you want to learn how to do."

Devonte pauses for a few seconds before blurting out, "Fly the STC!"

"Interesting, lucky for you I am a Transportation Specialist and would be more than happy to teach you everything I know about flying an STC."

"Well, what are we waiting for?" Devonte asks with enthusiasm.

"Calm down Devonte. Tell you what, meet me in the Hanger in ten minutes."

"Why not now?"

"You still have a mess to clean up. So, when you are done with that, come find me in the Hanger." Scott begins to walk away when he stops and turns around saying, "I'm serious, Devonte, clean this up!"

Devonte watches as Scott walks away down the hallway. He then takes a deep breath and marches into the Rec. Room.

Xavier stands on the ceiling, his hands clasped together tightly. His eyes closed shut, he breaths slowly and deeply as he meditates. After about an hour, Xavier releases his adhesion and descends to the floor. He takes a quick glance at the clock. Seeing the time, Xavier hastily runs out of his room. Within minutes, he reaches the door to the Lab.

He inputs his security code and enters the room. Upon entering, he notices a team of Technology Specialist frantically working at a table in the middle of the room. Xavier creeps closer to get a better look and sees that they were discussing the crystal from Mercy Gardens.

"No, no you've got it all wrong!" a Specialist bellowed in frustration. "This is not a diamond, it's a sapphire."

"Get over yourself, man. Just because you were elected lead Specialist of this project doesn't always make you right," another Specialist snaps!

"It's a quartz," Xavier interjects.

The room grows quiet as everyone turns their attention towards Xavier. A slow clap can be heard from the second floor. Xavier peers up to see Adam applauding him.

"You all need to take notes. That was very impressive, Xavier...meet me in the R&D room."

Xavier bypasses all the remaining Specialists and walks up the stairs to the Research and Development room. Upon entering, Xavier sees Adam sitting on the edge of a desk typing on a holographic keyboard that was projected above his right wrist. Just then, an image of the quartz appeared on the screen mounted to the back wall.

"You were correct in your assumption as to this being a shard of quartz. However, my readings are showing significant differences down on the molecular level."

"What are you saying Adam?" Xavier questions casually.

"It means that this is no ordinary shard of quartz. Based on my findings and some research, I found on common minerals, I would say that what we have here is synthetic quartz."

"Come to think about it, I have heard about

synthetic quartz. It was very prominent about fifty years ago."

"You are right again. However, there is more to it. Synthetic quartz, unlike natural quartz, must be manufactured. It is said to be a very involved process to produce these minerals. One of which is extremely rare to find nowadays.

What sets this apart from quartz or any other mineral is the fact that once it hardens it is almost unbreakable. It is even tougher than diamond."

Xavier slowly paces the floor; back and forth as he walks in front of the screen. Having been stumped, he turns to Adam and ponders, "What use would Nova have for a shard of synthetic quartz?"

"That, my friend is the problem. Despite our best efforts we have yet to ascertain their true ambitions. Quake's flighty attack pattern just doesn't make sense to me. Everything that Nova has done recently has been just…random!"

Xavier pauses to think to himself. He snaps his fingers in assurance! "Adam, what if they are attempting to harness the piezoelectricity? Like how scientist used to do fifty years ago."

Adam sits back and gives some thought to Xavier's prognosis. "You have a great point, Xavier," he says in admiration. "They could in fact be trying to harness the piezoelectricity. But I hypothesize that because this is synthetic quartz, that the amount of piezoelectricity would be much greater than if they used any other crystal.

Lady Luck has smiled at us, Xavier; we hold here an asset to Nova. I'll lock this away in the vault for now."

Adam gets up and walks over to a large metallic unit seated in the rear of the room. He swipes his ID card and presses buttons until the unit opens. He places the synthetic quartz on a shelf and locks the vault back. As he walks back towards Xavier, he keys into his keyboard and shuts off the screen. He motions for Xavier to follow him; the two head downstairs to the Grid.

"I must say that was very impressive stuff back there, Xavier. You have a good head on your shoulders. Now we have to get started tracking those jamming beacons."

"How many have we found since we started?"

"Sadly, only three. Nova has them hidden really well!"

"Adam, if they can tap into our coms, then why can't we tap into theirs? Maybe what we should be doing is figuring out a way to listen in on their frequencies."

Adam gets excited as he states, "Xavier, that's brilliant! This way we can finally figure out what they are up to and what are Quake's ambitions. So, let's not waste any more time; we need a point of access like yesterday, so let's find one!"

Chapter 12

Subject 62

Weeks after their last mission, the boys are summoned to the briefing room. Inside waits Kimberly, Jessica, and Janet. Dillan stands at the Grid alongside Richard who impatiently strokes his platinum beard. His eyes locked firmly on the Grid.

"Great, now that you boys finally made it, we can get started. Thanks to Gizmo, we were able to hack into the frequency that Nova used to hack our coms," Dillan states arrogantly. "We picked up some interesting chatter that can prove to be very useful. Listen up!"

Dillan accesses the audio file, *"What was that*

noise!?"

A chill slowly trickled down Xavier's back as he softly proclaims, "That's Stargazer."

"One of the rejected subjects has disappeared."

"What do you mean disappeared?"

"Disappeared, you know gone, ghost, he left, gave us the slip-"

"Save the jokes Hardwyre. How could you be so careless?"

"Calm down Scarface, subject 62 suffered from an irregular regulation. He will be dead in no time if his body doesn't have a substantial amount of the formula."

"You fool, you let one of our failed subjects escape! Taking with him everything he knows about our operation! Hardwyre, if subject 62 is not found and terminated you will have a lot more to worry about than an irregular regulation."

"How would I even know where to start looking for him? I mean seriously, I'm a hacker not a hunter!"

"Believe me Hardwyre, we are painfully aware of your inability to tap into your primal instincts. Why not check the records and search for a place of origin?"

"It says here that we acquired him from some place in Nebraska named Lionel's Creek."

"Very well, that is where we will start our

search...get back to work, Hardwyre!" Suddenly, the audio file cuts out.

Dillan proceeds to pull Lionel's Creek up on the Grid. "From the looks of it, Lionel's Creek isn't that big of a town. But I suspect finding this guy will not be so simple. When you get there, your mission is simple, find the target and extract whatever information you can on Nova and their plans."

"But what about Stargazer?" Marcus questions.

Dillan takes a deep breath then exhales before saying, "If you should run into Stargazer, you are to abort the mission. You all are not ready to face him yet. Last time he was playing, but this time there won't be any games." The room grows cold and still for a few seconds. "Sorry, if that wasn't what you wanted to hear. Nevertheless, we are sending team 352 along with you to increase the chances of you finding this Subject 62. Dismissed."

Later in the hanger everyone sits on the STC and waits for Scott to start the engine. Marcus slowly rotates his left arm working the joint in his left shoulder.

"How is it?" Xavier asks

"It's still sore, I can't put too much stress on it."

"Hopefully we won't run into too many problems."

Before long, they were skyward approaching

Lionel's Creek. Scott lands in a local football field and lets them out. Once everyone has disembarked, the STC ascends into the air. Everyone then crowds around Marcus; they wait for his thoughts on the situation.

"I think since the town is not too large, we should be able to cover more ground if we split up."

"Yeah, but we don't even know what this guy looks like," Jessica responds.

"True," Marcus says. "Chaos, you have the ability to sense energy. If this guy had dealings with Nova, then no doubt he has to be a meta-human right?"

"What's your point?"

"My point is that he would give off a greater energy signature than a human. I need you to scan, and if you sense anything out of the ordinary, that's the direction we will start searching."

"I will do my best, but you guys have to remain still. If I pick up your signature we could run the risk of going in the wrong direction."

Janet closes her eyes tightly as she concentrated on the energy around her. Everyone else became still and silent. Her head pivots to the left then to the right as she follows the fluctuating energy signatures. With her hand, she pointed out into the distance. "That way," she says while opening her eyes.

"I didn't pick up any meta-humans, but there

was an unusual signature coming from that direction."

"Unusual how?" Marcus questions.

"It's different from anything I have ever sensed. It's almost inhuman; I can't explain it. It's just different."

"The recording did refer to this guy as 'Subject 62'. Maybe whatever they did to him tampered with his energy signature," Xavier proclaims.

"Whatever the case is, we need to find this guy without drawing too much attention to ourselves. It has been my experience that the humans don't really care for us." Marcus states out of aggravation.

"River, what about a disguise?"

"Great idea, ShaXdow, but how would we go about that?"

"Simple, we take that company van over there by those doors," Xavier says as he directs their attention towards a service door to the rear of the field. "Someone drives, and Chaos can ride in the passenger seat to continue tracking. Everyone else should fit in the back-"

"I'll drive," Devonte blurts out in excitement!

Marcus shakes his head in disbelief as he says, "So much for splitting up. Whatever I like it, let's go before we lose him."

On the streets of Lionel's Creek, Teams 407

and 352 pursue Subject 62. Devonte is at the wheel; his armor shrouded by a thick jacket he found in the back of the van. Janet also wears a thick cotton jacket as she clasps tightly onto the door. All the while the others ride in the back amidst the wires and electronic devices that occupied the space around them.

As Devonte makes sharp turns and short stops, his teammates in the back were being thrown around. Janet attempts to concentrate on the road ahead.

"Which way now, Chaos?" Devonte questions as he completely turns his head towards her.

The van swerves into oncoming traffic. At the last possible minute, Devonte catches his mistake and veers back into his lane. Drivers slams on brakes and begin to blaze their horns.

From within the back of the van, Marcus calls out, "Kid! Do I have to take it from here?"

"No…no I got it."

"Well keep your eyes on the road then," Marcus shouts! After another ten minutes, the van was pulling up to a train station. Marcus instructs Devonte to pull around to the rear of the station.

"We're close, the target is somewhere in that station."

"We need to trap him somehow," Kimberly says as she maneuvers some junk in the back.

"Starbolt is right, and I know exactly how to handle this," Marcus states confidently.

"Just one problem, we are going to be

surrounded by humans." Janet proclaims.

"Crap, you're right…unfortunately we are going to have to overlook them just this once."

"Are you sure that is smart?" Janet says with skepticism.

"It doesn't matter, either we sit here and waste time talking or we do what must be done and go in there to get Subject 62. I am going to roll with the latter. Now you and I will take point, ShaXdow and Starbolt will be our back up. That leaves DaRock and Plasma here at the van. We are going to scare him right into your hands, so be ready!"

As Marcus and Janet walk through the train station, the civilians clenched their luggage tightly in apprehension.

"Talk to me Chaos, where's our guy?"

"Over there sitting by himself."

"Ok, remember stick to the plan," Marcus states calmly.

Sitting on a bench was a man pale in complexion. His appearance is that of someone with a history of substance abuse. He holds his head down with his face in his hands.

Marcus and Janet casually sit on either side of him. "This doesn't seem like the best place to hide for a man in your shoes," Marcus says.

The man remains still, his eyes wander

searching for a place to run through the spaces between his fingers. Abruptly, Subject 62 jumps up from the bench and takes off running through the station. Marcus and Janet are hot in pursuit; they keep a safe distance of 20 meters between themselves and Subject 62.

As he scurries through the station, Subject 62 finds his path blocked by Kimberly who stands at the entrance. Knocking over civilians, Subject 62 quickly changes direction and heads for an emergency exit. This door was located at the rear of the station. Pushing past people and knocking over luggage, Subject 62 races to the exit.

Closer and closer he comes to the door. Subject 62 is almost to the door when it swings open. Xavier is standing on the other side. Subject 62 panics and slides to a stop; he crawls to his feet and continues to run. Giving it one last shot, he runs to a nearby service entrance. On his way he pushes over a civilian and hurls their luggage at his pursuers.

Frantically, he bursts through the doors and scans the area. Much to his surprise, he notices a van that belonged to a local electric company parked by the wall. He rushes to the van and snatches the driver's door open. He jumps in, but before he had a chance to start the van he is grabbed and pulled into the back.

"River we got him," Jessica says while Devonte holds Subject 62 down.

Not long after, the others regroup in the van and Devonte drives off towards the road. Eventually he flees the main road and follows the train tracks south to an old railyard. Upon arrival, Marcus and Xavier lift Subject 62 from the van and escort him into the old rail station.

Devonte and Jessica stay close to the entrance to keep watch while Kimberly and Janet follow Marcus and Xavier inside. Subject 62 kicks wildly trying to free himself from their grasp. They find an old chair and sit him down on to it. Every time he tries to get up, Marcus forces him back down.

Janet pulls the scepter that hangs from her back; she uses it to summon a three-headed dog. Transforming the scepter into its whip form, she wraps the end of it around the neck of the middle head like a leash. The three-headed canine growls viciously as Janet walks it closer to Subject 62.

He starts to freak out as the Cerberus gets closer, "Ca… ca…call off your dog, I'll talk! I'll talk!"

Marcus instructs Janet to pull her Cerberus back. "Subject 62, we need some answers. Nova is up to something, and we need to know what it is."

"What makes you think I have anything to tell you?"

"If you had no valuable information then there was no reason to run. Now believe me, we are the good guys, but I wouldn't have much of a problem letting 'fluffy' over here play with you like a chew toy!"

"Good guys…come on. He is wearing a mask, and she is threatening me with some demon mutt! And yet you want me to believe that you are the 'good guys'." Subject 62 chuckles softly to himself. "News flash kid, there are no good guys! It's what you want versus what they want. Simple as that."

"Scum like you join up with Nova to help them oppress humanity!"

"I did what I had to do. Quake promised all of us that if we enlisted in his new project, we would be able to get whatever we want."

"So, you were desperate."

"So, what, if you had to go through the things I did you'd be desperate too!"

"You mentioned a project, what is it exactly?"

"It's called Project Acceleration."

"What is Project Acceleration?"

"Quake found a way to give normal humans like me powers like him. He along with that sniveling weakling Hardwyre created what they call the accelerated formula. They inject it directly into your neural network via five NARU patches."

"What's a NARU patch?"

"From what I recall, it stands for Neural Anesthetic Receptacle Unit. They place them in five key spots on the body," Subject 62 says while pointing to the back of his neck.

Marcus examines the patch closely; he can tell it has been tampered with. "These patches-"

"Yes, they hurt like crap! But the worst part is the injections. That formula is something serious let me tell you," Subject 62 proclaims trying to be comical. "There are five parts to Project Acceleration. I only made to phase 3. Throughout each phase, you are to receive constant injections of the formula to help regulate the primary procedures.

The accelerated formula is an advanced narcotic. Too much of it and you could risk becoming dependent on the stuff. Now that throws everything off track, because now your body will need more of it just to stay regular. At that point it causes you to have an irregular regulation like me, Subject 62 says somberly. "If you have an irregular regulation, they stop you wherever you are in the project, then they put you down...like a dog. I have seen many guys get taken out like they were nothing. So, I said, 'screw that' and escaped the first chance I got."

Subject 62 gets quiet for a minute. Finally, he breaks his silence saying, "Thinking about it now I should have just let them kill me. Sitting here as your body slowly becomes defective from lack of formula really sucks!"

"What else...there has to be more than just human testing. What is Quake really doing?"

"You honestly think that Quake would waste his time telling me their plans. To him I am nothing more than a number! To him I'm a dead man already."

There was another awkward silence between them. Marcus stares at Subject 62; he can see the desperation in his eyes.

"Fine...he's looking for some guy, that's all I know! If you guys really are the good guys, then you must understand that I was a victim. You got to let me go."

"Right, you were a victim," Marcus replies sarcastically. "A victim of circumstances. You wanted power, but instead you got helplessness." Marcus instructs Janet to have her Cerberus watch Subject 62 as he pulls Xavier aside. "What do you think ShaXdow?"

"I'm not sure. He seems to be sincere in his story about this Project Acceleration. And as far as Nova looking for someone-"

The howling of the wind interrupts Xavier's monologue. Shortly after, there was a buzz in their communicators, followed by the service van slamming through the wall. Jumping in separate directions, everyone just barely avoids being smashed. Subject 62 takes this opportunity to make his escape.

He runs outside amidst the howling winds and swirling dust. Placing one hand in front of his face, he begins to trot towards a set of decommissioned train cars. There is a pop in the air. Subject 62 suddenly falls to the ground. He had been shot in his leg. The intense pain from his wound causes him to release a series of violent shrieks!

Footsteps can be heard marching on the gravel below. Subject 62 musters up enough will power to start to crawl toward the train. With every inch, he crawls, the footsteps come closer. Steps grow harder, and the noise gets louder. From nowhere, Subject 62 is kicked in the ribs forcing him to roll onto his back in agony.

As he lies on his back, he stares down the barrel of a gun clasped firmly in the hands of Twister. "Now why would you go and run away like that?" Twister patronizes. "I bet you are just itching to die. It must suck knowing your body is literally killing itself. Hardwyre tells me that his formula is like a drug or something…I forget, that guy annoys me."

Subject 62 launches a glob of spit form his lips, hitting Twister right in the face.

"Clever, that's real smart! Piss off the guy with the gun," Twister says sarcastically as he wipes his face. "Thank you for making this so easy for me. Once I get rid of you, I will be rewarded for fixing Hardwyre's mistake and finally get the darn respect I rightfully deserve! Good bye Subject 62-"

Devonte tackles Twister to the ground. They wrestle with one another while Jessica pulls Subject 62 away. Twister uses a powerful gust of wind to force Devonte up into the air. Both men draw their gun and fire; the bullets collide in mid-air.

Devonte lands on the ground forcefully and rolls into cover as Twister gets to his feet. Devonte rests his back on a slab of concrete; periodically he sticks his head out to watch for Twister. He looks to his left to see Jessica nestled behind a train with her bow drawn. Devonte nods to her, then she leans out and fires one plasma bolt at Twister.

Jessica struggles to secure Subject 62 as he continues to panic frantically. He clasps his leg right above the gunshot wound.

"Calm down! We are not going to let him kill you."

"Sweetie, you're wasting your time. There is nowhere I can hide that is safe. And you kids aren't enough to protect me."

"Oh really," Jessica says as she leans from behind cover and launches more plasma bolts at Twister.

Devonte waits for his opening and takes two shots at Twister who is now hiding in an abandoned train car. Devonte and Twister exchange shots at each other from behind cover. Jessica periodically leans out and fires plasma bolts at Twister.

"DaRock, he is freaking out over here! I'm going to have to move him!"

"Alright I will keep Twister busy. Move now!"

Jessica grabs Subject 62 and pulls him away

from the battle. Twister sees her and uses a strong gust of wind to blow a train right at her. Jessica attempts to speed up to avoid the train, but to no avail. Kimberly jumps to the rescue and puts herself in between Jessica and the oncoming train. Kimberly rotates the wind around her body continuously until it forms a barrier.

Upon contact, the train is diverted skyward where it flips on its side before plummeting to the ground. Having grown frustrated, Twister begins to blow wind at violent speeds that it literally cuts through the metal of the train!

Kimberly increases her focus, enlarging the size of her barrier. Twister heightens the pressure until Devonte shoots at him, making him lose concentration. Kimberly forcibly expands the radius of her barrier until it reaches Twister. The force of the wind blows Twister against the wall and sends Devonte flying away from the fight.

Twister struggles to remove himself from the wall. His eyes look left, then right until he notices a broken rail spike sitting amidst the dirt. He summons a tornado that lifts the rail spike and flings it at Kimberly and Jessica.

The large jagged piece of metal cuts through the air violently. The closer it gets the less Kimberly can concentrate. She loses concentration completely and braces for impact. Jessica drops her bow and focuses her energy to her hands to blast the spinning projectile right out of the air. Suddenly she catches a glimpse of Subject 62 trying to escape. The brief diverting of her attention resulted in her missing the only opportunity to strike.

Their bodies tense up; when directly in between them, Xavier appears from his teleportation. With a powerful static charge coursing throughout his sword, he can cut the rail spike in half with little effort. The two halves of the spike shift into separate directions, avoiding both Kimberly and Jessica.

"Are you two alright?" Xavier asks as he examines them for injuries.

"Yeah, thanks for the save," Jessica replies as she stares at him.

"What about Subject 62?" Kimberly inquires.

"Let him go, we need to move, Chaos is picking up multiple energy signatures in this area." Xavier says as he helps them up and they prepare to make their move.

Twister falls to the floor and starts to crawl until he falls out of the train. "I will not be beaten by a child," Twister says as he raises his gun at Xavier. Janet then wraps up his arm; she gives it one great tug and pulls Twister to the ground. Before he has a chance to move, his eyes were drawn to Marcus, who had his blade extended just centimeters in front of Twister's face.

"This time you're coming with us!" Marcus states confidently.

In the meantime, Devonte struggles to find his way back to his partners. As he wanders amidst the weathered train cars, he can hear faint footsteps behind him. Unexpectedly, he turns around with his gun pointed straight out in front of him.

"Oh, it's you. Look that was cool and everything but next time can you watch where you direct that thing. Anyway, where is Twister?"

"He's right over here, c'mon," Kimberly says while rushing past him.

"Hey, wait up," he shouts as he pursues her!

She makes a sharp turn behind some debris. Devonte finally reaches the debris, but there is no sign of Kimberly anywhere. Just then Twister comes charging full speed at Devonte. He attempts to tackle Devonte but is thrown into a sharp piece of rooted debris. Upon collision a gash is cut on Twister's arm. Devonte pulls out his gun once more and walks up to Twister.

With the barrel just inches from Twister, Devonte states, "Yeah, you're not so tough now! Where's all that noise you were talking to Subject 62? You aren't crap, now you come-" Devonte suddenly stops his rant as he witnesses Marcus subduing Twister in the distance.

When he brings his attention down, he was now looking at Kimberly. Confusion and doubt swelled up inside of him. "Wait a minute, how did you-" Devonte watches in shock as the body in front of him shifted and rearranged itself. It turned out to be a teenage girl.

Her hair was long and pine in color; her skin was tan and smooth. She gazes at Devonte with her piercing green eyes as she slowly stands up. Devonte keeps a steady aim on her with every move she makes.

"Who are you?" he questions.

She responds by saying, "I'm Rebecca." Without warning, she goes for Devonte's gun.

Having been caught off guard, Devonte unknowingly squeezes the trigger letting off one shot. Rebecca grabs Devonte and swings him into a slab of debris headfirst.

Chapter 13

Femme Fatal

As they prepare to secure Twister, a gunshot can be heard within proximity. Marcus walks away from the group into the direction of the gunshot. His right-hand was clamp firmly around the grip of his double-ended blade. He steps into the opening where he can see Devonte kneeling down on the ground.

"DaRock, what was with the gunshot?"

"Sorry I was still dizzy from being thrown over here. I was walking when I tripped and fell and cut myself on the rock over there. I guess my gun went off by mistake."

"Whatever just get yourself together, so we can get out of here. Chaos is picking up a lot of energy around us. I'm trying to avoid an unnecessary fight if I can…so let's go!"

Just as Marcus turns around he sees Devonte shuffling towards him with his hand on his head. "What, how did you-" Marcus repeatedly turn his attention between the two Devontes.

"River…wait! It's me! I'm the real DaRock!"

"Screw that, I'm DaRock!"

"Enough! Both of you better start making sense, or I'll haul you both in for detainment!"

"I give up, this is not fun anymore. Besides I want to play a new game!" Devonte says, as he wipes the blood from his arm and reverts back to Rebecca. "What do you think boys, am I pretty? Daddy says that I'm the prettiest!"

"No! He says I'm the prettiest," A girl shouts from atop a train. She looked identical to Rebecca; instead her hair was pink and short.

"We're triplets. That means we are all the prettiest," says a third identical looking girl with medium length blue hair. She walks slowly towards Marcus and Devonte; in her hands she held onto Subject 62 and was dragging him across the dirt.

"Plasma?" Devonte questioned suspiciously.

"That's not Plasma," Marcus replies.

Rebecca walks up to her blue haired sister, "Alexis" she says in frustration. "These guys are no fun to play with. Daddy didn't let us bring our toys and Uncle T won't let us use his!"

"Remember Rebecca, before we had guns,

people would fight with sticks and stones or sharp pieces of piping used to induce a slow death."

Marcus and Devonte look at each other in confusion. Just then their teammates run up behind them.

"Friends of yours," Xavier says.

The pink haired sister flips off the train and lands next to her sister. "There are six of them and only three of us."

Jennifer, what game should we play now?" Rebecca asks as she pushes the long strands of hair from in front of her face.

"Why are you asking her, she couldn't even hurt a fly," Alexis says as she tightens her grip on Subject 62. "I say we play a little game of keep away."

Jennifer rejoices as she said, "Yes, I love this game! We can be like those three really pretty private detectives from California!"

"Right, and our mission is to locate the package," Alexis says as she punches Subject 62 in the face. "Now that we have the package we have to keep it away from the evil assassins."

The Atlas Operatives look on in disbelief.

"Enough of this kiddy crap. Get out of our way," Marcus snaps!

"Wait, what about me? You can't just leave me here. They'll kill me!" Subject 62 hollered hysterically.

"You said you were a dead man either way. So why should we-"

"Chaos, that's enough. You know we can't do that. Unfortunately, we are going to have to play their stupid game, so we can secure Subject 62. Besides, it's only three of them," Marcus states confidently.

"Really? Then why am I still picking up at least a dozen energy signatures?"

Marcus remains steadfast as he scans their surroundings.

"Don't worry, you were never going to win. We just wanted to have a little fun before we destroyed you all," Rebecca says as she stares at Marcus with her piercing green eyes.

"Rebecca? Something is missing, something important...a name. We need a name for our group. Something like what those detectives had," Alexis said as she flung Subject 62 to the ground behind her.

"How about...the Mirror Sisters?"

"The Mirror Sisters...I like it!" Suddenly, multiple copies of Alexis jump out into the open. There were exactly one dozen copies of her. "Ok, come and play!"

Marcus takes a glance over his shoulder at his teammates to give them the conformation to attack. Everyone charges at the nearest clone to him or her except Marcus who runs at the original. As he runs full speed at her, Jennifer jumps on top of him to intercept him. He manages to throw her off. She twirls gracefully through the air.

When she lands, Marcus can see that her hands have begun to glow a bright red. She kneels and places her hands on the ground, creating a swirling red vortex.

Out of the vortex rose up a near perfect replica of Marcus. The skin was pale and devoid of all color, and its eyes were full and black. With every minute movement, Marcus made the doppelganger mimic simultaneously.

Xavier and Kimberly stand back to back as they face off against a swarm of clones.

"Remember what you learned during our sessions. Let your opponents defeat themselves. We need to maintain control of this fight at all times, so we don't get overwhelmed."

"Right," Kimberly responds as she takes down two clones. "They just keep coming!"

"That's ok, just keep fighting," Xavier replies while knocking back a few clones.

Meanwhile, Rebecca joined the fight and is in pursuit of Devonte. She lands a series of hits on Devonte as he was preoccupied with a group of clones. His body falls to the ground where he was then trampled by the clones. Rebecca stalks him and waits for the clones to finish their attack.

Devonte freezes the ground around him and causes the clones to slip around. Rebecca takes the opportunity to attack. She steps onto clone after clone to avoid the ice until she reached Devonte. She wraps her legs around his neck, and using her own natural momentum, she flips him through the air.

When he regains his composure, he jerks his body upward until he was standing. He sees Kimberly fighting a cluster of clones. She gets knocked down and he rushes to her aid. As he runs up, he shoots out a flurry of ice freezing the clones where they stand.

He reaches down to help her up but stops as he realizes it was a trap. Rebecca reverts to normal and takes a giant swing at Devonte's head with a broken piece of metal. The attack is deflected by one of Kimberly's daggers. She rushes in with a spin kick, one of which Rebecca dodges with relative ease.

"Regroup with Xavier; he just ran after Twister. We will take it from here!"

Devonte nods in compliance and runs off after Xavier. As he runs, he ducks to avoid three clones that were just blown away by Jessica.

At the other end of the field, Marcus is trying to fight Alexis and Jennifer all the while his doppelganger attacks him. *I can't keep this up. They will have to finish this fight without me. Time to make these brats play my game*! Marcus rolls to the side launching a fireball into the distance. The doppelganger mimics him only for its fireball to fly towards the Mirror Sisters.

They scatter to avoid the attack. Seeing his opening, Marcus gets to his feet and sprints away from the fight. His doppelganger was in hot pursuit!

Jennifer attempts to follow him but is stopped by Janet and her Cerberus. The three-headed hound fires fireball after fireball at Jennifer. She flips and twirls nimbly avoiding every projectile.

"Aww, he's so cute! I want a puppy," Jennifer swiftly runs up to the Cerberus and slid underneath its attack. She pets it on the head, then flips backwards until she was about ten yards away. Again, she places her hands on the ground summoning the red vortex. This time a doppelganger of the Cerberus rose up out of the vortex. "I wonder if daddy will let me keep him!"

She witnesses Janet striking the Cerberus with her whip, so she picks up a chain and strikes her Cerberus. It lets out an ear-piercing roar followed by a volley of fireballs.

As Kimberly faces off against Rebecca, and Janet battles Jennifer, Jessica is still swarmed by clones. They all pile on top of her as the real Alexis walks up with a broken pipe in her hands.

"Tag you're it," Alexis says playfully as her clones' bombard Jessica.

A bright, green light begins to escape through the openings amidst the mound of clones. A wave of green energy sends all the clones flying away. Jessica ascends into the air; a bright green aura surrounds her hands and feet.

"No fair, you can't fly! That's cheating!"

"Grow up already," Jessica says as she rains down a barrage of plasma energy at Alexis.

"Oh, I see! You want to play dodge ball too? Ok my turn." Alexis summons some clones that combined their efforts to launch one clone skyward at Jessica. She blows that clone back down to the ground, completely unaware of the second clone coming from behind her. It wraps its arms around her and slams her to the ground. Then the clones pile on top of her once again.

Marcus fights diligently against his doppelganger, but to no end. For every attack he initiated, the doppelganger counters with the same attack. After a while, Marcus starts to slow down. The wound to his shoulder starts to get the better of him. His doppelganger, however, continues its relentless assault. It was throwing Marcus around the field with ease.

He attempts to fight back, but his shoulder completely gives out on him. The doppelganger then begins to target Marcus' injured shoulder with strikes and submission maneuvers.

Kimberly struggles to land a hit on Rebecca as she redirects every attack. Rebecca lands precise strikes to Kimberly's abdomen. After each attack,

Kimberly would try to retaliate with a much more forceful attack of her own. She finds herself wasting too much energy and uses the wind to put some distance between Rebecca and her.

Memories of Xavier's voice telling her to maintain control starts to come back to her. Kimberly takes a deep breath, then slowly exhales. Her gaze is fixed on Rebecca as she prepares for her attack. Rebecca throws a series of punches at Kimberly; she manages to dodge all of them. Kimberly's stance changes; she now has a more balanced stance that closely resembles Xavier's.

Rebecca comes back with a combination attack that ends with a hard knee to Kimberly's abdomen. Kimberly topples over in pain, but quickly shakes it off. She regroups with just enough time to avoid a heel kick. Kimberly waits for Rebecca to attack; she has her hands raised slightly in the defensive position. Every time Rebecca attacks, Kimberly hits right back.
The tension has now diminished significantly as Rebecca starts to slow down from exhaustion. Kimberly stands firm as her foe slowly creeps backward.

"This was fun! Sadly, I have grown bored of this game. But don't worry, we can play again next time. Bye!" Rebecca rushes off into the distance leaving Kimberly to succumb to her fatigue.

In the meantime, Jessica continues to blast

through the waves of clones. The real Alexis jabs at Jessica with the pipe, causing her to fall to her back. She rolls to the side as Alexis tries to impale her. Jessica flips continuously as Alexis repeatedly swings the pipe at her.

With each swing of the pipe, Alexis grows increasingly upset, "No fair! Stay still," she shouts while summoning more clones.

The swarm converges on Jessica in overwhelming odds. She blasts them back, but the clones continue to spawn. Jessica attempts to get airborne but is unable, due to lack of energy. She pants heavily as the clones continue to swarm. Finally, she diverts her attention to the real Alexis. Jessica takes off running towards Alexis ignoring the swarm of clones that surround her.

She gets about five yards from Alexis when she launches a plasma energy sphere at her. Without losing any momentum, Jessica flips backwards and draws her bow. While in mid-air, she fires one plasma bolt straight at her energy sphere.

Soon as she lands, she is bombarded with clones. Alexis moves out of the way of the energy sphere just as the plasma bolt makes contact. The resulting explosion sends Alexis flying. Her concentration is broken, and the clones disappear leaving Jessica beaten on the ground.

Jessica struggles to sit up; she grabs her bow, mentally preparing to use what energy she has left.

"It would be nice to keep playing, you are fun to play with! But like daddy says, 'All good things must come to an end'. So, bye, bye for now!" Alexis staggers to her feet and chases after her sister into the distance.

Lastly, Janet straddles her Cerberus as it battles Jennifer and her Cerberus. Jennifer strikes the beast on its side, causing it to swipe with its massive claws. The claws make contact knocking Janet off her Cerberus. The two beasts lock up and engage in a vicious dogfight. Janet watches as Jennifer skips along the ground, all the while spinning the chain through air.

Janet cracks her whip twice in anticipation of Jennifer. Jennifer whips the chain at Janet. Their weapons tangle, and they both start to pull. During their struggle, Jennifer is able to pull Janet in close enough for an attack. Janet rolls out of the way and trips Jennifer with the chain.

Jennifer twirls her legs through the air and she spins to her feet. She jumps over Janet's whip and unleashes a flurry of strikes at her. Only able to defend, Janet tucks her arms in to absorb the blows. It's only when Jennifer gets distracted at the sight of Janet's Cerberus locking its jaws around the neck of her clone, did Janet have an opportunity to retaliate.

Janet summons two glowing pigmies that are hairless and reddish in color. They let out a shriek as they begin to chase after Jennifer. She flips backwards continuously to avoid the rabid creatures. They chase her to a dead end and lunge at her. One manages to grab a hold of her; she fights with all her might to get the beast off. She then flings the creature into the other just as they release their energy in the form of an explosion! Having only been caught by the shockwave, Jennifer is thrown to the ground.

As she lies on the ground, her summoned creatures faded away almost instantly.

Across the field, Marcus has been pinned to a wall by his doppelganger. Just as the clone is about to strike, it fades away leaving Marcus resting up against the wall. He lets out a sigh of relief. *They did it*, he thinks to himself.

Janet walks over to Jennifer. She has now turned her whip back into scepter form. She stands over Jennifer and examines her. Suddenly, Jennifer jumps up and trips Janet and rushes to an empty train car.

"I had a lot of fun, but I'm tired and I miss my daddy. Try to survive until next time so we can play again." Jennifer vanishes between the trains as she runs after her sisters.

The other members of Team 352 eventually regroup at Janet's location. Jessica places her hand onto Janet's shoulder and gives her a warming smile. Soon after that, Devonte walks up followed by Xavier who is supporting Marcus on his shoulder. Marcus grabs a hold of his left arm as it rests at his side.

"Is everyone ok?" Marcus inquires.

"Nothing a little rest and relaxation can't fix," Jessica states. "A better question is… are you ok?"

"Yeah, I'm fine," Marcus, says in agonizing pain.

"What was with those girls? They looked like teenagers, acted like children, yet they fight like seasoned warriors. It was hard for me to fight the green haired one. Most of the time I couldn't even read her moves, she made it difficult to defend against her," Kimberly says in frustration.

"Where is Nova getting these people from?" Devonte asks. "Hey, where is Subject 62?"

Everyone takes a glance at his or her surroundings. There was no sign of subject 62, only man-sized footprints in the dirt leading off into the distance.

"Looks like he escaped," Xavier answers.

"Let him go, we got what we came for. Besides Scott is on his way and I don't know about you, but I don't have another fight left in me," Marcus says, as he slowly rubs his arm.

After a couple of minutes, Scott picks them up, and they make their way back to base. Upon arrival, they report to the briefing room where they find Commander Maximus and Richard hovering over the Grid. They report their findings about Lionel's Creek; and when they are done, they are sent on their way to recuperate.

Chapter 14

The Verdict

Inside the Atlas Infirmary, Marcus sits on the edge of one of the beds. Victoria was examining his file. Impatiently, Marcus takes periodic glances at his shoulder, he attempts to move it, but fails. He looks around at some of the other members of Atlas that are lying in the various beds.

Victoria places his file down beside him on the bed as she states, "You are very lucky." She grasps his arm and slowly rotates the joint.

Marcus' face scrunches up in pain. "And how

do you define lucky?" He says as he pulls his arm away from her out of pure instinct.

"After all of the stress you have put this arm through since the initial injury, you only have minor nerve damage."

"So, what does that mean?"

"It means you retain use of your left arm. However, you must give it substantial time to heal. So, unfortunately, as of this moment you are confined to base per my prognosis."

Frustration consumes Marcus, "Whoa! You can't do that!"

"You need to calm down, you are disturbing the other patients!"

"Screw them, this is about me! You can't keep me out of the field they need me. If I have to fight with one arm then so be it, but I can't just abandon them."

"Marcus, you need to think rationally. Without proper rest, another battle like the one you had yesterday will severely damage that arm."

Marcus looks disappointed as he sluggishly stands and shuffles towards the door. With his hand around the knob, Marcus stops and asks, "How long do I have to be here at base?"

"For at least three weeks."

Marcus neglects to respond; he only slams the door behind him. He makes his way to the Living Quarters where he marches to David's room. Upon arrival, he knocks on the door three times. It was not too long after that David opens his door.

"Marcus, what's the matter?"

"I need you to do me a favor."

David looks at Marcus and can see the obvious frustration. "What do you need me to do?"

"The doctor has confined me to base for three weeks. Can you convince her to let me stay on active Operative duty?"

"Marcus, you need to rest, and if the doctor has you confined to base, well, that's the way it has to be." David pauses for a brief second, "I know this is not what you want to hear, but it is what's best for you. Remember what we talked about that day in the Battle Arena."

"Well, what about Xavier and Devonte? What are they supposed to do for three weeks while I'm out?"

"None of you are Elite ops yet so they cannot operate on the field without a team leader. We will just have to find something for them to do around the base. But as of right now, Team 407 will be strictly used around the base. At least until the three weeks are up."

"David, I know we had that talk a couple of days ago, but I'm not the type to sit around and do nothing-"

"Marcus, I have something that I need you to see. Please come in," David says as he walks Marcus into his room.

Inside David's room, everything is clean and neatly positioned in its proper spot. He takes Marcus over to a small table tucked in between the bed and the wall. On the table is a picture frame with a picture of a woman in a floral sundress standing in the shallow waters of a beach.

"She is very beautiful, who is she?"

"Selena Hernandez, she is my girlfriend."

"Hernandez…like Hector Hernandez, Brick?"

"Yes, she is Hector's younger sister. I have known them pretty much all my life. We grew up together." David picks the picture up and admires it. "Selena does not have powers, so therefore she can't protect herself like I can. Imagine if I were to push myself so hard that something happens to me. I would no longer be able to protect the one thing I can't live without.

I know about you and Trish, just think about how she would feel if you didn't listen to reason and got yourself hurt, or worse. I can tell you right now, she wouldn't be happy."

"He's right you know," a voice said from the doorway. Commander Maximus walks inside and stands directly in front of Marcus.

"A big part of what we do in life has to do with rising above ourselves. Putting the needs of others before our own. That is what Amir Robinson believed we at Atlas were chosen to do. We must realize that sometimes what is best for the people we fight for may not always be something we are happy with.

Victoria informed me of her prognosis; I figured you would come to David, so I decided to make a visit. I see a lot of great potential in you and your friends. What intrigues me about you, however, is that you remind me so much of myself. You're bold, brash, heavy-handed, and so passionate to the point where you make reckless decisions.

About six years ago, I too was an active Operative. Although my duties as Commander were most important, I still had responsibilities as an Operative. My last mission, I will never forget it.

I was to accompany some of our younger Operatives, as the mission required us to liberate a convoy of captured meta-humans. It was Team 321, which is Quazar, Brick, and Gizmo. There was Stargazer and myself; he was already an Elite Operative and that mission marked his one-year anniversary with Atlas.

The mission was going according to plan until Quake and some of his Nova ops ambushed us. Somehow Quake managed to turn the captives against us. He not only talked the captives into fighting for him, but his words got to Stargazer as well. Quake had always had a way of manipulating people, even when we were younger. He prayed on Stargazer's narrow-minded ambitions and corrupted an already tortured soul.

In his retaliation, Stargazer injured me in the leg. Thank goodness for David stepping in and fighting Stargazer.

When we returned to base, the doctor at that time examined my leg and confined me to base so that I could recover. I didn't listen to him and wind up messing up my leg up so bad that I now must walk with a cane. Being that I had lost a great deal of mobility, I had no choice but to give up my responsibilities as an Operative and become a full time 'stay at base' Commander.

My point in all of this is that I don't want you to make the same mistake I did. Do not let stubbornness cost you an arm...or worse. I admire your passion and recognize your potential, and I don't want to see you throw it all away for nothing."

Marcus takes a seat on David's bed; his head hangs low as he ponders on Commander Maximus' story. He looks up at David and Maximus, his face contorted with conflict. "Fine, I will let it go. I'll take it easy for the next three weeks."

"That's the spirit, now go on and get some rest. I will personally deliver the news to your teammates," Maximus says as he smiles softly.

Marcus gets to his feet and shakes both men's hands. Then he flees from the room.

Maximus pats David on the shoulder once Marcus was out of sight. "I never told you how I think you made the right move bringing those boys here. They have so much potential, and as long as we continue to nurture them, we may have found the answer to beating Nova once and for all."

"Commander, what are we going to do with the other two?"

"Nurture them as well, this is a time of rest for them also."

"So, it is," David responds proudly.

"See you at the next Council meeting, David. You take care, I'm going to deliver these messages." Commander Maximus states as he turns and walks out of David's room.

Over in the Lab, Xavier sits at a table in the R&D room where he is examining the file on synthetic quartz. As he reads silently, he hears the door opening. "Hey Adam, I took a look at the, -" Xavier turns his head towards the door. "Oh, it's you, Commander. How can I help you today?"

"Busy working hard I see."

"Yes sir, I was just doing some research on synthetic quartz."

"Right, Adam told me that you helped him figure out that the crystal was actually synthetic quartz. He also told me that it was you that gave us a way to hack Nova's coms. Thanks to that, look at all the information we acquired yesterday."

"Something about that still doesn't sit well with me. He talked too easily, and I still don't completely trust the information he gave us either."

"Try not to over think it. You gave us a much-needed advantage. And because of it, we now know more than we knew before…and that's all that matters."

"I guess so."

"Listen, I needed to tell you that you and your team will be working primarily around here for the next three weeks."

"If I may ask, why the change in duties, sir?"

"The doctor wants Marcus to stay at base for the next three weeks so that his arm can heal up. So, until that time is up, he won't be able to go out into the field, likewise neither will you or Devonte."

"I understand. I've got a lot of work to do as it is. Seems like a better time than any to catch up on it."

Commander Maximus takes a hard look at Xavier. "You know, looking at you, you remind me of someone I met once before."

Xavier looks puzzled as he replies, "Really?"

"Yes, do you have another family member that is a meta-human like you?"

"Well, according to my father, my grandfather had powers."

"That's it, your grandfather. You remind me a lot of your grandfather," Maximus states with confidence.

"You knew Grandpa Ian?"

"Knew of him is more appropriate. Your grandfather was a hard man to find."

"Yeah tell me about it. I haven't seen him since I was thirteen. He just stopped showing up."

"I'm sure you heard the story of how I became Commander. Well, my first major assignment was to restructure and increase our operations. So, I went around looking for meta-humans who would join our cause. We had heard about your grandfather's legendary achievements while he lived in Japan. We found out he was living in Mercury, North Carolina, and made a special visit to the house."

Xavier looks intrigued as he recalls a conversation with his parents. "Right before I left home, my father mentioned something about Atlas coming to see Grandpa Ian."

"Indeed, we came to see if he would join us and help us stop Nova and his followers."

"Well, what did he say?"

"Your grandfather's words verbatim were, 'your petty squabble means nothing to me. You should spend more time securing your future and less time chasing your past.' He wasn't the most cordial individual I have had the pleasure of meeting, but nevertheless his words stuck with me. That brief monologue your grandfather gave to me helped make me a better leader."

"Grandpa Ian inspired me to become a ninja. The style of Ninjutsu teaches you how to adapt. To a ninja everything can be and is a potential tool. I wanted to be versatile so that I can effectively complete my task. Grandpa always had a way out of a situation; he was my hero."

"So that's the reason behind your decision?"

"Yes. When Grandpa Ian was not staying with us, he was living in Japan. Every time he would come home, he would bring with him two things, a toy sword and stories. He told me so many stories that I learned more about how to understand a culture from him then I ever did in school."

"Was your grandfather a ninja?"

"It's complicated. He used the style but denied the label."

"That's very interesting. Well, I enjoyed this talk. I will leave you to your work." Maximus starts to walk towards the door. He stops as Xavier's voice speaks out to him.

"Thank you."

"What for?" Maximus questions.

"For giving us a chance. I know the rest of the Council didn't want us around at first. You believed in us and we won't let you down."

"You are more than welcome, but there is really no need to thank me. I was just doing what I thought was best for my team. You can say I was securing our future by letting go of the past. Give yourself some credit. You boys earned the right to be here."

"You said you see my grandfather in me, but I see him more in you."

"I believe he and I shared a common goal. Life has taken us down two different paths." Maximus walks out of the room, leaving Xavier with a smile on his face.

In the Rec. Room, Devonte sits with Janet; they wait for Kimberly to arrive. Janet summons a glowing pigmy onto her lap. She scratches it on its head causing it to let out a minute squeal of satisfaction.

"So…what is that thing?" Devonte asks doubtfully.

"This is what is called a 'kami'. It's a type of pigmy that specializes in self-detonation."

"Detonation, like a bomb!"

"Yes, like a bomb. Only these don't explode. They can store massive amounts of energy, which they release all at once. It leaves them severely drained, so they are instantly sent back to the Echo."

"Why would you summon it here? There has to be rules against that."

"Calm down Devonte, you aren't in any danger. The self-detonation is strictly a defense mechanism. The pigmy will not release its energy unless provoked."

Within minutes, Kimberly joins them at the table. "Sorry I'm late. I was just finishing a project."

Before Devonte had a chance to respond, he notices Commander Maximus walking towards the table. As Maximus gets to the table he says, "Devonte, may I have a word with you out in the hall?"

"It was nice knowing you Devonte," Kimberly says whimsically.

Devonte gets up from his seat. His palms become sweaty, and his mind begins to fabricate reasons why Maximus wanted to see him. He follows Commander Maximus out into the hall. When they stop, Devonte snaps!

"I'm sorry, I didn't think it was a super big deal. It's not like I meant to break the STC!"

"Devonte calm down, I didn't come here to reprimand you. Wait…you broke an STC?"

"Not completely…I only knocked one of the wings off."

"You were flying without a license. When was this?"

"About two hours ago…" Devonte says hesitantly.

Commander Maximus prepares to yell at Devonte, but instead throws his hands up saying, "You know what, forget it."

Maximus regains his composure, "Marcus has been

confined to base for the next three weeks to rest and heal up. You and Xavier are to remain here as well."

"Yes! Three weeks off! I needed a vacation. I got my butt kicked by a little girl yesterday and let me tell you-"

"This is in no way a vacation. Unfortunately, we don't get vacation time around here. Even though you won't be out in the field, I do expect you to find something constructive to do with your time."

"Aww, come on sir, why can't I just rest?"

"You can't just rest because evil doesn't rest. Look Devonte, you are a good kid with a lot of potential, maybe even more than your friends. Your problem, however, is that you lack the necessary focus needed to reach that full potential. I bet you spent your whole life just coasting along, never doing more than you had to, or just not stepping up at all."

Commander Maximus can see the disappointment in Devonte's face. "I'm sorry...it was not my intention to upset you. I just don't like to see such potential go to waste. You remind me of myself when I was your age-- so carefree and innocent. Unfortunately, there comes a time when we all must grow up.

My father sent me away to the military so that they can instill some discipline in me. He did that, so I would not squander my talent. I require the same from all of you because you may not see it, but I see just how vital you are to this team. That's why we push you guys so hard. Tell me Devonte, why did you join Atlas?"

"I joined because Xavier and Marcus joined, and I didn't want to be left out. In case you haven't noticed, I don't do well on my own."

"Nice try, but I don't buy that. You have a reason for joining, and when you are ready to talk, I'll be ready to listen."

"I'm starting to see why you are the boss, and I respect that. But please don't tell anyone I said that. I still have a reputation to maintain."

"Very well. Your secret is safe with me. I expect you to find something productive to do around base over these next three weeks. Oh yes, you will be fixing the STC you damaged." Commander Maximus turns to walk away; he trots steadily down the hallway until he exits the building.

Chapter 15

Loose Ends

Two weeks and four days later Marcus and Xavier are up early that morning in the Battle Arena. Marcus was demonstrating his new ability to fly while Xavier looks on from the bleachers. As he sits idly, Xavier drapes a towel over his head like the hood of a jacket. Marcus struggles to maintain his flight and begins to descend from exhaustion.

"So, what do you think?" Marcus inquires as he slowly rotates his left shoulder. "I first noticed I could do this back home. So, I have been trying to figure out how to perfect it."

"That's very impressive. We have had our powers for quite some time now, yet we still have no idea of how much we can do."

"I hear you. Hey, do you want to get another round in? I still have to work out my shoulder."

"I would, but I can't. I'm already late for my shift at the lab."

"That's right, you and Trish work with Adam. Is she still there now?"

Xavier nods as he states, "She should be. She usually waits until I get there to leave."

"Well, I'm coming with you. I want to see her, and not to Mention, I need you to show me how to use the Grid."

"No problem let's go."

Marcus follows Xavier out to the lab. They make a quick stop by their rooms to change clothes. Within minutes, they were at the door to the lab. Xavier inputs his code and opens the door.

The double titanium plated doors slide apart, revealing the inside of the lab. Xavier takes Marcus up to the Research and Development Room.

They find Trish sitting at the computer, her attention locked on the screen. Marcus creeps up to her very slowly and places his hands over her eyes in playfulness. "What are we looking at?" he asks.

She turns around to face the two boys. "You are late Xavier."

"My apologies, Trish. We were training. I

guess we lost track of time."

"I hope you didn't hurt him too bad, Xavier. I still have a use for him," Trish says while grabbing a hold of Marcus' hands.

"Ha ha, very funny babe, enough of the jokes. What are you looking at?"

"It's the case file on the Regal Nevada Mission given to Operatives Hotstreak and Slipstream."

"Isn't that the mission where Nova wiped out a lot of former Operatives?" Xavier questions.

"Yes, that's the one. Apparently, the mission was a set up. Hotstreak and Slipstream were sent to aid in pacifying a group of meta-human extremists who were violently protesting in Regal, Nevada. According to Hotstreak, the protesters were Nova ops in disguise, and in all the commotion, he and Slipstream were separated. That was the last check in before Hotstreak later called in a 'code red'."

"What is a 'code red' again, I forgot?" Marcus asked.

"A 'code red' is the signal for immediate assistance while one is out in the field. There are different colors depending on the severity of the situation, with red being the most severe. Likewise, we have similar signals for around here at the base."

"So, Nova managed to force Hotstreak to call a 'code red' in order to bait as many of us in one spot as possible." Marcus states.

Trish grips the mouse tightly as she scrolls down the page. "Apparently, the coms went silent until Operative Burner made his call warning us that it was a trap."

Xavier sits on the edge of the table; a glare of curiosity consumes his face. "Who is Burner?" he asked.

"Give me a second," Trish said as she brought the file on Burner. "Mark Titus call sign Burner was an Elite Operative and Transportation Specialist. He served with Atlas for three years. Before that, he was a small-time criminal who was arrested for failing to give up his accomplice in a bank heist.

He spent eight months in prison, and once he got out, he was recruited by Atlas. He would serve as team leader of Unit 402 alongside Hotstreak, who was his nephew, and Slipstream. Burner powers were full body combustion and heat resistant epidermis. So, not an Elementalist but something close to it."

"So, what separates regular meta-humans and Elementalist?" Marcus inquires as he pulls up a seat.

"From what I gather, the apex genes in normal meta-humans are less developed than an elementalist."

"Basically, when the apex gene forms, it only partially forms in normal meta-humans. Whereas the apex gene in an elementalist has been fully developed. Thus, that's how things that are powers to a meta-human can be obtained as an ability to a elementalist," Xavier says confidently.

"So, elementalists are more powerful by default?" Marcus questions.

"That's one way of looking at it. The way I see it, elementalists have the most untapped potential. It makes sense why they are so sought after."

As Xavier finishes speaking, Trish navigates back to the file on Regal, Nevada. She skims the file once more with her eyes. "What are we to do if this is to ever happen again? Somehow Nova knew exactly how to compromise us."

"Stargazer!" Xavier says in enlightenment.

"What, what are you talking about, Xavier?" She asks.

"Stargazer used to be an Elite Operative for Atlas. Meaning that he went through the training, learned all calls-"

Marcus interrupts, "Then defected to Nova, taking with him everything he knew about our operation."

"Exactly Marcus. I think Stargazer had a big hand in everything that happened in Regal, Nevada."

Squatting behind a desk, Hardwyre finds himself reconfiguring his computer. He plugs in three translucent colored wires before returning to his seat. He restarts the device with one hand while lifting his goggles onto his forehead with the other.

"I'm just saying, we spent all this time looking for ONE guy! He better be worth it."

Cordell stands stately and motionless behind him. Hardwyre gives him an uneasy glare.

"You know sometimes I question why I work with you guys. I mean I must be the most normal person here. Think about it. You got three genetically altered five-year-old girls, a scientist turned militant leader, an ex-criminal with an unhealthy lust for destruction, some punk kid with a serious 'beauty and the beast' complex, a living demon, and you!"

Cordell is unflinching at Hardwyre's attempt at disrespect.

"Compared to you all I am-"

"A sniveling, spineless, weak, strongly opinionated excuse for a homo-sapien," Cordell states calmly. "Hardwyre, when we found you, you had nothing. It was Lord Quake who saw fit to spare you. He saw a mind as keen as his own which is why we brought you back here.

One would think you would show a greater amount of appreciation for one man's selfless generosity, yet you openly question everything. Consider yourself highly fortunate that we still have use for that brain of yours or we would have fed you to Rampage long ago!"

"Yeah, right, my mistake." Hardwyre says in a panic. "Anyway, I finally managed to narrow the search down to two facilities."

"Excellent! We are now one step closer to achieving our goal."

"Is Quake here on the island?" Hardwyre asked.

"Yes, wait here for my return." Cordell vanishes only to reappear moments later with Quake and the Mirror Sisters.

"Hardwyre, Cordell tells me that you have news that will satisfy me."

"Yes, Lord Quake, I have found our guy. After rerouting the power, I was able to broaden my search. What I found were numerous red herrings, but after a bit of hacking, I found our little friend. As we speak, I am logged onto a secure AstroTec server. They have a directory with the names of all their employees and what field they specialize in.

Our guy is one Dr. Felix Maldune, a geneticist. He is also the author of one very important piece of literature in which you so desperately seek."

"I am pleased with your findings, Hardwyre. I will speak with Dr. Maldune personally to see if we can't work out an agreement."

Hardwyre pauses for a moment before stating, "So this book...where did you hear about it, because I have checked the Internet hundreds of times, and I haven't seen a single glimpse of it?"

"Hardwyre, if I could obtain the knowledge that I seek simply from downloading it from some website, do you think I would waste so much effort looking for one man? The search alone has taken way too much time as it is. You should have done this from the start."

"Quake, once Atlas catches wind of this they are bound to try and stop you."

"You fail to realize that Atlas are just pawns to me. Every time they think they have gained the upper hand, I make my next move. They are blind to the scope of my ambitions...let them come!"

Cordell steps forward and places his left hand on Quake's shoulder, "My lord, it is almost time for the seal to be reapplied. I can feel the hold weakening. I will reapply it at once."

"Do not bother, Cordell, I think our boy has earned some time to stretch his legs. How long before the seal is completely broken?"

"My predictions say we have another four hours at most."

"Very well, Hardwyre, prep me a transport. I want to leave first thing in the morning."

"Daddy, can we come along too?" Jennifer says in a soft voice.

"Of course, my darling. I would not have it any other way. Besides I can't do this without you." Quake starts to walk towards the door when he stops. "Hardwyre, I need an update on Project Acceleration. We can't afford to have another 'Subject 62' situation. You need to be more careful with how you take care of my subjects. Another mess up like that and we just might have to start looking for your 'permanent' replacement."

Quake leaves the room, followed closely by Cordell and the Mirror Sisters. Hardwyre is left to work in solitude; he clenches his fist tightly generating a minute surge of electricity. Out of frustration, he slams his fist onto the desk, knocking over the keyboard.

Chapter 16

Resurrection

The next morning, Devonte is in his room looking through a pamphlet that Scott gave him. His body draped across the edge of his bed. *Man, this is a lot of information in such a small book*, he thinks to himself. His focus is broken due to a knock at his door. "Yeah, yeah it's open."

Scott walks into the room to find Devonte reading the pamphlet. "My goodness," he says. "Here I was thinking that you wouldn't actually read that book. So how is it so far?"

"Boring, extremely boring! You know what this has been one of the most boring experiences of my life. I mean all you do is talk and show me stuff.

You only let me fly once and look how that turned out."

"Yes, you knocked the wing off the STC and almost died."

"Yeah, but that's because you won't ever let me practice!"

"Devonte, you weren't supposed to be flying that STC at all. I had a lot of heat on me for letting that happen."

"Whatever, I'm done with the stupid book anyway. Here you go…" Devonte says as he hands Scott the pamphlet.

Scott backs off the subject and turns to leave the room. "One day you will come to appreciate everything I have tried to teach you," Scott says as he closes the door behind him.

Devonte lies back in his bed with his head resting in his hands. He slowly inhales only to exhale seconds later. Devonte is lost in his thoughts for about forty-five minutes. Finally, he gets up and walks to his bathroom. He throws hot water on his face; the water cools down upon contact with his skin.

He takes a long look into the mirror, his eyes filled with doubt and frustration. He leaves the bathroom and returns to his bed. There was yet another knock at his door. "Scott, look about what happened."

Devonte stops as his door slowly creeps open revealing Marcus on the other side.

"Devonte, the doctor has cleared me for active field duty again. So now we can start going on missions.

"Finally, it's about time!"

"Glad to see you are excited, because I was sent here to get you. They need us for a mission right now, so suit up and meet me in the Briefing Room ASAP!"

Devonte begins to jump for joy; his frustration turns into excitement. Before he knew it, he had slammed the door in Marcus' face and races to get ready. After about twenty-five minutes, everyone gathers in the Briefing Room. Richard has accessed the Grid and was streaming information from Cornerstone Alley, California.

"Welcome back, boys. It's time for you to get back into the groove of going on missions. For this mission, Team 352 will accompany you.

We received a distress call that Nova had broken into an AstroTech Lab and is tearing the place apart. The call came in about a half an hour ago, so we have already lost a lot of time. Your mission is simple--- get in and drive them out. Now go, the girls will meet you at the STC.

The boys hastily exit the Briefing Room and rush to the Hanger. As planned, Team 352 met them at the STC and they all board the aircraft. While in the air, Marcus and Kimberly have a side conversation about their plan.

"From what I hear, this is a big facility. They said that Nova was concentrating all its focus on one building. We might make it in time to prevent more damage," Kimberly says optimistically.

"I hope so, it's been too long since my last mission. I'm itching for a fight."

"So, what do you suggest we do?"

"It's too early to tell. We are going to have to wait until we get there."

It was not too long after that, the STC was landing in the courtyard of the lab. Smoke was escaping from several holes in the building. The teams exit the craft and gather by a statue. Scott lifts off and flies away.

"Chaos talk to me," Marcus says.

"I am picking up multiple signatures coming from inside that building. They seem to match the ones from Lionel's Creek."

"Then let's hurry!" Marcus, responds.

They sprint towards the main entrance. They carefully trek through the shattered doorframe. As they walk through the desolate lobby, they come across a frightened employee cowering under the reception desk. Jessica bends down and extends her hand to aid the employee.

"Stop! Please, you said you would leave me alone if I told you where he was!"

"Sir, calm down, you are still in shock. We are here to help!"

"No! You can't fool me, you were just here!" Marcus walks over to the man and pats Jessica on the shoulder signaling her to step aside.

"Sir, I need you to tell me which way they went. We can still stop them…but we need your help."

The employee breathes heavily as he stares at Marcus. There is a brief pause until he speaks out saying, "They went to Dr. Maldune's office on the third floor. Hurry, there may be a chance to save him!"

Marcus signals for everyone to proceed on to the target. They bypass the broken elevator and run straight to the stairs. Xavier is the first one up the stairs, at which time he bursts through the door and into the hallway. There is an eerie stillness to the air. The only noise is high pitch beeping that periodically echoes through the hallway.

Xavier checks the directory on the wall. He sees that Dr. Maldune's office is down the hall and around a corner. It is nestled in the far corner at the end of the corridor. He takes off running followed closely by his teammates.

Within seconds, they are approaching the door to the office. From the outside, the door looks undisturbed, showing no signs of forced entry. Suddenly, there is a loud thud that rings out from inside the office.

Before anyone has a chance to react, the door

bursts open and out flies a body. The shriveled up lifeless corpse hits the wall with a loud thud before it descends to the floor.

Everyone looks on as a man walks out of the office. His hair is blue and slicked back into a small ponytail. His face is aged to that of a man in his mid-forties. His skin is tan and firm. He wears a nice designer suit with his left hand tucked into his pocket. The Mirror Sisters flanks him as they walk up and stand in front of the group.

"The humans have the gall to deem themselves the dominant species. Yet their will breaks like glass. You waste your time trying to save humanity. You fight with all your might, and yet their minds are never swayed."

"Who are you?" Marcus questions.

"I am the embodiment of the essence which will change this world. I am Quake!"

Everyone becomes motionless except for Jessica who seems to be in shock. Her shock swiftly turns to anger as she yells, "You bastard! How did you survive? I thought they hunted you down and killed you!"

"My word…can it be. Is it you...Jessica? You have grown up to be so beautiful. You look even more like Maria now then you-"

"Don't you dare say her name! You lost that privilege a long time ago."

"I admit I have made some questionable

choices in my past. Much as you have made the wrong choice in which side you fight for. But it's ok, because you are my child and I will steer you in the right direction. Now come back home my little Jessica. Come back to your father!"

Her teammates look on in shock from this startling revelation.

"My father died that day with my mother. Tyrell Martinez is dead to me. You are nothing but a piece of filth. I will make you suffer like I had to suffer!" Jessica charges head first at Quake.

Xavier attempts to grab her, but she blasts him back with a plasma sphere.

Jessica propels herself forward at great speeds driving Quake into the wall. Before she could make another move, the Mirror Sisters gang up on her. The others rush to her aid, they manage to fight back the Mirror Sisters and pull Jessica away.

Quake grasps firmly onto her arm. As his skin rests up against hers, she could feel her energy fleeing her body. With one last tug, Xavier pulls Jessica free, and they fall to the floor. Quake's hands and feet begin to glow a bright green as plasma energy escapes his limbs. He takes a glance over his body admiring his new abilities. Marcus launches a fireball at Quake, who reacts by forming a barrier around himself and the Mirror Sisters.

"Evolution favors the strong, and I am the next stage of evolution."

"Talk all you want. You are not leaving this hallway," Marcus says as he summons fire into his palms.

"You might have given my subordinates trouble, but you are powerless to stop me!" Quake starts to fire plasma spheres at them to distract them. "Can't you see just how inferior you six are to me? Atlas strings you along with hopes of some delusional future in which humans accepts us as their equals. The blind leading the blind...pitiful. I fight for a more realistic future, one in which humans and meta-humans live united under one rule...mine!"

"You say we are delusional, you have a dream that will never come true. No one would ever hand over this world to you," Marcus snaps!

"On the contrary. You already have...Marcus. Yes, I know exactly who you are. You and your friends are nothing more than pieces to a puzzle, pawns in a game I designed. You think I am not in control, yet even Atlas is at my beckon call. My influence is far reaching...I have people in positions just waiting for the right moment to put my plans into action. Now that I have the good doctor's knowledge, I am one step closer to reaching my goal."

Quake stares hard into Marcus' eyes saying, "You and your friends denounce your allegiance to Atlas. Agree to serve under me and take your place where you truly belong."

"Bite me!" Marcus snaps in anger.

"Have it your way. There are others. If you wish to live side by side with them, then you shall die how you live!"

Quake launches a massive wave of plasma energy sending the Atlas Ops flying. They crash through the wall and wind up landing back in the lobby. Then Quake and the Mirror Sister descend into the lobby. They rush outside as Atlas tries to collect themselves.

Once everyone is up, Marcus orders for them to follow Quake. As they come outside, they find that they are too late as Quake is on the ramp of his cruiser. He turns to face his foes as the craft slowly rises into the air.

"Humanity is weak. It is us who should be the dominant presence. It is our birthright…the world is not what it once was, and you all have a lot to do with that. By partaking in these pointless heroics, you are not winning their trust. You are deepening their hatred. Such potential wasted on a fool's errand." Quake pauses briefly as the craft continues to ascend. He looks down at Jessica and said, "You were right about one thing…Tyrell Martinez is dead, and with him all of his petty attachments. You may be my daughter, but you have made your choice. I spared you once…the next time we meet, I will not afford you the same generosity."

As Quake walks aboard the Nova cruiser, everyone on the ground launches a flurry of attacks at him. The cruiser takes off into the air.

"Scott, we need you now!" Marcus yells into his communicator. "Guys, we have to catch that cruiser-"

Marcus is interrupted by the sound of an engine in the distance. They watch as another cruiser approaches fast, suspended from the hull via cable was a giant canister. As it gets closer, it releases the canister and continues to fly off into distance. The giant metal container plummets to earth at such speeds that when it finally touches down, it sends out a micro shockwave knocking everyone over.

As the dust settles onto the earth, Atlas find themselves staggering to their feet. They all lock their eyes on the giant canister as it begins to rock side to side. There are a series of loud, violent thuds coming from the inside of the canister. Everyone braces themselves for the unexpected as the canister thrashes around violently.

Soon the lid comes bolting off the canister, and flails wildly through the air before landing just feet in front of Devonte. It topples over onto its side. Out of the darkness of the canister, crawls a very lanky Caucasian male.

Devonte lets out a sigh of relief, "Really that's all that was in there. Come on I'm bigger than that guy."

"I think I will eat you first," the boy says as he stands."

Devonte stops laughing, "Wait, what did he say?"

"I said," as the boy begins to violently transform into a giant hairy beast, "I think I will eat you first."

In the distance, the STC approaches fast. Seeing this, the beast plunges his razor-sharp claws into the hull of the canister. With a flick of his shoulder, he hurls the container skyward. Before Scott had time to react, the canister smashes into the cockpit of the STC. It begins to spiral out of control while plummeting towards the ground.

"We have to save him! Starbolt, DaRock move now!" Marcus shouts.

Kimberly uses her control of wind to form a small tornado to slow the descent of the STC. Devonte blows out a sheet of ice to brace the STC as Kimberly lowers it to the ground. The craft hits the ice with a thud and slides along the surface before coming to a stop thirty yards away from the group.

The beast turns his attention towards the STC. Giving it little thought, Marcus lunges forward ramming his shoulder into the beast's chest. The impact only pushes the beast three feet backwards. Marcus yells for everyone to run for the STC. He stands his ground against the beast as his comrades' hurry to the fallen STC.

Kimberly, Devonte, and Janet sprint for the STC, while Xavier follows carrying Jessica.

Marcus begins to blow fire at the beast; the flames seemingly have great effect on it. Once there was enough safe distance between his teammates, and him, Marcus attempts to run for the STC.

"Not so fast. You will be Rampage's first meal," Rampage says angrily as he flings Marcus in the other direction.

Marcus bounces on impact with the ground, his armor absorbing most of the fall. He gets to one knee and radios in to Xavier to have them take off without him! There was no response; Marcus stands up as straight as he could. "Hey freak show, I'm over here!" Marcus shouts at Rampage.

Meanwhile on the STC, Devonte carefully moves Scott from the pilot's seat and onto a bench in the back. There was an injury to his ribs from where the massive canister pierced the hull of the STC. Scott struggles to catch his breath as he clasps tightly onto his rib cage.

"Calm down Scott. You need to relax," Devonte says. "We are going to get you out of here."

"It's getting harder…to breath," Scott says while trying to sit up.

"What are we going to do? Who will fly the STC now?" Kimberly states frantically!

After a moment of hesitation, Devonte finally says, "I'll do it." He pats Scott on the shoulder, "I'm sorry, for earlier. I didn't mean what I said. But right now, I have to fly this thing, or we won't make it."

Devonte heads up to the cockpit.

"This is insane. You don't know how to fly an STC!"

"I've done it once before."

"Ok, and how did that turn out for you?" Kimberly questions.

"I crashed...but we don't have any other options now do we? If River can't hold off that monster and we're still here, then we are all screwed. It's best to try and get out of here while we can...not to mention we have an injured man onboard who needs assistance fast."

"We are not leaving him. We fly low and give him a chance to catch up."

"Yes ma'am, boss lady," Devonte says whimsically. "ShaXdow, a little help here please. The ignition is shot; I need a jump-start."

"I'm on it," Xavier says as he walks up to the console. He pulls off some paneling and grabs ahold of some wires. With one good charge, the engine of the STC jumped on with a boisterous roar.

Kimberly settles into her seat; she and Janet look after Scott, while Xavier attends to Jessica.

In the courtyard, Marcus is being slapped around by Rampage. Every attack he attempts to land has little affect against Rampage's thick skin. Marcus ducks a swipe from Rampage's razor-sharp claws. As he rises, he swings his right arm with all his might and punches Rampage in his massive jaw. Without reacting, Rampage slaps Marcus up into the air then follows it up with a drop kick.

The force of the kick sends Marcus flying into a slab of concrete. His head slams hard against the wall, leaving him motionless. Rampage lets out a loud roar before he gets down on all fours in a canine like position. Taking such great strides across the courtyard, it only takes seconds for Rampage to reach Marcus.

Having gotten about five feet away from him, Rampage lunges at Marcus, who instinctively rolls out of the way. Rampage slams into the wall head first, his body wobbles unsteadily.

Marcus slowly staggers to his feet; he shuffles towards Rampage to capitalize on his mistake. As Marcus goes for his attack, Rampage snatches him up and hoists him over his head. Rampage puts Marcus in his mouth; his razor-sharp teeth begins to carve out holes in the alloy of Marcus' armor.

Marcus yells violently from the pressure of Rampage's massive jaws closing in around him.

"Sorry...I'm not on the menu," Marcus shouts as he lands a hard elbow to the crown of Rampage. The blow makes Rampage loosen his grip on Marcus, and he falls to the ground. He blows a stream of fire from his hands propelling himself backward, putting some ground between Rampage and him.

As he slides back, he launches fireballs at Rampage. The fire surrounds Rampage causing him to lose sight of Marcus. Marcus gets to his feet and starts to hobble towards the STC, which was hovering nearby.

Within the fire, Rampage sniffs heavily picking up Marcus' scent. He gets down on all fours and jumps straight through the flames. He rapidly closes the gap between Marcus and him. Having seen this, Marcus starts to pick up the pace until he breaks into a full sprint. He races across the courtyard with Rampage hot on his heels. Marcus forces fire from the soles of his feet and takes to the air.

For a moment, he fights to maintain his altitude until finally he levels out. Rampage attempts to grab him, but misses. Having failed in his attempt to grab Marcus, Rampage veers off course. He runs towards a group of buildings.

As Marcus soars through the air, he fights to keep level. Finally, he reaches the STC where he falls onto the hatch. "Take off! he shouts."

Devonte ascends straight up, allowing Marcus time to get secure. Once Marcus gets to his feet, he takes a glance over his shoulder. His gaze directed towards the ground. He turns back around and starts to walk inside the STC. "I don't see him, I think he ran-" Suddenly, Marcus is snatched out of the STC where he and Rampage drop towards the ground below.

Xavier breaks into a run and leaps from the STC. He concentrates extremely hard and disperses into electrical energy. He reforms above Marcus only to grab him by the hand. Rampage continues to fall as they teleport away.

Seconds later, they reappear inside the STC. "Close the hatch," Xavier shouts!

Devonte closes the hatch, and the STC cuts through the air. Meanwhile Rampage hits the ground with such force that his body forms a huge crater.

He rises to his feet and watches as the STC escapes into the distance. He lets out a thunderous roar that is heard for miles. Suddenly, his wrists start to glow; large stone handcuffs form around his arms. Chains shoot from the earth and bond to the handcuffs.

A dark energy emits from the chains; reacting with Rampage; the energy causes him to revert to normal. Once he is weak and frail, the chains retract, pulling him to the dirt.

"You said I could be free," Rampage says in a hushed tone.

"The fate of your freedom rest with how effectively you serve Lord Quake," Cordell says as he appears next to Rampage. "It was you who lost control. It was you who turned your claws on your teammates. Instead of an execution, Quake felt imprisonment would serve as a more substantial punishment. You have no one to blame but yourself."

Rampage quietly replies, "Some would welcome death over rotting away helplessly in a dark hole with nothing but your thoughts."

"When we found you, you were wandering that dense forest like a mindless animal. A myth used to scare children from going into the woods. You owe me your life for it was I who gave you back the one thing you desperately wanted...your humanity."

"I'm a monster, always have been. What you did was give me the power to choose my meals."

"To get your freedom, you must fulfill your obligations. There is no other way, "Cordell says while summoning a swirling vortex around Rampage.

As he descends into the vortex Rampage begins to chuckle wildly. Cordell waits for a strong gust of wind to stir up the dust. And once the dust settles Cordell had vanished.

Xavier stands in front of the Council, his arms tucked away into the depths of his pockets. There was a momentary silence in the room.

Richard speaks up, "In your debriefing you all mentioned something about Quake. What was it exactly?"

"Quake mention something about Atlas being at his beckon call. He said his influence was far reaching, and he has people in places ready to put his plans in motion."

"That's insane. No one here at Atlas would ever side with Quake," Neim blurts out!

"Don't be so naive, little brother. We cannot forget about Stargazer. He was our finest Operative at that time, and yet he could be poisoned by Quake's twisted tongue. This is a problem we can't take lightly," Arthur states.

"I agree, but Quake speaks in riddles. We will have to figure out some way to deal with this problem without raising too much of a fuss. Identifying a Nova supporter will not be easy."

Commander Maximus stands with his eyes locked firmly on Xavier. "You seem uneasy. This is not like you."

Xavier rubs the back of his head to stall his response. "Plasma, I mean Jessica…is Quake's…daughter." He lets out a feint sigh of disappointment.

Commander Maximus looks unsurprised at this startling revelation.

"Wait...you knew?" Xavier says doubtfully.

"There is a lot of pain in her past. I was aware; however, I didn't think it would ever become an issue. Tell me, how did she react?"

Xavier hesitates for a second, "She went ballistic. I tried to stop her, but she shot me down. She was confused; she said she thought he was dead."

"That is what we thought until eventually he resurfaced as the head of Nova. When Jessica joined, I felt it best to keep the truth from her to spare her more pain."

Richard blurts out, "Commander, don't you think you should have shared this information with us. Protocol states-"
Maximus cuts him off, "Protocol is nothing more than guidelines. Sometimes you have to follow your heart rather than your orders." Maximus looks at Xavier, "You seem to follow your heart a lot. You want to protect those close to you and to do that you have to be willing to bend."

"I am worried about her and want the Council to watch her. Make sure she doesn't try to do anything reckless. Today proved that she is not ready to confront him yet." Xavier says in confidence.

"We will do what must be done. You have our word that we will keep an eye on her." Commander Maximus states. "You did the right thing bringing this matter to us, but now we must convene in private."

Xavier turns towards the door, his heart heavy with conflict. He goes to open the door when Commander Maximus says, "Do me a favor, and make sure Marcus gets his rest. He's a great Operative, but that stubborn side will be his undoing."

Xavier pauses for two seconds before saying, "Yes sir." He opens the door and lets it slam shut as he exits the Council Room.

Chapter 17

Frustration

Staring at the clock that hangs on the wall, Marcus slowly rubs his abdomen. *This is the second time I have had to lie in this bed. I'm going to have to take it easy for a while*, he thinks to himself.

Suddenly, the door creaks open and Xavier walks inside. He sits next to Marcus as he says, "Hey Marcus, how are you feeling today?"

"Better, the doctor said that I could get out in about a day or two. You know, once the swelling goes down."

"That's good. It's probably for the best that we all take it easy."

"Xavier, have you been in to check on Scott?"

"As of matter of fact I just came from seeing him. He is in the next room; the doctor says he has a few broken ribs and some swelling, but he will make a full recovery. Devonte is in there with him right now."

Marcus sits up straight in his bed, his head tilted back against the wall. "Hard to believe it has been almost a full six months since our first encounter with Nova. Now it seems as if that is all we ever do." Marcus stares blankly at the Infirmary ceiling. "The other day, when I was fighting Rampage...a feeling came over me. For the first time in a long time, I was actually scared."

"Marcus it's ok. Fear is a natural human emotion. I feel scared every time we leave the base."

"No, you don't get it, Xavier. You weren't the one fighting him. You weren't the one put into a situation where nothing you did seemed to work. Rampage made me feel...powerless!"

"Yet you made it back in one piece. When I jumped after you guys, I looked into his eyes. They were filled with much pain and frustration."

"Much like my own..."

"I wouldn't compare yourself to a creature like Rampage. His frustrations are primal, whereas your frustration is internal. You get mad at yourself for things like having to spend so much time in the Infirmary. And you are right, you shouldn't have to be in here all the time. I should be lying right there

next to you…I should have helped you fight him."
Xavier drops his gaze in disappointment, "I'm sorry."

"Marcus looks at Xavier, "It's ok, you were where you needed to be."

"Had circumstances been different, we could have taken him. But something tells me we will cross paths again."

"And when we do…I won't be afraid to do what I have to do," Marcus proclaims with confidence.

Xavier takes a subtle glance at the clock, "Marcus, I hate to cut this short, but I am late for my lessons with Kimberly. I will be back later to check on you and Scott."

The two boys shake hands before Xavier gets up and leaves the room.

Devonte stands amidst a crowd of young ladies. They were all enthralled by the story he was telling.

"Yeah, they came at me. It was like twenty of Nova's toughest, most ruthless guys."

"Well, what did you do?" One female asks as she leans on his shoulder.

"What did I do…baby, I beat them all with one of my awesome techniques. One move took out all thirty of them."

"I thought you said it was twenty?"

"My mistake. I meant thirty. Yeah it was thirty. Anyway, after I took them out, I had to find this scientist, but when I got to him, he was dead. So, I fought the villains to the point where they had to turn tail and run. You know, with the help of my teammates…not that I needed them, but because I am not selfish, and I value their skills."

Suddenly, Devonte is woken up; he had fallen asleep at the edge of Scott's bed.

"Kid, if you are tired why don't you go relax. I'm fine, you don't have to spend the whole day watching over me."

"How long was I out?" Devonte asks as he wipes drool from the corner of his mouth.

"About thirty minutes…you know one for every Nova warrior you knocked out on your last mission."

"You heard that…huh?"

"Have you always talked in your sleep? Never mind just go on and enjoy the rest of your day. I'm ok. I appreciate you checking in on me. When I get better, I am going to give you a full lesson on how to fly the STC. We're going to work on getting you certified…that was very impressive what you did the other day."

"Thanks Scott, I will stop in tomorrow and check on you." Devonte leaves the Infirmary and heads directly to the Rec. Room.

He scans the room until he sees Charles and

Kenny sitting at a table in the corner. He casually walks up to their table and pulls up a chair. As he sits down, Charles glares at him as he takes his seat.

"Hey guys, where are the girls?" Devonte asks.

"Not here obviously. Janet went to get Kimberly from the Battle Arena, and no one has seen Jessica since you guys got back from your mission the other day. Whatever, I don't care anyway," Charles says as he looks away in frustration. "Can you believe that it has been a week since our last mission? Yet you three get to go on all the missions you want," Charles states sarcastically. "We are just as good as you guys...maybe even better. And I'm not the only one who feels this way...Kenny is too nice and wouldn't ever say anything to rock the boat, but he feels the same way!"

Devonte looks over to Kenny whose face was riddled with conflict. "What about Trish? Does she feel the same way?"

"Heck if I know. That girl is so distant, I wonder if she still realizes that she is a part of our team!"

"What Charlie means is unless we are on a mission, we hardly ever see her. She stopped coming to our mandatory training session, and the lack of communication really hurts the whole group dynamic thing...and it shows...a lot."

Devonte sits back in astonishment, "If that's

the case, why haven't you gone to the Council about it?"

"Go to the Council and do what!" Charles snaps. "Those has-beens spend more time running their mouths then actually solving anything! Personally, I don't even see the need for a council. It's their fault we are always stuck at base! If you ask me, I think we should get rid of the council, get rid of its members, and get rid of Commander Maximus-"

"Ok Charlie, I get it. Just calm down-"

"Calm down, calm down! That's easy for you to say. You still get awarded missions even after all of the bone-headed pranks you pull." Charles gets up from his seat, "Mark my words, Devonte, there is a change coming. It's time for the Council to wake up and see the truth before it's too late." Charles takes a long slow inhale before saying, "I need some time to cool down."

He starts to walk towards the door when he notices Kenny getting up to follow him. "I need to be alone, Kenny," he says, causing Kenny to stop in his tracks. Charles disappears into the hallway leaving behind Kenny and Devonte.

"Charlie once said that it would be better if we could pick our own teams. It's not that we don't like our team...it's just...it's complicated."

"I bet, but whatever, this will all blow over and you guys will be back out there in no time," Devonte says positively.

"I hope so," Kenny says reluctantly.

Across the complex inside the Battle Arena, Xavier stands next to the bleachers. Draped across his right shoulder was a harness that securely holds his katana to his back. After a few minutes of waiting, Xavier starts to walk towards the exit. Suddenly, Kimberly emerges from the locker room area; her hair still damp from washing up.

"We had a good session today. You are getting better with your balance between your powers and physical combat," Xavier states.

"Thank you…I think I might come back and practice some more later. It sucks that today's session was cut short."

"Again, I apologize. I forgot I have to get to my shift at the lab. As it was, I got a late start today having to check on Scott and Marcus."

"No, it's okay, I understand. How is he by the way…Marcus I mean?"

"He's doing fine. He's a fighter; it's going to take a lot more to keep him down. He should be back to his old self by tomorrow."

"That's good to hear. I felt really bad letting him fight Rampage alone."

"Me too, but he made it out ok and that's what truly matters. Next time we won't let him do it by himself."

"Agreed!"

Kimberly wraps her arms around Xavier and gives him a hug. When she releases him, she hurries towards the exit and vanishes in the doorway.

Xavier continues to walk towards the exit when he remembers that his sword is still strapped to his back. He returns it to the weapons closet and leaves for the lab. As he approaches the lab, he catches a glimpse of Jessica walking through the hallway. Without hesitation, he walks up to her and says, "Hey, Jessica."

"Oh…um hi," Jessica says dolefully.

"Is everything ok, no one has seen you since we got back?"

"I've been better, Xavier. I just need some time to myself."

"Well, if there is anything I can do to help-"

"I said alone…I don't need anyone's help, especially not yours! Do you know that I have been placed on observational lockdown because of you?"

"Me, what did I do-"

"Oh please, Xavier, you are one of the smartest guys I know. Don't pick now to play dumb!"

"Jessica what did I…" Xavier stops at the realization of his mistake.

"Figure it out? Because you had to go and open your big mouth about my dad, the Council has restricted me from leaving the base. They said you told them everything, and that you wanted them to watch me. I don't need a baby sitter!"

"No...no it wasn't supposed to happen like that. I was worried about you and wanted them to watch over you. I was only trying to help, honest."

"Yeah, you did a great job with that. I don't need you to worry about me. Why don't you just mind your business and worry about yourself!"

There was a brief exchange of glances between them; Xavier could see the overwhelming disappointment in her eyes.

"Jessica...I'm sorry...I just didn't want you to do anything reckless."

"Stop...just stay away from me Xavier, I mean it." Jessica brushes past him and continues to trek down the hall until she disappears in the distance.

Xavier stands motionless in the hallway as people scurry past him. As people walk by him, Xavier can hear their judgmental tongues flicking away at him. For a moment, he feels a pain that he had not felt since he left home from Mercury, North Carolina. For the first time in a long time, Xavier felt like an outsider.

He stares blankly at the floor until Trish taps him on his shoulder. He lifts his head towards her, "Let me guess, you heard that?" he asks.

"Yeah, don't worry she is upset now, but she'll get over it, then things will go back to normal."

"I doubt if things will ever go back to normal. To be honest, I don't see them getting much better either." Xavier lets out a big exhale before stating, "Nevertheless, there is work to be done," Xavier says as he shuffles past Trish and into the Lab.

The next morning in the Battle Arena, Marcus and Xavier are engaged in a sparring session. Marcus lands an elbow to Xavier's forehead sending him collapsing to the floor. Marcus backs off his assault and helps Xavier up and onto the bleachers.

"What is with you, Xavier, you have been acting like this all morning? You usually see that move coming…you're not still worried about Jessica, are you?"

"I screwed up Marcus. I never should have said anything to the Council about her relationship to Quake."

"I will tell you like you would tell me; you have to stop beating yourself up. You made a tough call, you did what you thought was right. That's all anyone can ever ask of you. If you ask me, I don't think she is angry with you, as much as she is really upset about the whole situation in general."

"How can you be so sure?" Xavier questions with doubt.

"Take it from a guy who has had a lot of anger related issues. Majority of the time, I was never mad with one person. I was just…mad."

Xavier sits silent with his chin resting on his

fists. "I have to make this right…I have to find some way to clear her name."

"Bro trust me, you need to let this one go. Give her some space, and when she is ready to talk to you, she will."

"Yeah, I guess you are right," Xavier says while getting to his feet. He assumes his fighting stance and the two continue the session.

They train for another two hours and can get some rest before they were summoned to the Briefing Room. Devonte meets them outside and they walk in together. On the inside, Richard stands alongside team 718; they were gathered around the Grid.

"Team 407, we picked up another transmission from Nova's coms. Trish discovered it this morning. So, here it is. I will give you the short version. Nova is receiving a shipment of weapons from an unknown launderer. It is rumored that these weapons were derived from the stolen compound you lost to Twister. The exchange is going to take place late this afternoon. You six are going to be there to intercept the weapons. According to Trish, the exchange is happening somewhere in New Jersey. I don't need to tell you how crucial this mission is. If we can find out who Nova's suppliers are, we can cut them off."

Charles slams his fists onto the table, "Why are they here! We can handle this without them!"

Richard snaps back by saying, "Boy, you

would be wise to check your ego at the door. It can get you into a lot of trouble. I have summoned them because knowing that we have enough manpower helps guarantee that the mission will get completed... correctly! Now no more discussion, you all have about another three hours until the exchange you better get prepped."

After about an hour, everyone meets geared up and ready to go at the Hanger. Instinctively, Devonte walks towards a vacant STC.

"Hey kid, remember we have another pilot for this mission," Marcus states.

Devonte stops at the realization that Scott was still in the Infirmary. He quickly shakes it off and rushes to the group.

They board an STC and take to the sky. The mood is somber; everyone keeps to themselves for the duration of the trip. They land atop a hill overlooking what was said to be the destination for the exchange. The STC pulls off leaving them to stake out the complex.

Dusk approaches as the sun sets on the horizon. A calm soothing stillness rolls down the length of the hill. Marcus and Xavier sit atop a rock with their gaze locked on the complex.

"What's taking so long? We should have made our move by now!" Charles says impatiently.

"Pipe down, Blaze! We have to wait for the right moment to advance. Besides no one has even shown-" Marcus abruptly stops speaking as he watches a Nova cruiser fly over the complex. "Everyone gets down!"

They all lie prone, the black of their armor casting no shadows in the darkening sky. The Nova cruiser lets out one Operative, and then it ascends skyward. It speeds off in a hurry leaving behind a trail of smoke.

"ShaXdow, isn't that the same guy from the youth center?" Marcus asks in disbelief.

"It is; if I recall he is called Screech."

"Look there, a truck just pulled around back. Now is the time to move. We have to secure whatever is in that truck."

Charles crawls up next to Marcus, "Is it time to move, or are we going to wait for an invitation?"

"Listen Blaze, I want you and ShaXdow to go on ahead and get into position. Solara and I will be right on your heels. DaRock and Storm will bring up the rear and provide cover."

Before Marcus has a chance to finish his statement, Charles takes off down the hill. Marcus shakes his head in disappointment; he looks over to Xavier and gives him a casual nod of acknowledgement. Xavier makes his way down the hill after Charles.

Within minutes, they were creeping alongside

the shadow of the complex. Xavier takes a quick glance at his surroundings; he can see the rest of his teammates are now in position.

"Blaze, what do you see?"

"They are just standing around talking. I don't see any weapons…unless they left them in the truck."

"Something about this doesn't feel right," Xavier complains.

"Good, you stay here and figure it out. I'm going for the truck!"

"Blaze wait," Xavier says while reaching out for Charles.
He is unsuccessful in his attempt. Charles rushes around his foes towards the truck. He keeps his body tucked low under the shipping crates that litter the area. Xavier watches as Screech turns his attention away from the men and toward him.

"It never fails, if given the right motivation, people will do whatever you want them to. Even if that means coming to their death!" Screech boasted.

Just then the back of the truck opens, and out jumps about eight men with weapons. Charles just barely has time to duck behind cover.

Volleys of bullets are sprayed through the air. Frantically, everyone jumps for cover; Marcus shouts for Devonte and Kenny to give them cover fire. They lean out and fire back at the truck giving Marcus and Trish an opening to move up.

In perfect synchronization, the men put their

guns away and pull out melee weapons. "Delta, begin the assault!" Screech shouts.

Delta unit charges towards the Atlas Ops, making sure to stay in formation as to present a more opposing threat.

Charles jumps out and tackles one of the men, they wrestle around on the ground. Xavier tries to make his way over to Charles but watches as Kenny breaks out from cover and runs for Charles. Kenny manipulates the electrical energy around him to help traverse the terrain faster. Within seconds, he was able to cover a twenty-yard gap.

Delta forces the rest of them to regroup, everyone runs towards the truck. Kenny and Charles however were still engaged in a fight.

With both of his swords in hand, Charles expertly deflects a series of oncoming attacks. He then surrounds his blades in fire as he glides his arms through the air, twirling his blades and slashing his opponents. Charles arrogantly mocks his opponent as he knocks them to the ground. "What, too hot for you?"

Devonte and Xavier attempt to fight their way back to Charles and Kenny. One member of Delta strikes the ground with his fist. Xavier and Devonte are forced to separate as they jump out of the way of a shockwave. As Devonte hits the ground, he rolls backwards and fires off three shots. The frozen bullets tear through both shoulders and the right knee of their attacker. The Nova operative drops to the ground in agonizing pain. Xavier already in mid stride is closing the gap between Charles and him.

Unaware of the impending attack from the rear, Xavier continues to run. Charles glances past Xavier and sees a member of Delta preparing to take aim. With precision timing, Charles forces Xavier out of the way and takes the hit instead.

Having been shot twice, once in the chest and the other in the abdomen, Charles falls to his knees.

Enraged at what he just witnessed, Kenny lets out a loud cry and zaps over to Charles. He looks him over once, then turns around and stares angrily at Delta. He zaps over to them, but once he comes to a stop, he was blasted against the wall by Screech's sonic vibration.

Seeing this, Charles summons what strength he could and sprints at Screech. Before Screech has time to react, he is tackled through a wall into a dark room.

Xavier tries to follow but was intercepted by Delta. As Kenny lies there dazed on the floor, Devonte runs over and covers himself and Kenny in an ice shield. Marcus and Trish regroup to provide cover for them.

Amidst the darkness, Charles lies in severe agonizing pain; he fights with all his might to get to his knees.

"Does it kill you to know you were never

going to leave this place? You all walked right into your own extinction," Screech's voice rang out from within the darkness.

He blasts Charles with his sonic vibration. "I am the leader of Delta, the most highly trained and deadliest group of meta-humans to ever come out of Nova. We are trained to dissect our targets piece by piece, where you all are playing hero in a battle you have yet to understand."

"You may be right about one thing…up until now I have just been playing around. But now the fun stops and the real battle begins. I hope you're ready…I'm going to break every bone in your body!"

"You are powerless to hurt me. I cannot feel pain. My mask pumps a sedative into my body, which dulls my nerve receptors. Physical trauma does nothing to me!"

Screech blasts Charles two more times, leaving him splayed out across the ground. In his mind, Charles begins to reminisce on all the things that matter to him.

"I wanted to become the best so that I could protect everyone that mattered to me. I was too late to save my brother or my uncle. However, if I can inspire my friends to finish what I could not…well, that's ok too."

Charles' eyes bursts into flames as he stands up. Fire rushes from the soles of his feet to the top of his head rapidly until finally it shoots out against the floor and ignites the entire room.

Surrounded by a blazing inferno, Charles turns to face Screech. With every step he takes, the heat from his body burns the ground.

Screech rushes at him and launches a powerful right hook that spins Charles completely around. Afterward, Charles lands a punch of his own. Screech grabs him and lifts him up over his head, then forcefully slams Charles to the floor. Stomp after stomp, Screech mashes Charles' face into the ground.

Charles manages to turn his body just enough to catch Screech's foot and trip him up. Charles lands a series of kicks to Screech who stumbles back towards the wall of fire. As he comes forward, he hits Charles with a straight punch that sends him flying backwards into a piece of machinery.

Upon collision, a jagged metal fragment breaks off the machine and hits the floor alongside Charles.

Screech picks Charles up off the ground and lifts him into the air. With Charles feet off the floor, the two men are now face to face. Charles slaps Screech in the face with the jagged piece of metal. Screech slowly looks back at Charles who now wears a smirk on his face.

Screech emits a sonic vibration, but suddenly stops. He throws Charles as he doubles over in pain. Just then, he notices his mask had been cracked and the sedative was escaping through the hole in the glass. Screech picks up the jagged piece of metal in frustration and shuffles over to Charles.

Before he could use the sharp chunk of debris, a pillar of lightning springs up from the ground. It launches him into the air; by the time he hits the ground, another pillar shoots up, then another. The pillars of lightning continue until the final one launches Screech from the structure and out into a ravine at the bottom of the ridge.

Kenny zaps over to Charles and cradles him in his arms. Devonte immediately rushes in and puts out the fire. The others follow quickly.

"Charlie…Charlie come on man, speak to me!" Kenny shouts as he shakes Charles' body.

There is no response until Charles lets out a feint cough. "Kenny…I'm sorry…I guess I wasn't as strong as I thought."

"No…no Charlie you are. You are the strongest guy I know."

"It's ok…I'll be ok. I understand it now. I understand that this is a war and we all have a part to play in it. No one person is more important than the other. I only wish I would have realized that earlier."

"Charlie…no stay with me!"

"Kenny…no matter what you find yourself forgetting, always remember that you…"

"Charlie…Charlie!" Kenny says at the realization of Charles' passing.

Kenny breaks down into tears and weeps over

Charles' body. Trish turns her head and cries into Marcus' chest as Xavier and Devonte stand in silence with him.

Chapter 18

Uprooting Evil

Late the following afternoon, Marcus and Devonte find themselves in the Gym; they are doing their reps in silence until Devonte drops the dumbbells. They hit the ground with a thud and bounce slightly. Marcus stops his crunches and sits up and looks at Devonte.

"Why do we keep doing this?" Devonte says as he stares at the floor.

"Doing what?"

"Why do we keep pretending like everything is ok? Charlie is dead, Marcus…and we have been at death's door a lot ourselves. It's very hard to deal with it all, and I'm not sure I can keep this up much longer."

"Not a day goes by when I don't have the same feeling. At times it does seem hopeless to keep fighting…I can't believe I'm saying this, but Charlie said something that was true and made a lot of sense. This fight is bigger than just one person, and everyone has a part to play in it."

"What are you saying?"

"I'm saying that Charlie's fight ended yesterday, but not ours. He paid a heavy price to make sure that we can continue to fight…as a team. I never cared very much for the guy, but he has earned my upmost respect. He went out fighting for what he believed in…and that's us!"

Devonte looks at Marcus with doubt in his eyes, "Ok…we keep fighting, but we never lose sight of our goal…no matter how bad things get."

"I couldn't have said it any better myself, kid."

Later on, amidst the silence of night, Xavier is perched on the ceiling of his room lost in deep meditation. His body and mind were still; the only sound that could be heard was the stillness of his breathing.

A faint sound rings out from within the hallway. It was extremely minute, yet it was loud enough to pull Xavier from within the confines of his thoughts. He detaches himself from the ceiling and lands on the floor without a sound. *It's the middle of the night, no one should be this active this late*, he thinks to himself.

He creeps up to the door and places his ear on the hard surface. He listens as the sound of footsteps hasten past his door. He backs away from the door and waits for four seconds before he slowly opens his door. He peers into the hallway only to catch a glimpse of a shadow as it rounded a corner.

Partially closing his room door, he hurries after the shadow. From the Living Quarters out towards the Garden, Xavier follows this mysterious assailant. Xavier finds a perfect spot to hide and watches as the assailant disappears into the Garden. His eyes widen in shock as he sees clearly who walks before him.

The following morning at a quarter to noon, Xavier rushes to the Rec. Room. Upon his arrival, he scans the room until he finds Devonte sitting with a group of girls. He casually walks up to him amid conversation.

"So, I rolled out of the way. I rolled like three-" Devonte stops as he notices Xavier, "Hey, what's up?"

"Sorry to interrupt, but I need to speak with you immediately."

"Come on, Xavier, I know I'm awesome, but I

can't be there for everybody," Devonte says whimsically.

Xavier stands motionless, unimpressed at Devonte's attempt to impress the group of girls.

"Right...excuse me ladies."

Devonte walks over to another table with Xavier where they sit with their backs to the wall. They face the crowd but speak loud enough that only each other could hear.

"So, what's up, Xavier...I think this group actually likes me."

"Fascinating, I have something important I have to tell you."

"Oh, that reminds me, I have something to tell you too. Remember back in Chicago when that fat guy stepped on my favorite board. Well with Marcus' help, I developed an alternative mode of transportation. I call it my perpetual ice slide, and it's awesome. I propel myself forward using my ice, I can even ride it in the air!"

"That sounds amazing, but this is serious," Xavier says.

He leans over to Devonte and whispers into his ear. Confusion consumes Devonte as Xavier explains the situation.

"Are you sure?" Devonte questions as Xavier pulls back.

"I spent the rest of the night trying to convince myself otherwise."

"This is insane, first Charlie, now this. You know a lot of people are saying the Jessica might be a traitor or something. What do we do?"

"We…I have to tell the Council, but first I'll need evidence."

"Yeah, you have fun with that…have you told Marcus yet?"

"No…that's where I'm headed next. Is he still in the Battle Arena?"

"No clue, you might want to check his room first," Devonte says.

Xavier gets up and leaves the Rec. Room; he heads back to the Living Quarters. He walks up the stairs to their floor and he notices several Medical Specialists rushing past him. Out of curiosity he follows them through the hall until David stops him. Xavier watches as the Medical Specialists run into Kenny's room.

"Xavier, I'm afraid you can't go any further," David says as he blocks Xavier's view of the room.

"What happened…is Kenny ok?" Xavier asks hesitantly.

"Kenny…is gone. He was found with a stab wound to the abdomen." David looks away with unease. "There was no sign of foul play; I'm guessing he took Charlie's death real hard."

Xavier looks at David in doubt, "Wait, you think he did this to himself, I'm not sure I buy that."

"Not the point. We will have to wait for the

official statement to be released. In the meantime, I need you to stay away from this room."

Xavier slowly backs away and heads back outside where he runs to the Battle Arena. When he gets inside he, notices Marcus panting in the middle of the floor. Xavier walks hesitantly towards him.

In his mind his thoughts are cluttered in confusion. He takes a moment to think about the situation. He stands unmoving with his eyes locked on the floor. He jolts back to his senses as Marcus calls out to him. "Xavier…Xavier! Hey, what's the matter with you?"

Xavier looks unsure as he answers, "I need to talk to you. I'm just trying to process it all myself first."

"What are you talking about?"

Xavier goes on to tell Marcus everything he had discovered within the last couple of hours. After hearing him out, Marcus stands up and looks Xavier right in the eyes.

"Are you kidding me…I don't believe you Even still, you are up at the dead of night yourself. You were obviously mistaken."

"Who else could I have been looking at?"

"Anyone, just not who you think. I get it, Jessica is mad at you, people are talking about a supposed traitor, and you don't know how to let go and back off. So, you are going off on this foolish detective binge, making claims that you have no right to make. Now I am truly sorry about what happened to Kenny, but that other thing, you can forget about it."

Xavier looks content as he backs away from Marcus. He turns and walks towards the exit. He gets a few feet from the door when he stops, "You were right, it was foolish of me to come to you this way. But when you find out the truth, I wonder if you will be strong enough to do what must be done?" Xavier says before disappearing into the light of the outdoors.

At about midnight, Xavier sits in the darkness of night. He uses his static adhesion to secure himself above the window of what used to be Kenny's room. He carefully peers through the window just as some Operatives were leaving the room. Without a sound, Xavier enters the room via the window.

He moves cautiously as to not disturb the crime scene. Not even five minutes later, he finds something that peaks his curiosity. The couch had been drug across the floor, leaving marks on the ground. Xavier kneels to examine the marks; he places his hands on the ground to brace himself.

Under his hands he can feel the rough grains of dirt. He lifts his palm up to eye level. He can see the faint shimmer of tiny fragments of minerals. He pulls out a small plastic bag and dusts the dirt off his palm into the bag. He reaches back down and gathers up another handful of the dirt.

He sits back on one knee and takes a long hard look at the outline of Kenny in his final moments. Xavier notices that the outline was looking towards the closet. Xavier turns his glance to the closet that sits slightly ajar. Slowly, he steps towards the closet when he hears an unusual cracking sound coming from the floor.

He takes two steps backwards then kneels on his knees. He takes his hands and presses them against the floor. As he applies pressure, the cracking sound rings out once more. Xavier glances at the door for security, he can tell he is running out of time. He electrifies the tip of his finger and uses the electricity to cut along the seam of the floor paneling.

As he lifts the paneling, he reaches his hand in and pulls out a flash-drive that was hidden within. He slowly lowers the paneling and eases his way back over to the window. Once outside, he hastily maneuvers to his own window and goes inside.

Xavier pulls out his personal computer and places it atop his table. He pulls out the flash-drive and inserts it into his computer. Revealed were countless video files organized in chronological order. Xavier spends a few minutes watching some of the videos. Each video was a recollection of a day in Kenny's life.

After about four videos, Xavier scrolls down

to the end of the list. The final video was the shortest on record and was recorded the night before, right before Xavier heard footsteps in the hallway. He moves the cursor over and clicks on the file.

"It's late November...the 23 I guess. I haven't slept since Charlie died yesterday. That whole mission continues to play repeatedly in my head. He was always misunderstood; no one knew the real Charlie except me. He was my friend, the only true one I ever had. Not like Trish...something about her never sat right with me. Everyone is calling Jess a traitor but I think it's Trish. I followed her around all day; she just conveniently does everything by the book. So, I thought...I caught her in the lab about an hour ago. She was downloading files onto some data chips. I wanted to confront her, but I know I'm not good enough to take her alone. So, I ran back here and started this video, I'm going to take it to the Council in the morning.

I know Jess is innocent. Trish is the traitor among us. Not to mention, it just so happened that she was the one who picked up the transmission to a secret deal that turned out to be a trap.
Charlie...I'm not as strong as you were, I'm not even as brave...but I have a duty. I have a duty to keep my teammates safe even if that means-"

The sound of knocking can be heard in the background. *"Kenny...Kenny are you in there?"*

"It's her, I got to go-"

The video suddenly cuts out, and Xavier is left shocked and speechless. He sits back in his chair and remains motionless for a couple of seconds. He closes his computer and hides the flash-drive and bag of dirt.

The next morning, Marcus sits atop the edge of his bed, his eyes locked on a small table. On the table were three picture frames. In his mind, thoughts of what Xavier said to him begin to surface.

Hastily he shakes off his internal conflict. Marcus leaves his room and heads out towards the lab to meet Trish.

He stands outside the door for fifteen minutes before she was done. Finally, she emerges; in her hands are a stack of books. Marcus smiles at her and offers to carry the books. She obliges, and they walk together to the Rec. Room.

Along the way, Marcus discusses his frustrations with Xavier.

"I'm surprised to hear such accusations come from Xavier. He is a logical thinker. This doesn't seem like him. I have no reason to betray you guys, and as far as catching me at the garden…I always go there when I'm sad. One of my teammates died…I needed a minute to grieve."

"Babe I know, and that's what has me irritated. He knows better; why is he acting like this?"

As they reach the Rec. Room, Trish pats Marcus on the shoulder and says, "You know what you have to do. The question is will you do it?"

"I don't know. A lot has happened in a short amount of time. Maybe I'm just overreacting," Marcus responds hesitantly.

After about an hour of relaxation, Marcus gets up to go find Xavier when suddenly, he appears in the doorway. The two share an intense stare down for a couple of seconds before members of the Council walk up behind Xavier.

Xavier slowly walks up towards Marcus and Trish. Conversations begin to stop as Xavier moves through the Rec. Room.

"Xavier, what are you doing?"

"Marcus, it's time for you to see the line in the sand." Xavier hesitates for a moment. "Trish... is not what she appears to be. Charlie and Kenny are dead, and it is all her fault."

Just then two operatives come into the Rec. Room and walk up to Trish. They take her by the arms and escort her out into the hallway. Marcus attempts to stop them, but Xavier prevents him.

Marcus looks angrily at Xavier, "Xavier you're wrong... you are wrong about this!"

"Marcus please listen, you know I wouldn't do something like this without evidence."

"Evidence...what evidence?"

"Last night I went to Kenny's room to see if I could find any clues. I found two things--- dirt and a flash-drive. The dirt matches that of the dirt left by Trish after she activates her powers-"

"What does that have to do with anything!" Marcus shouts.

"It's not ordinary dirt. Moving forward, on the flash-drive I found videos of Kenny. The last recorded video he says how he saw Trish downloading files onto data chips in the lab. He sneaks away to record the video…and at the end you can hear her call out to him from the hallway. All of this happened right before I heard footsteps in the hall."

"No…no this is not right; Trish can't be a traitor. I think you got this all wrong, Xavier!" Without warning, a transmission comes in to Richard that Trish had escaped custody.

Marcus stands there in disbelief; he looks over to Xavier who states, "If there were no reason to run, why would she run…" Marcus stares Xavier in his eyes before he brushes past him.

Marcus races out into the hallway. He looks down the hall in both directions. He takes off running past dozens of people. Marcus hurries to the one place he knew she would go.

He burst through the doors of the Garden to see Trish standing in full uniform with a bag thrown over her shoulder.

"What…what are you doing?" Marcus says in disbelief.
Trish ignores him and continues to secure the bag around her shoulder. Marcus walks up and grabs her

by both arms in an attempt to talk to her. She breaks free and quickly morphs her arm into a thorny vine and takes a swipe at Marcus. He jumps back in just enough time to avoid getting hit. The thorns tear a hole in his shirt.

"Xavier was right, but why? Why would you betray us? Whatever Quake told you it isn't true!"

"You don't get it, none of this was real...it was all just another mission."

"So, you were with Nova from the beginning?"

"My mission was to infiltrate Atlas HQ and monitor you and your friends. After Stargazer and Screech were driven away by a group of teenagers, Quake took notice. He sent me here to gather as much Intel on you three as possible. He also wanted data from your hard-drive."

Marcus stands there in shock, his fist was balled up tightly out of anger. "So, you and I were nothing more than a distraction?"

"I needed you to trust me. What better way to do that then to have you fall in love with me."

"Everything Xavier said about you was true. You are the one who killed Kenny, and you set us up on that mission. And Charlie-"

"That wasn't supposed to happen. That mission was orchestrated by Lord Quake to get rid of you three. After he revealed himself to you, and you turned down his offer to join Nova, he devised this plan. You all were supposed to die, and I was to go missing. This would take care of you three, give me cover for returning back to him, and leave Jessica with the burden of being suspect number one in the 'who is a traitor' crisis. Everything was going perfect until that idiot Charles decided right then that he wanted to grow a spine."

"You used us…you used me."

"Get over yourself, this is bigger than you and I. Quake is going to save this world from itself."

"You will not get away with this."

"What are you talking about, I already have," Trish states with a sadistic smirk on her face.

Just then a vine shoots up from the earth behind Marcus. Without warning, Xavier teleports into the garden. He pushes Marcus out of the way.

The vine coils itself tightly around Xavier's whole body. With the momentary distraction, Trish takes the opportunity to make an escape. To stop her, Marcus launches a fireball at her. The intense ball of heat misses its mark and sets some flowers ablaze. He turns his attention to Xavier who shouts, "Forget about me. You have to stop her…go!"

Marcus hesitates before he rushes after Trish. When he steps outside, he can see Trish sprinting across the field. Marcus takes to the air and flies after her. Trish manipulates the earth and launches roots from the ground; they start lashing out at Marcus.

In the air, he maneuvers from side to side,

avoiding the roots. Marcus launches fireballs at Trish who was then blown into the trees by the force of the blast.

Marcus lands just feet from Trish who was brushing the dirt off her uniform.

"You are so selfish. All you care about is how I lied to you. What about the bigger picture?"

"Stop it! You know what we fight for…who we fight for."

"Quake wants the same thing…you should come with me, then we can be together." Trish can see that Marcus is flustered with anger. "Nova is winning this war, to stand against us is suicide."

"I'm bringing you back. You are going to answer to the Council for your crimes."

"My, my, aren't we the model Operative. Secure the target, and bring them in," Trish mocks. "You have your orders, and I had mine."

Trish throws a right cross at Marcus as he tries to deflect the onslaught; however, her hits are slightly too fast for him to defend against. She goes for another punch but is thrown into a tree. As she lies on the ground, she tunnels into the dirt and comes charging at Marcus. He watches as the ground beneath his feet starts to rumble faintly as Trish gets closer.

Once she was in position, she springs out from the dirt; her hands are morphed into sharp mineral blades. She twirls her body through the air and slashes at Marcus. He jumps back and reaches behind him as if to grab his blade. Having realized that it was not on his back, Marcus gets into a defensive position. As Trish swipes at him, Marcus ducks and dodges her attacks. He blocks her attack and tries to land a few hits of his own.

She anticipates his attacks and hits him with a bicycle kick. The attack spins him around three hundred sixty degrees. After the rotation, Marcus catches Trish with a fireball. The blast forces her back into a tree. As she lands on the ground, she places her hands on the dirt. Within seconds, sections of the surrounding trees broke into her husk creatures.

They surround Marcus who ignites his hands in preparation.

"It didn't have to be like this. You could've died with your friends rather than by yourself."

Trish takes off running as her husks close in on Marcus. He starts to fight back with all his might, and after a couple of minutes, he destroys the last husk. He takes off after Trish who has run about a mile and a half. Marcus catches up to her and stops her on the edge of the cliff. There was a runoff that led to a sixty-foot drop.

"Looks like this is where we go our separate ways."

"There is nowhere for you to go. You would never survive that drop. Just hand over the bag and turn yourself in."

"Here," Trish takes the bag off her shoulder and dangles it over the edge. "It's your choice, me or the bag!"

Trish jumps over the edge and flings the bag to the side. Marcus jumps off the edge after the bag, but he misses by mere inches. Having spent a great deal of energy, he could not fly to stop himself. Seemingly out of nowhere, he is caught by Xavier who has been following them, and at the last-minute teleports to save his friend. Xavier grabs a hold of the bag that has been slung around an old eroded tree stomp protruding from the cliff side.

They watch as Trish stands on what looks to be nothing. Just then, an aircraft uncloaks itself. Trish had landed on top of a Nova cruiser. She stares long and hard at Marcus before the hatch opens revealing Stargazer standing on the ramp. Trish blows Marcus a kiss just as she enters the cruiser. It turns around and zooms off into the distance.

Eventually Xavier and Marcus climb back up to the ledge. As Marcus climbs, Xavier extends his hand in assistance. Marcus takes a firm grip and allows Xavier to pull him up onto his feet.

"Thanks...Xavier," Marcus says as he stares off into the distance. "She had us all fooled right from the beginning. She was planted here to watch you, Devonte, and myself. After the battle at the youth center, she said Quake took an interest in us." Marcus pauses for a second, "It all makes sense now, how he knew my name. Trish had been leaking information to him-"

"Via the channel that I hacked. While we thought we had an advantage, Quake was still one step ahead of us." Xavier states.

"She used it to try and have us killed. She told me that it was supposed to be us that died on that mission, not Charlie. Then she was going to disappear making a clean getaway. Leaving Jessica labeled as a traitor.

I feel so foolish; I should have seen this coming. I should have believed you, and I'm sorry. I can't help but feel somewhat responsible for what has happened today." Marcus clenches one fist tightly. "No matter how long it takes, I will stop her. She will pay for this."

Marcus walks off towards the base, his eyes filled with frustration. Xavier follows closely behind him, periodically looking over his shoulder. As they approach the base, they can see the garden had been burned down. Commander Maximus, Richard, and David wait for them at the entrance of the building. Without saying a word, Marcus hands over the bag and continues to walk inside.

"She got away sir," Xavier states. "She was picked up by a Nova cruiser. Stargazer was onboard."

"Were you able to ascertain the reason for the betrayal?" Richard questions.

"According to Marcus, she was a plant, put

here to gather intel on Marcus, Devonte and myself. She was also here to steal information from our hard-drives."

"At least you secured our files," Richard says in relief.

"Sir, with all due respect, I wouldn't celebrate just yet. Trish has near perfect recall. She can remember almost everything she has either seen or heard."

"Then Quake has the upper hand once again." Commander Maximus breathes slowly; in his heart were feelings of confusion and disappointment. He looks at David and says, "We need to do a full system restore, back up all of our data, then wipe the servers. From there we will have to reconfigure the systems, put up new and stronger firewalls, as well as limit who has access to the secure files." Commander Maximus rubs his brow in frustration. "We lost three Operatives in the last two days." He slams the tip of his cane on the hard ground cracking it with ease. "Quake is slowly chipping away at our foundation."

"What is he trying to prove?" David asks.

"Nothing, he means to break us…break our will. He wants to tear us down piece by piece. He won't stop until we have either given up or have been destroyed."

"I will contact Adam and have him get started on backing up the hard-drives." David states as he heads back inside.

Commander Maximus looks down towards Xavier, "That was some fine work you did. For her to have made it this long means she was skilled at covering her tracks."

"Yeah, well she got careless. Up until now she has been in control of the outcome, but when people started snooping around, she became desperate. To simply put it, she got sloppy."

"Well, nevertheless, we have to keep moving forward. Our mission is the same it has always been. Besides this is not the first time we have had an Operative jump ship to another team-"

Stargazer stands with his arms folded across his chest as Quake speaks to Trish. She sits on the other end of the desk with her hands tucked under the table on her lap.

"It has been a while since the last time we sat face to face."

"Indeed, it has, Lord Quake. I believe it was when you were giving me my orders after you rescued me from those BCI dogs."

"The humans attempt to comprehend the magnitude of our abilities. The ones that can't, try to keep us in cages like animals. Once I reach completion, they will see that we cannot be contained. Your work precedes you. Welcome to my armada…"

"Solara, my call sign is Solara. I believe in

making a good impression, so I brought you this."

Stargazer's eyes open wide as Trish places the shard of synthetic quartz on Quake's desk. Quake smirks as he gazes upon the synthetic quartz.

"Stargazer see to it that Cordell gets the synthetic quartz. Solara and I need to speak about our next move."

Stargazer walks up to the desk and snatches the quartz off the table. He slowly walks towards the door before seeping into darkness.

Chapter 19

State of Emergency

Sunrise approaches over the horizon; the light climbs up the length of an STC. Devonte sits atop the STC lost in his thoughts. In his hand clenched tightly was a rock, and at his side sits one of his guns. He begins to examine the rock closely. He tosses it repeatedly into the air. After about thirty seconds, he hurls it into the distance. Waiting no time at all he pulls his gun and shoots the rock out of the air.

"Twenty-five yards…not bad," a voice comes from down beside the STC.

Devonte takes a glance down towards the ground. Much to his surprise, he sees Janet standing there. In her arms cupped tightly was Zoe, and she was squirming in playfulness. Devonte turns his body towards her, letting his feet dangle over the edge.

"Hey, how did you find me?"

"I ran into Scott and he told me where you were."

"You were looking for me?" Devonte questions.

"Yes, why do you sound so surprised?"

"Well, you usually don't notice me unless we are with the others."

"If you haven't noticed, our little group of friends just became two guys smaller. I don't know about you, but I don't want to lose any more friends."

"Me neither…I don't want to lose anyone ever again."

Janet looks deep into Devonte's eyes; she can see his sadness. "You seem upset," she says.

"I'm fine, it's just times like this make me think of my sister." He hesitates momentarily before saying, "She went missing some time ago and the cops gave up the search. To them, my parents, and everyone else, she is dead. But I know that she is still alive somewhere out there. She is a Coleman, and we are survivors."

"How do you intend to find her?" Janet asks. "Whatever way possible. She is my top priority-"

"And the reason you joined Atlas," Janet interjects.

Devonte looks away into the distance, "Am I wrong for coming here?" He asks solemnly.

"Everyone has their reasons for coming to Atlas. Using the resources around you to help you find your sister is not wrong. If anything, it makes you human." Janet places Zoe down onto ground and watches her scurry along the ground. "We have these powers and sometimes we forget that we are still human."

"Human or not, I won't stop looking no matter what! I could always use some help, that weird thing you do with your eyes can be handy. I mean it found Subject 62, so no doubt it can find Sarah."

Janet chuckles to herself. Devonte smiles from ear to ear at the realization of her laughter.

"Do you mean my ability to sense energy?"

"Yeah, can you do that and help me find her?" Devonte asks out of desperation.

Janet bends down and picks up Zoe. "If I do find her, then what? Are you going to leave?"

"Of course not, whether you like it or not you are stuck with me," Devonte says jokingly! He starts to laugh as Janet walks away. What he couldn't see was the smile on Janet's face as she walks back inside the hanger.

Standing at the foot of his bed, Xavier examines the flash-drive from Kenny's room. He twirls it through his fingers before placing it in a locked box. The black metallic box has a strip of tape on it with Kenny's name written on it.

He takes the box and walks out of his room and down the hall. Once he reaches the first floor of the Living Quarters, he can see Jessica approaching him in the distance. He makes a quick right turn and exits out of the front door. As he walks alongside the building, he can hear her call out his name.

He stops in his tracks; his head hangs down slightly in uncertainty. Finally, he turns around, "Hey," he says dolefully.

"Can I talk to you for a minute?" she asked hesitantly.
Xavier nods in compliance, he puts a warm smile on his face.

"I've had some time to think about it, and I want to apologize for how I yelled at you."

"Don't worry about it. I'm sorry for all the trouble I caused you. I was only trying to help, honest."

"Yeah, I know, and I appreciate it. You are a good person, Xavier, and a great friend."

"Thanks Jessica. So, has the Council lifted their decision yet?"

"As of yesterday, I am free to fly," Jessica says while letting out a few giggles. She stops laughing as she notices the black box nestled tightly under Xavier's left arm. "What's with the box?" she asks.

Xavier lifts the box out in front of him to

show Jessica what was inside. He opens the lid to reveal a hollow void of nothingness. The one and only thing that was in the box was Kenny's flash-drive.

"What's that?" she questions.

"It's a flash-drive; I found it the other night in the floor of Kenny's room. There are videos on it…recordings if you will. Each from a different day in Kenny's life."

"It's just so crazy you know, everything that has happened over the last few days. I mean it can't possibly get any worse than it is."

"I hope not, but something tells me there is darkness on the horizon. I don't know what it is, but…" Xavier shakes off his confliction. "You know what, let's not worry about that. I prefer to think positive rather than negative." He smiles at her, "It's good to see you smiling again. I wish I could stay longer but I must get this flash-drive to the Council. See you around Jessica," he says as he slowly walks away smiling.

She waits for him to walk away, "Whatever's coming, we can face it together," she says loudly.

"Agreed," Xavier states as he gives her a reassuring thumbs up. Steadily, he continues to walk to the Council Room where he drops off the black box.

The Chosen: Breaking Bonds

Marcus stares hard at a picture of Trish sitting amidst the flowers of the gardens. In his mind, constant flashbacks occur of all the good time he and Trish spent together. Just then, he ignites the picture and watches as it burns. The ashes fall into a garbage can atop a mixed-matched bundle of trash.

He collects the bag and exits his room, where he strolls quietly down the hall with the bag slung over his shoulder. There was a vacant stare on his face. Totally unaware of his surroundings, Marcus runs into Kimberly knocking her to the ground.

When she falls, she let go of the folder in her hands. Having realized his mistake, Marcus lets his bag fall to the floor, and he helps Kimberly up. He reaches for her folder, but before he could touch it, Kimberly frantically grabs it.

"I'm sorry, I wasn't looking where I was going," Kimberly states apologetically.

"No, it's my fault, I had my mind on other things. I guess I wasn't paying attention."

Kimberly looks at Marcus' face; she could see that he was very upset.

"How are you holding up?" she questions with care.

There was no response at first. Eventually Marcus breaks his silence saying, "I have had my share of bad breakups, but this is different. Usually, I get over it quick, and I move on. This time it's different; this time it's personal!

No matter how long it takes, I will find her, and she will answer for what she has done. If not to me, then to the Council!"

"Revenge comes at a high price. They say when one seeks revenge they should dig two graves--- one for the person you are seeking vengeance against, and the other for yourself."

"To me, it's not revenge…it's justice! She lied to us from the beginning and put us all in danger. If you ask me, she can burn right along with Quake!"

"You're frustrated, I get that. But don't let her get in your head, or else she will have won. She will have broken you to the point where you could do something reckless. I don't want to lose you, too…I mean we can't afford to lose anybody else!" Kimberly looks away trying to hide her tears.

Marcus looks on in understanding; he inhales and lets out a great sigh. He places one hand on her shoulder and says, "I take it they were good friends of yours," he says respectfully. "I'm sorry for your loss. I guess I got caught up in my own pain that I couldn't see that everyone around me was suffering too."

"They were good people, and that witch just…how could she do that without any sort of guilt," Kimberly proclaims in sadness.

Marcus lets go of Kimberly, "I'm not really sure what to tell you, but she hurt us all." Marcus forms a slight smirk as he states, "If Xavier was standing here, he would say something like we need to use the pain of loss to make us stronger, or something like that."

Kimberly finally gets herself together, wiping her face dry from the tears. "I'm sorry, I didn't mean to do that."

"Do what?" Marcus questions.

"I didn't mean to cry like that."

Marcus begins to laugh softly; his laughter causes Kimberly to turn red from embarrassment.

"Don't worry about it. Everyone has a right to grieve for the ones they have lost."

Her embarrassment left her, and she looks on in admiration.

"You don't have to apologize, I would have done the same thing. Unfortunately, I do not have the luxury of crying. I have to remain strong for my teammates."

"Maybe you don't have to. Xavier and Devonte need their friend more than they need a leader. You shouldn't keep things bottled up inside you, it's not healthy.

My father taught me a technique to help circulate the body's natural flow of energy. Believe it or not, negativity on the mind can disrupt the flow of one's energy."

"By any chance, would you mind teaching me this technique?" Marcus inquires.

"Yes, of course. We can start whenever you are ready."

"Thanks," Marcus says softly.

Two days later, team 407 was in the Battle Arena in a group sparring session.

Devonte glides around on his perpetual ice slide, firing a volley of ice projectiles down at both Xavier and Marcus. While dodging the ice, the two continue their sword fight. Swinging twice, Marcus is able to knock Xavier to the ground, at which point he ignites both ends of his blade and flings it at Devonte.

The superheated steel cuts through the ice slide, which resulted in Devonte plummeting to the hard floor. Marcus attempts to go for his blade but is rendered motionless by unexpected bolts of electricity. Xavier then teleports and catches Marcus' blade before it hits the ground. Devonte releases a sheet of ice that races across the floor towards Xavier.

As the ice approaches him, Xavier begins to spin Marcus' blade around his body creating a dome of electricity. The unstable heat from the electricity holds the ice at bay. Suddenly, the blade shoots from within the dome. It rotates rapidly through the air. Having regained his mobility, Marcus leaps into the air with such precision to grab his blade in mid rotation and releases a brief tornado flame that sends Devonte flying backwards.

As Marcus comes to a stop, he notices Xavier running straight towards him. They engage in close quarters combat until their focus is broken by a loud ringing alarm from the timer on the wall.

Once the ringing ceased, the only sound that can be heard was the sound of the boy's heavy panting. Marcus stares at Xavier who stares back at him. The two shake hands and make their way over to Devonte who sits on the floor. The ends of his braids were dripping wet with sweat.

They all clean up and exit the locker room. As they walk back into the main room of the Battle Arena, they begin to joke amongst themselves.

The fun suddenly stops as they see David staring at the TV monitor in the control room. As they get closer, they can see the disbelief and frustration in his eyes.

"David, the session is over, we were going to go back to our rooms. David are you ok?" Marcus questions.

"Hold on, look," David says as he diverts their attention to the TV.

The boys turn their heads towards the screen just as David raised the volume.

"We are coming to you live, just hours after a devastating meta-human showdown took a turn for the worse. What started out as a battle between two meta-humans quickly turned into a terror attack on the citizens of this great nation." On the screen was footage recorded from a personal video camera.

"My fellow Americans do not look at this as

another presidential campaign but look at it as a transition into the next stage for this great nation," President Carmichael states.

The crowd responds with thunderous applause, the video camera flailing around as the operator gave a round of applause. As President Carmichael continues his speech, the cameraman turns his attention to the top of a nearby building. Off-screen, a voice rings out saying, *"What is she doing up there?"*

Alexis stands motionless on the edge of the building. She expertly maneuvers down the side of the building and into the crowd. One by one, the people in the crowd become frantic as they scurry away from Alexis. Security jumped in her way to halt her advance. She takes little time to defeat them.

More armed men run up and begin to shout at her to lie down and surrender. In the meantime, down by the podium the ground begins to tremble. From within the earth, roots spring up and dismantles the podium.

A loud shriek rings out, *"No...no...no...run!"*

The camera falls to the ground where it is kicked and trampled on by the fleeing crowd. When it finally comes to rest, its lens was focused on what used to be the podium.

"It's Trish," Xavier says.

On the video, Trish can be seen standing over the first-lady. *"She won't be defeated so easily. You all are powerless to stop people like her. That is why we of Atlas go out of our way to keep you safe.*" Trish starts to fight Alexis with the giant roots.

She uses the roots to pick up massive chunks of debris and hurl them at Alexis. Cries of terror can be heard off-screen. She continues her assault, but suddenly stops.

She turns her attention to the humans, "*For years, we have fought for you filthy, ungrateful, selfish, humans, and still you hate us. Nothing we do is good enough; we will no longer stand beside you. Now you lie beneath us…in the dirt…where you belong.*"

Just then the video cuts out. Everyone stands there in silence as the news continues to play. "*We have reports of several casualties, and many injured, among which was First Lady Carmichael. We have also received word that the President will make an address later this evening-*"

David shuts off the TV; he sits back on the console. He slowly inhales only to exhale moments later. He looks over to the boys who were caught motionless in suspense. He focuses his gaze on Marcus, whose nostrils start to flair in anger.

"What was that?" Marcus snaps wildly. "What are we going to do, David? We have to do something!"

"I agree something must be done. However, nothing can be done at this moment except wait."

"But David, if we just sit around more people will get hurt."

"Listen. You three go back to your rooms. I am going to meet with the Council." David says as he walks past them and out of the Battle Arena.

Later on, that early evening, the boys are all gathered in Xavier's room. They wait for President Carmichael's address.

"How long do we have to watch the news, this crap is depressing," Devonte says while laying upside down on the edge of Xavier's bed.

"Quiet down Devonte, this is important. We have to be patient."

"Xavier, I'm going to have to side with the kid on this one." Marcus interjects.

"Shh… look it's coming up next," Xavier says while lifting his hand.

The local news continues to play for another few minutes before a live camera feed began to stream the Presidential address.

"Earlier today, our national security was compromised by the radical acts of these domestic terrorists. These…meta-humans think that just because they can lift a car or fly like a bird, that they have the right to do so. Every man, woman, and child special or not must be held accountable for their actions."

A man can be heard screaming, *"Bring back the MRA!"*

"Once our allies, it would seem that Atlas have now become our primary targets. Their negligence and lack of regard for mankind has cost the lives of many and injured many more. Among those was the one person that means the world to me. My wife, First Lady Carmichael, was hospitalized and now lies in intensive care with several lacerations, and some severe bruising as well as internal bleeding. My fellow Americans no longer will we have to live in fear of these meta-human barbarians-"

"Yeah, bring back the MRA!"

"History has shown us that locking them away won't solve our problem. I stand before you today with a more permanent solution. I have here the plans for America's latest defense against meta-humans. Ladies and gentlemen, I give you...the Alpha Human!"

The crowd goes ballistic as a series of blueprints begin to show on the massive screen behind the President.

"They are built with a flexible alloy that was designed by our leading engineers to maneuver fluidly revealing a built-in arsenal. This alloy is super lightweight and flexible giving the machine more human-like movements. An advanced AI system allows the Alpha Human to adapt to situation in real

*time. It was built to withstand the hardest conditions;
simply put, it is the unrivaled answer to meta-
humans.*

*These are just concept designs; however, we
do have three prototypes that I think are ready for
their first test. If Atlas doesn't want to turn
themselves in, then we will round up every meta-
human we can find until they do!"*

The President walks off stage as the crowd
serenades him with loud cheers and thunderous
applause.

Xavier turns off the TV and throws the remote
onto his bed.

There was an eerie silence within the room.

"Robots," Devonte says jokingly! "He plans
to fight us with Robots?"

"Kid take this serious please. Xavier, do you
think David was watching?"

"Most likely, but we need to find him."

They all get up and leave the room and rush to
the Council Room.

"That's suicide," Richard shouts!

"What else would you have us do? The longer
we wait the more innocent meta-humans will be
hunted."

"David, I understand your frustration, but
right now our top priority is here. The President is a

politician; he's manipulative not stupid. He will do nothing more than capture them. And once we are back on our feet, we will deal with this situation-"

"Stop. How can you even believe that the nonsense you speak of is ok? Amir Robinson put this team together all those years ago because he believed that we had to rise above who we are to do what we had to do."

"Now is not the time to be naive, David. We were framed; our reputation no longer matters. We have to be smart right now… we are still trying to regroup from losing data to that little girl."

"You make a valid point about needing to regroup, but I have a duty to fight for the innocent. We have more than enough manpower to do what needs to be done around here, as well as stand up to this new threat."

Without giving Richard a chance to respond, David leaves the Briefing Room and walks down to the Council Room. He reaches the door at the same time as the boys.

"David, did you watch the news?" Marcus inquired.

"I did, and I'm working on a plan as we speak. If you boys are up to it, I could use your help."

"You don't even have to ask. We are with you until the end," Marcus says firmly.

"Good, wait here, I have to speak with Commander Maximus. I'll be out in a few." David opens the doors and walks into the Council Room.

Commander Maximus sat alone at the round table. On the wall the TV was turned to the news. The volume was muted. David calls out to Commander Maximus.

He responds by saying, "We have to make our move. The longer we wait, the worse the situation will become."

"How should we handle this, sir?"

"Unfortunately, we are going to have to contact Agent Newman."

"Great, do we not have any other options?" David asks in uncertainty.

"None as peaceful as this. Agent Newman is our only voice right now."

"Yes, but that guy is shifty. From what I have seen he isn't pro meta-human. I'm not too sure he has our best interest in mind."

"Morally conflicted he is; however, Agent Newman is duty bound to be our liaison. All we can do now is hope for the best and plan for the worse."

"Commander are you sure about this?"

"No, but what are our other alternatives? I will arrange for you two to meet tomorrow."

David nods in accordance and turns to walk out of the room.

"David, watch yourself. Be prepared for anything."

"Yes sir, understood." David exits the room;

waiting for him were the boys. They look on in determination as David gives them a nod of acknowledgement. "I have a plan," He says.

Chapter 20

Project Alpha Human pt 1

Down on the streets of Fortune City, New York, stands a man clad in an all-black suit. His tie blows in the wind as he stands next to an abandoned vehicle. In his left hand, he holds onto a mobile phone with a firm grip.

Suddenly, in the distance, he sees an STC coming his way. Neglecting to slow down, the STC zooms across the sky above him. David jumps from within the STC and freefalls to the ground. He lands precisely in front of Agent Newman.

"Very bold entrance for 'America's most wanted'."

"Save it Newman, you know why I'm here."

"Ah right, you came here to convince me that

yesterday didn't happen."

"I'm here to clear our name. We were framed!"

"Very likely story," Agent Newman states. "Who would want to frame you?"

"One of our Operatives turned out to be a plant from another organization. She betrayed us earlier this week and went back to Nova-"

"Nova? What the heck is that?"

"I thought the NRD would have looked into them by now. Anyway, she was not, and is not affiliated with Atlas. You know better than a lot that we would never attack innocent humans."

"Apparently, I don't. I have done my job tirelessly to keep the peace between Atlas and the US Government. My hands are tied, and there is nothing else I can say that can change that!"

The conversation continues as people look on from the shelter of the massive skyscrapers.

"You can go to your leader and fight for us!" David proclaims.

"You don't get it. This is not like that time in Dallas. I can't just walk up to President Carmichael and ask for another pardon. Whether or not you were framed no longer matters the American people have had enough of you meta-humans abusing your freedom. Therefore, we who represent the will of this great nation will stop at nothing to keep its citizens safe."

David clenches his fist tightly in disgust. "Your system is corrupted! You want nothing more than to see us all wiped out. We, who are among the citizens you swear to protect."

"I don't see citizens, I see guests who have overstayed their welcome." Agent Newman stares hard into David's eyes. Just then the mutter of a helicopter is heard amidst the vast skyscrapers.

Now, hovering just above the conversation is a military grade helicopter. Tethered to its underbelly is a large metallic crate with the word 'Alpha' etched into the side.

"I have a duty to serve this country," Newman says while pressing a button on his phone.

Suddenly the crate is detached and plummets onto an abandon car. A ladder falls from within the helicopter, it lands within arm's reach of Newman. David looks on as Newman steps onto the ladder. The walls of the crate fall to the ground. Inside were three androids; there was one of female design, and two males.

Agent Newman clicks another button on his phone, activating the Alpha Humans. The helicopter begins to ascend as Agent Newman climbs the ladder.

"You had a duty to us as well," David says to Newman as he climbs into the helicopter.

Having finally turned his attention towards the Alpha Humans, David watches as they begin to move.

The Alpha Human model LIGHT steps

forward; it's body sleek and athletic. "*Scanning meta-human threat level…level ten detected. Execute 'purification protocol'*," it announces in its robotic voice.

Just then Alpha Human model HEAVY lifts its massive arms to reveal twin cannons housed in its forearms. It charges up energy for an attack; David stands unflinching and motionless as the HEAVY fires a sphere of pure energy at him. But before the energy could make its mark, a pillar of concrete intercepts it.

"*Compensating*," the HEAVY says, as it retracts the cannons and breaks out into a sprint.

Behind the pillar, David activates his powers lifting his body into the air. Now hovering inches from the ground, David glides to the side just in time to avoid the HEAVY smashing through the pillar. Once David moves, Hector jumps out and punches the HEAVY into a car.

Alpha Human model SWIFT attempts to provide some aid but is picked up by a strong gust of wind and carried away. As the LIGHT model starts to sprint at David, a stream of fire pushes it down another street.

The HEAVY rolls backward off the car, and then lifts it over its head. It uses it as a projectile and hurls it at Hector. Adam swoops in using his jetpack and blasts the car out of the air with the mechanical arms attached to the jetpack. It falls to the ground in pieces in front of Hector. Adam throws David his sword; he nods in appreciation. The HEAVY scans its opponents, forming tactics and strategies based on what it can see from the surface.

Out of its right arm, a jagged blade forms, and from its left arm, it forms a cannon. Out of its shoulders, rise mini cannons.

"*Compensating*," it says.

It opens fire from the mini cannons in its shoulder; Adam maneuvers through the air avoiding the shots. Hector runs directly at the HEAVY and punches it again. He does a series of close quarter combat techniques knocking the HEAVY towards David. As the HEAVY flies, it flips and lands on its feet.

"*Compensating*," the HEAVY says as it comes to a screeching halt.

David takes his sword into both hands and assumes his fighting stance. He and the HEAVY begin an intense sword fight. David blasts the HEAVY into the air at which point Adam grabs a hold of it and flies into the side of a building.

As it falls to the ground it says, "*Compensating*." Panels at the bottom of its feet shift to reveal thrusters. They ignite and the HEAVY flies back up towards Adam. The cannons mounted in its shoulder pivot and start to fire at Adam.

Adam activates an energy shield, which protects him from the cannon fire. Without warning,

David flies up after the HEAVY and hits it with yet another blast. He flies after it, attacking it with precise slashes from his sword. He cuts into the frame of the HEAVY; the heat from his attack disrupts the HEAVY's regenerative functions.

The HEAVY flips wildly through the air until it regains control. "*Compensating*," it says as David flies straight at it. The HEAVY forms a barrier in front of it.

David quickly changes course and begins to circle around the HEAVY. Adam charges up his mechanical arms for an attack. Once David is around behind the HEAVY, he glides his blade through the small of its back. The HEAVY snaps around towards David, leaving its rear vulnerable. Adam fires two unstable energy blasts that disperses into smaller energy blasts. The volley of energy bombards the HEAVY and send it plummeting to the ground.

Hector jumps into the air and wraps his muscular arms around the HEAVY and slams it onto the hard concrete below. Before Hector had a chance to do anything else, the HEAVY gets to its feet. It retracts its weapons as it says, "*Compensating*." Having now returned to its base form, the HEAVY takes a fighting stance. It starts to exchange blows with Hector, they brawl all along the street. Amid their scuffle, cars get damaged and trees are knocked down.

Hector knocks it into a car, with little effort it

snatches the door off and smacked Hector in the face with it. He falls to the ground where the HEAVY pinned him down.

"*Executing 'purification protocol'*," the HEAVY says as its eyes light up.

From within the air, Adam shoots a blast from the cannon mounted to his right forearm. The attack lands right in between the eyes of the HEAVY. This momentary distraction gives Hector enough time to summon minerals around his arms. He forces himself up and lands a hard-right hook on the HEAVY. They lock hands in a power struggle. The HEAVY starts to force Hector down to his knees. He responds by tightening his grip until he literally rips the HEAVY's arms out of their sockets.

"*Compensate-*"

"Compensate this…3," Hector says as he uses the arms to smash the HEAVY's head.

Adam fires down two energy blast as he shouts, "2!" The blasts react to one another and trap the HEAVY in a field of energy.

While the HEAVY was trapped in the field of energy, David zooms through the air directly at the HEAVY. As he closes the gap, he flings his sword into the air. He flips in the air and gathers massive amounts of energy in the palm of his hand.

"1," David says, as he slams his fist down onto the ground directly in front of the HEAVY. The result was a vast pillar of light and heat that shoots up past the tall buildings and into the sky.

As the light disappears, what remains of the HEAVY is nothing more than smoke.

The minerals fall from Hector's arms as he drops the only pieces that remain of the HEAVY. Adam lands next to Hector and retracts the mechanical arms into his jetpack. Finally, David stands up straight and lifts his hand into the air. With expert timing, he catches his sword and lowers it to his side as he glances back at his teammates.

Flailing wildly through the air, the SWIFT struggles to grab ahold of something. Finally, it manages to use the tendrils from its head to latch itself to a building. With arachnid like fluidity, the SWIFT crawls down the side of the building. It leaps from the third story and lands daintily on top of a streetlight.

It turns its attention down to the street where Janet stands motionless. Just then, a plasma bolt hits the light pole blowing it down. The SWIFT rides it all the way down to the ground. At the last second, the SWIFT rolls off the pole and stands just meters in front of Janet.

"*Scanning meta-human threat level…level two. Executing 'purification protocol'.*" The SWIFT shifts its left hand into a mini Vulcan cannon. Just then, Jessica launches two plasma bolts at the

SWIFT's feet. This gives Janet a chance to move out of the path of the Vulcan cannon.

The SWIFT then turns the Vulcan cannon towards Jessica, who sits strategically on a fire escape two blocks away. "*Compensating,*" it says as it shoots the support bars to the fire escape. Jessica jumps away and climbs up a neighboring fire escape. Seconds later, Kimberly runs out from behind cover. She plunges her daggers into the Vulcan cannon and flips the SWIFT into the air.

"Chaos, I'm bringing 'her' to you-"

"*Compensating,*" the SWIFT says as it unlocks the joints throughout its whole body. Having now gone limp, the SWIFT hits the ground like a ragdoll, absorbing very little damage.

"No way," Kimberly states in disbelief.

The SWIFT twirls its body and relocks it joints, then it bombards Kimberly with a combination of attacks. She goes flying back onto the pavement.

As the SWIFT stalks Kimberly, two pigmies rush out and pounce onto its back and leg. It flails violently to free itself from their grasp. Janet runs out and smacks the SWIFT across the face. It responds, "*Compensating,*" then its epidermis becomes thorny, causing the pigmies to let go.

The SWIFT activates lasers from its optics and destroys the pigmies. Just in time, Jessica runs up and jumps in front of her teammates and puts up a barrier. The SWIFT fires a continuous laser at the plasma barrier. "*Signal failure, Alpha Human HEAVY terminated*," the SWIFT states after several minutes of combat.

"What are we going to do? It adapts to our attacks," Jessica says excitedly.

"Well then, we need to give it too much to adapt to." Janet responds.

"Chaos is right, we need to hit it hard and fast. We are going to have to give it everything we have," Kimberly proclaims as she sits up off the ground.

"So, get ready then," Jessica says. "I'll hold it off for now."

"Wait for the right moment to strike. Chaos and I will draw its attention."

Kimberly and Janet wait a couple of seconds, then run out from behind the barrier.

The SWIFT sees this and raises both arms and says, "*Compensating.*" Its arms revert to the Vulcan cannons.

Before it had a chance to attack, Jessica says, "You need to pay attention!" she increases the force of her barrier, it forces the laser back into the eyes of the SWIFT. The backlash makes the SWIFT back away; its optics are disrupted.

Taking this opportunity, Janet summons two glowing pigmies that grab a hold of the SWIFT and releases their energy. The blast knocks it into an attack from Kimberly.

The SWIFT staggers backwards and glances

from side to side. Seeing nothing but static, the SWIFT spoke out, "*Compensating.*" Lights run along the shaft of the tendrils, making them seemingly come to life and squirm in place. The tendrils are now picking up sonar waves, which it uses to see its surroundings. It lifts the Vulcan cannons out towards the girls and opens fire.

They scatter and avoid the attack. With every move they make, the SWIFT directs its cannons at them.

"Chaos, we need to draw its fire!" Kimberly shouts into her communicator.

Janet tucks down behind a wall and inhales deeply. With much concentration, she summons a dozen pigmies and they scurry throughout the street. The SWIFT turns its attention to all the pigmies. One by one, the SWIFT dispatches the pigmies. This causes Janet to summon her Cerberus. The multi-headed canine leaps from behind cover to pounce on the SWIFT.

The tendrils pick up the movement and the SWIFT avoids the attack. A few of the tendrils shift in appearance as the SWIFT spoke out, "*Compensating.*" It begins to generate a whistle-like noise that irritates the Cerberus.

The hound hops about in pain, its mouth now filling up with fire. Janet rushes out and wraps her whip around a section of the tendrils and yanks vigorously. This causes the SWIFT to teeter slightly.

It lifts it left arm at Janet, at which point Jessica fires two plasma bolts from down the street.

Using its tendrils, the SWIFT detects the plasma bolt, and can step out of its way. Unknowingly, it steps right into an attack from Kimberly who cuts the tendrils off the SWIFT's head.

As a result, the high-pitched whistling stops, and Janet runs out and jumps onto the back of the Cerberus. She commands it to attack, at which point it jumps all over the SWIFT. After a series of attacks and two fireballs, the SWIFT is sent flying through the air.

"Plasma get ready," Kimberly shouts as she sticks her daggers into the SWIFT. She swings it around and begins to attack it.

Miraculously, the SWIFT can retaliate after losing power in its optics. "*Compensating*," it says for the last time. It forms two blades from its arms. But before it had a chance to do anything, a Kami tackled it.

Janet shouts, "Starbolt move!" at which point the Cerberus launches a fireball from its massive jaws. Kimberly runs as the mass of fire collides with the pigmy, resulting in an explosion. The blast sends the SWIFT flying backwards down the street; as it approaches Jessica, she releases her attack. She forms a giant plasma sphere that she uses to obliterate the SWIFT. With much concentration, Kimberly uses her wind to keep the force of the attack contained to the

SWIFT.

As the pieces pile up in the street, the SWIFT is finally destroyed. Jessica stumbles back, as that last attack drained her of tremendous energy. Kimberly helps her up; afterward Janet comes up behind them riding on the back of her Cerberus.

"Is it finally over?" Jessica inquired.

"For now, the rest is up to them," Kimberly says confidently.

Chapter 21

Project Alpha Human pt 2

With his arms locked tightly around the LIGHT, Marcus carries it through the air in a stream of fire. At great speeds, he slams it into a car. As Marcus lets go, his body rolls over the roof of the car and into the street. Once he starts to stand, he watches as the car begins to compress around the LIGHT.

Marcus slowly pulls his weapon and joins it together at the handle. He listens as the metal frame of the car becomes brittle.

"*Compensating,*" the LIGHT says as it forces the car off itself, the pieces fly everywhere.

Marcus twirls his blade in the air then plunges it deep into the concrete. He kneels behind it just as a fragment of the car zooms right at him. When the attack was over, Marcus stands up slowly.

Seemingly from out of nowhere, Devonte strolls in on his perpetual ice slide and flanks the Alpha Human. He pulls both guns out and points them towards the LIGHT. "Let's see what you are made of, bucket-head," Devonte says playfully.

"*Scanning meta-human threat level…level four. Executing 'purification protocol'.*"

Marcus gets into his fighting stance and takes a few good breaths.

The LIGHT turned its right arm into a razor-sharp sword, and it forms a cannon out of the left arm. It wastes little time running full speed at Devonte. As Marcus tries to move, the LIGHT begins to fire the cannon at him. He twirls his blade in defense against the blast.

Devonte opens fire as the LIGHT pursues him. When the frozen bullets collide with its body, the LIGHT starts to slow up.

"Yeah, hurts don't it!" Devonte proclaims.

"*Compensating,*" the LIGHT states as its exterior hardens.

Devonte's eyes get bigger as the LIGHT continues its charge. When it finally reaches him, it says, "*Compensating,*" as it turns its limbs back to normal. It begins to perform close quarter combat on him, rendering his gun useless.

As Devonte is being beaten, a lightning kunai sores through the air and hits the LIGHT in the face.

The detonation causes it to stagger backwards; Xavier teleports in with a slash attack from his sword. The attack sends the LIGHT back towards Marcus, who starts attacking it. Xavier pats Devonte on his shoulder; Devonte gives him thumbs up.

Marcus is battling the LIGHT when Xavier runs up to join the fight.

Seeing this the LIGHT model says, "*Compensating.*" With expert precision, it performs a flip kick hitting both Xavier and Marcus. When it comes to rest on its feet, it forms another blade out of its right arm. It slashes down at Marcus, but is deflected by Xavier, who teleports at the last second.

The two begin to battle in one on one sword combat. The Alpha Human has been programmed with countless fighting tactics, thus making it increasingly difficult for Xavier to overpower it. Marcus brushes himself off and runs into battle. Aware of the impending attack, the LIGHT says, "*Compensating,*" and turns its left arm into a shield.

It hoists the shield up in defense against Marcus. As Marcus and Xavier battle with the LIGHT, Devonte lifts his guns again and waits for the right moment to shoot. He takes three shots, which are deflected by the shield.

The LIGHT slaps Marcus away with one great swing from its shield, and then follows it up with a thrust kick, sending Xavier flying into a pole. The force from the impact bends the pole.

Devonte continues his assault, causing the LIGHT to focus on him.

"*Compensating*," the LIGHT says as it breaks out into a full sprint at Devonte. In mid stride, the LIGHT notices Marcus coming directly at him. In response, it forces its blade into the ground and spun itself, kicking Marcus forcefully in the ribcage and back onto the ground.

It stops and returns to its feet; lifting the shield up in front of it, the LIGHT continues to sprint at Devonte.

Devonte fires shot after shot until he was no longer able to fire. His guns lock up in mid shot. Devonte thinks nothing of it and drops the guns. He forms the large ice fists and attempted to attack the LIGHT. However, he is gored into the side of a building where his body goes limp.

As the LIGHT stands over Devonte prepared to strike, it is pulled by Xavier who used some wire to act as a lasso. He tugs with all his might. The LIGHT goes flying back where it lands in front of him. Soon after that, Marcus rushes in and stops right behind the LIGHT.

Just then, the fight stops momentarily as everyone notices a pillar of light ascending skyward.

"*Signal failure, Alpha Human HEAVY terminated!*"

Marcus goes in for the attack. The LIGHT blocks his attack with the shield. Xavier starts to swing his sword at the LIGHT; expertly the LIGHT can fend off both attackers. As they are fighting, Marcus plunges one end of his blade into the shield and it comes out the other side; he then struggles to pull the blade free from the arm of the Alpha Human.

The LIGHT rotated its whole forearm as it stated, "*Compensating.*" The blade snaps, leaving the bulk of it still lodged in the LIGHT. It then rotates its body three hundred sixty degrees, swinging both blades. Marcus ducks, but Xavier gets cut across the face as he tries to step out of the way of the attack. The LIGHT then fires a shockwave that sends both boys flying away.

Xavier sits up; his mask is cut and stained with blood. He watches as the LIGHT tries to shift its left arm back to normal but was unable to because Marcus' blade is disrupting its functions. A brief memory of the blueprints plays back in his head.

"River are you seeing this?" Xavier questions. "Your blade is preventing it from changing its arm."

"Well, what are you suggesting?"

"I am going to make it vulnerable, then when the core is exposed...we strike."

"Core...what are we talking?"

"It's probably some unstable mass of energy that can redirect power at any given moment. Thus, allowing it to adapt instantaneously."

Xavier gets back up to his feet and throws one lightning kunai at the LIGHT. "We need to stop it,

River, no matter what happens," he says.

The LIGHT charges at Xavier and the two engage in a sword fight once again. Xavier lands cut after cut on the LIGHT to find its weak spot. The LIGHT knocks him to the ground and tries to stab him, but Xavier cuts at its leg making it stumble. Xavier rolls out of the way and rolls back onto his feet. The LIGHT comes up vertically with the blade stuck in its arm. Timing it precisely, Xavier flips out of harm's way.

The LIGHT goes for another attack when it suddenly stops, "*Signal failure, Alpha Human SWIFT terminated.*"

Xavier sends an electrical current through his sword as he states, "It's time for a full system shutdown!" With his sword, Xavier rips through the chest plate of the Alpha Human LIGHT.

The heat from his electricity disrupts the LIGHT's regenerative functions. It staggers back, grabbing at its chest.

"*Damage…critical. Must seek repair unit,*" it states as it tries to escape.

Once the Alpha Human turns around, Devonte, who has clasped his hands together, clobbers it with his ice fist. He then forms ice around the LIGHT's limbs and begins to beat on it.

Finally, Devonte can land an uppercut, which sends the LIGHT soaring backwards. When it stands up, it rocks unsteadily from side to side.

"Damage…critical, compensating."

Before it could do anything, Xavier lodges a lightning kunai into the wound in the LIGHT's chest plate. It explodes, blowing off the chest plate entirely. Marcus then flies straight at the LIGHT; he twirls what was left of his blade and shoves it into the glowing core as he lifts it skyward. Once they were high enough in the air Marcus looks at the LIGHT, its face is cold and emotionless.

"The game ends here," Marcus says, as he yanks his blade out from within the Alpha Human. With one final swing, he severs the LIGHT's head from its body. Marcus begins to freefall but is forced down towards the earth once the core imploded in on itself. The shockwave rumbles the streets below. Marcus flails uncontrollably as he hastily descends towards the ground. Down on the street, Devonte creates his perpetual ice slide and rides it up the side of a building. Once he got enough momentum, he jumps off into the air where he grabs Marcus. The two boys land onto another ice slide and ride it down to the street.

As they come back down to the street, debris from the LIGHT falls from the sky, including its entire head unit. Xavier waits for his friends to land; he wipes two fingers across his cheek. He sheaths his sword and walks up to his teammates.

"Well…we did it. Meta-humans are safe once again. At least for now," Marcus says as he places both hands on the shoulders of his friends.

Just then teams 321 and 352 walk up and surround the boys. They all embrace one another in happiness until they hear the mutter of a helicopter. In the distance, Agent Newman pilots a helicopter towards them. David steps forward and instructs everyone to wait there. He takes to the skies and flies directly in front of the helicopter.

Newman is forced to hover rather than land. "You have always been a persistent lot. I would have been disappointed if this had gone any different."

"You put innocent humans in danger just to draw us out into the open!" David snaps sternly.

"They were warned. Regardless, it was a necessary sacrifice to get the data we needed."

"What data?"

"Come on now Quazar, you didn't think we would put so much at risk with three untested prototypes without having some sort of fallback plan. The 1.0 models were flawed, but they offered great results."

"Why are you doing this, Newman? Why turn your back on us now...when we need you the most? What do you stand to gain by hunting down meta-humans?"

"I'm just following orders. Besides you and your friends got careless. You are too trusting; just because someone smiles in your face doesn't mean they won't stab you in the back. So, because you messed up, I must put my neck on the chopping block! Well not anymore. You guys have the powers, then why not trying to clean up your own mess for once!"

David watches as Newman pulls off and flees the scene. Slowly, David descends to the ground. He lands next to Hector, who puts his hand on David's shoulder. David proceeds to tell them everything that was said in his conversation with Newman. Soon after, the STC was landing in the middle of the street. The hatch opens and Scott calls out to them to get in.

Later that evening team 407 as well as David and Commander Maximus gather in the Briefing Room. The boys sit at a table in the corner, while David and Commander Maximus stand by the Grid. The TV was on to the global news station.

Commander Maximus lowers the volume remotely from the Grid. "Today was a hard-fought victory. You three have come a long way since we first met. You managed to overcome every obstacle that you faced."

"Yeah, but in light of recent events…was it worth it? The humans hate us now more than ever," Marcus states doubtfully.

"Indeed, the journey that we chose to embark on here at Atlas seems foolhardy at times. The humans fear us, and because of that fear, they hate us. But nevertheless, our goal remains the same, to achieve harmony between humans and meta-humans."

But what if they don't want harmony," Marcus blurts out. "What if what mankind wants is to see us wiped out?"

"Then we stand until the last man falls. But never will we force our ideals on them. Corrupted souls liken unto Quake see things just the opposite. They want harmony, but harmony through chaos! Fear is motivating, and Quake aims to rule by using that fear.

Whether for us or against us, the humans remain a very vital factor in this fight. Unfortunately, the actions of Nova consistently set back the progress we have made over time."

"In order to stop that from happening, we are going to have to get rid of Nova…permanently," Xavier proclaims.

"I agree, but something tells me that Nova will be laying low for a while. If they know us as well as they think they do, then they know that we will be gunning for them next!"

Xavier stares long at the TV; he tells everyone to pay attention to the screen. Everyone diverts their eyes to the flat screen on the wall as Commander Maximus unmutes the TV.

"This just in. Several high-ranking officials have verified today's battle in Fortune City as a military training routine. Reports say that the blame for the attack on the President was deemed a case of

mistaken identity. Reports say the one who attacked the conference has no affiliation to the organization known as Atlas, but instead was an imposter. President Carmichael is investigating all aspects of the Government, from the military, to groups like the CIA and NRD. The President says that he will not rest until the real culprits are brought to justice before the American people. Stay tuned for more on this developing story."

The room grows quiet. Everyone sits still in shock. Commander Maximus turns off the television; a slight smirk crept across his face as he says, "Newman…you son of a gun."

Just then, an alert went off on the Grid. David examines the alert, "It's an encrypted message…from Newman," he says while accessing the message.

"If you just watched the news, then I can probably assume that you are wondering what happened. It turns out there was something I could do. I could buy you some time. I concocted a story that was to paint you all as victims. An unknown meta-human framed you. Now the President suspects the same could be with some of his own organizations.

You survived the Alpha Humans…whoopee! But those were only prototypes. The next batch will be the real deal. So, I suggest whatever you have planned, you better get a move on, because you only have about two years before these puppies start coming off the assembly line.

Three years I have been going to bat for this organization, and every time it gets harder and harder to keep them from knocking down your front door. I am a man who is committed to his work and will do whatever necessary to complete his mission. But unfortunately, a man must know when to hang up his tie...

You are out of the line of fire for now...but from here on out you all are going to have to clean up your own mess. Or find someone else to do it...I'm done!"

The message cuts out; David looks at Commander Maximus. Maximus stands firm as he proclaimed, "A man is bound by his duty, even if that means doing something he doesn't want to. You three did not know Agent Newman, but he was our liaison to the American Government. Newman was assigned this job; knowing how he truly felt about meta-humans, he took the job anyway.

As you just heard that partnership has come to an end. We are now on our own. From here on out, we are going to have to be extra careful how we handle situations. There is no doubt in my mind that we can do it. All of us together have the necessary talent to complete this journey. This has been a very special year. We have made new allies, we have also made new enemies. We forged just as many bonds that we have broken. But it's through the breaking of these bonds that makes us stronger."

Maximus walks up to the boys, David stands proudly behind his right shoulder.

"So how about it? Do you boys think you can handle the road ahead? Or would you like to go home?"

Xavier stands up followed by Marcus, then Devonte.

"What are you talking about? We are home," Devonte says confidently.

Epilogue

The sun is setting on Fortune City, New York. A military clean-up crew has been called in to secure the remains of the Alpha Humans. They scurry through the city picking up piece after piece. They dump them into containment bays.

"Careful with that, every scrap belongs to the US Government."

"Yes sir," a squad of soldiers' shouts in unison.

Perched on top of a small skyscraper is a figure shrouded in a black cloak, its shape was thin and petite. The figure watches as the soldiers' scramble to pick up the pieces. As she leans over the edge of the building, strands of her long-braided hair fall from within her hood.

Minutes later, the hooded female is down on

the street, where she stands over a charred mass of metal. The metal hunk was the burnt head unit of the Alpha Human LIGHT. With no one around, she bends over revealing a Nova uniform under her cloak. She toys with the head for a second until she was able to open it up revealing a processing chip.

She removes the chip and kicks the head down the street. As it bounces down the block, the soldiers run back down the street. When they get there, all that is left is the charred Alpha Human head.

End

Join our heroes again in
The Chosen: Road to Destiny

JACOB MAXWELL
Atlas Commander **Maximus**

Height: 5'9
Weight: 150lbs
Eyes: Blue
Hair: Brown

Intelligence: 7
Strength: 9
Speed: 5

Durability: 7
Fighting Skill: 7
Energy Projectile: 0

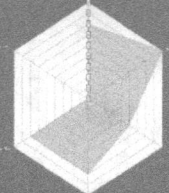

Jacob Maxwell possess the power of super strength. Jacob is an expert combatant and master strategist. He is admired by all of his subordinates due to his strong leadership and compassionate heart. He has been Commander of Atlas for almost 20 years. Jacob embodies what it means to be a true leader and does his best to groom the next generation of heroes.

DAVID GRAHAM

Atlas Operative Quazar

Height: 6'1	Intelligence: 7	Durability: 7
Weight: 210lbs	Strength: 7	Fighting Skill: 8
Eyes: Blue	Speed: 8	Energy Projectile: 9
Hair: Black		

David Graham uses an advance form of light energy. He is calm and level headed, he rarely gets upset. David's combat skills are unparalleled by anyone. The only person to come close is Kyle Turner. He is driven by the need to protect the world and those on it. David is kind hearted, strong, and very humble. He embodies what it means to be a true hero.

HECTOR HERNANDEZ

Atlas Operative Brick

Height: 6'8
Weight: 275lbs
Eyes: Brown
Hair: Brown

Intelligence: 6
Strength: 8
Speed: 6

Durability: 7
Fighting Skill: 8
Energy Projectile: 5

Hector Hernandez is an earth elementalist and one of Atlas' most effective operatives. He is former military and uses his vast knowledge of combat to train new recruits. Due to his size, Hector is perceived as intimidating, however he is one of the nicest people at Atlas. Hector is an expert at submission and close quarter combat. When on missions he prefers to fight and leave the talking to his lifelong friend David.

ADAM BAKER

Atlas Operative Gizmo

Height: 5'6   Intelligence: 9   Durability: 5
Weight: 140lbs   Strength: 5   Fighting Skill: 6
Eyes: Green   Speed: 6   Energy Projectile: 7
Hair: Brown

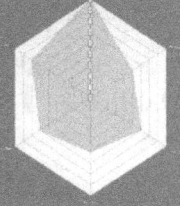

Adam Baker is a technopath and the smartest person at Atlas. He was one of the youngest interns at Astrotec which led him to Atlas. Adam is quick witted and very sarcastic at times. He prefers to take to the air when in combat. Adam spends most of his free time in the lab working on new technology.

MARCUS DANIELS

Atlas Operative River

Height: 5'11
Weight: 195lbs
Eyes: Brown
Hair: Black

Intelligence: 6
Strength: 7
Speed: 6

Durability: 6
Fighting Skill: 7
Energy Projectile: 8

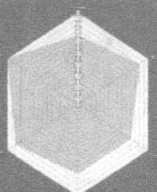

Marcus Daniels is a fire elementalist with a fiery temper. He is an expert combatant and strategy. Marcus is a naturally gifted fighter. He spends long hours honing his skills in the Battle Arena. Marcus is a very passionate person and this often influences his temper. Playing sports his whole life has made him a good team player as well as an effective team leader.

XAVIER EVANS

Atlas Operative **ShaXdow**

Height: 5'6   Intelligence: 9   Durability: 6
Weight: 165lbs   Strength: 5   Fighting Skill: 7
Eyes: Brown   Speed: 7   Energy Projectile: 7
Hair: Black

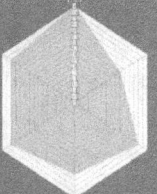

Xavier Evans wields the power of lightning and is an expert at stealth and close-quarters combat. He has also become an expert swordsman. Xavier is a natural born genius with an uncanny eye for engineering. He can operate and understand most aspects of technology. He has taken up an interest in the art of Ninjitsu like his grandfather before him. Xavier is kind hearted and easy to befriend. He is a natural born problem solver. He seeks clarity through meditation.

DEVONTE COLEMAN

Atlas Operative **DaRock**

Height: 5'9	Intelligence: 5	Durability: 7
Weight: 155lbs	Strength: 4	Fighting Skill: 6
Eyes: Brown	Speed: 6	Energy Projectile: 7
Hair: Black		

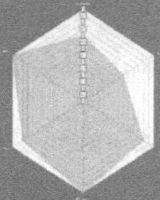

Devonte Coleman is a young ice elementalist and expert marksman. He is light hearted and often care free. Devonte has a tendency of pulling pranks on his fellow teammates. He sometimes gets himself into situations that he can't handle. Although Devonte lacks focus he uses the thought of finding his missing sister as motivation to keep him going. Devonte can be very social, often choosing to hang out rather than train.

KIMBERLY YOUNG

Atlas Operative **Starbolt**

Height: 5'5   Intelligence: 7   Durability: 4
Weight: 115lbs Strength: 4   Fighting Skill: 7
Eyes: Blue   Speed: 7   Energy Projectile: 6
Hair: Pink

Kimberly Young is a wind elementalist and an exceptional operative. Kimberly is shy and reserved. She was made team leader to help her boost her confidence and help her reach her true potential. She is very close to Janet as they have been close friends since High School. Kimberly is very nimble and is one of the fastest strikers in Atlas. She has become one of the top combatant after training with both Hector and Xavier.

JESSICA MARTINEZ

Atlas Operative **Plasma**

Height: 5'6   Intelligence: 6   Durability: 5
Weight: 120lbs   Strength: 4   Fighting Skill: 6
Eyes: Green   Speed: 7   Energy Projectile: 8
Hair: Blue

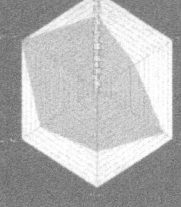

Jessica Martinez produces an unstable green energy known as plasma energy. Jessica is a gifted gymnast making her very agile. She took up archery when she was younger becoming an expert marksman. Jessica is a sweetheart and only loses her cool in extreme circumstances. She has developed a strong bond with her new teammates Kimberly and Janet. Jessica is a skilled fighter up close, however she prefers to fight from a distance.

JANET PETERSON

Atlas Operative Chaos

Height: 5'7 Intelligence: 6 Durability: 5
Weight: 120lbs Strength: 4 Fighting Skill: 5
Eyes: Green Speed: 5 Energy Projectile: 4
Hair: Black

Janet Peterson is a summoner. She is unique among the summoners as she can sense life force. Janet is a very soft spoken and introverted young lady, however she has a passion for all things living. She struggles with control over her powers therefore she tries not to get emotional. Janet tries her best not to lose control or the full force of the Echo will be unleashed.

TRISH ROBERTS

Atlas Operative **Solara**

Height: 5'7	Intelligence: 8	Durability: 5
Weight: 120lbs	Strength: 4	Fighting Skill: 7
Eyes: Green	Speed: 7	Energy Projectile: 3
Hair: Blonde		

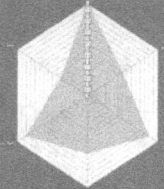

Trish Roberts is an earth elementalist with the gift of near perfect recall. She is strong willed and nurturing. Trish excels at fitting in with different groups of people. This is due to her family constantly moving from city to city. Trish is an expert combatant and gifted intellectual. She has had her powers since she was young, therefore she is more in tune with her powers than your average metahuman.

CHARLES MILLER

Atlas Operative **Blaze**

Height: 5'9   Intelligence: 5   Durability: 6
Weight: 165lbs   Strength: 5   Fighting Skill: 6
Eyes: Blue   Speed: 7   Energy Projectile: 8
Hair: Red

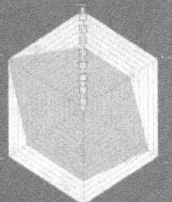

    Charles Miller wields the element fire. He is a cocky, self-absorbed teen with a fiery temper to match. Charles is a well rounded operative with mastery in combat and infiltration. He prefers to rush into battle head first and defeat his opponents with blinding offense. Though rough around the edges, Charles is good at heart.

KENNETH SCOTT

Atlas Operative Storm

Height: 5'7 Intelligence: 5 Durability: 5
Weight: 160lbs Strength: 5 Fighting Skill: 5
Eyes: Brown Speed: 8 Energy Projectile: 8
Hair: Blue

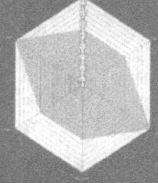

Kenneth Scott uses the element lightning and has become adept at precision shooting. Kenneth is a light hearted bundle of innocence. He suffers from short term memory loss and has to make recordings to himself so that he won't loose the memory. Kenneth struggles with self confidence which is the opposite of his best friend Charles Miller.

MARK TITUS
Atlas Operative **Burner**

Height: 6'3
Weight: 215lbs
Eyes: Blue
Hair: None

Intelligence: 6
Strength: 7
Speed: 5

Durability: 7
Fighting Skill: 7
Energy Projectile: 4

Mark Titus has the power of full body combustion. He was a very skilled operative and a very gifted transport specialist. Although Mark has had troubles in life, he remains one of the most dutiful men to ever walk into Atlas. Mark has a welcoming personality and became a mentor to many of the operatives, but none more important than his nephew Simon.

SIMON MILLER
Atlas Operative Hotstreak

Height: 5'10 Intelligence: 5 Durability: 6
Weight: 170lbs Strength: 5 Fighting Skill: 6
Eyes: Blue Speed: 6 Energy Projectile: 8
Hair: Red

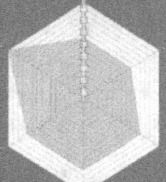

Simon Miller was born a fire elementalist with the ability to mold fire into whatever he desires. He struggles with close-quarters-combat so he uses fire whips to fight at a distance. Simon is very over confident and usually gets into more than he can handle.

EVA ALLEN

Atlas Operative **Slipstream**

Height: 5'8	Intelligence: 7	Durability: 5
Weight: 120lbs	Strength: 4	Fighting Skill: 7
Eyes: Orange	Speed: 7	Energy Projectile: 5
Hair: Blue		

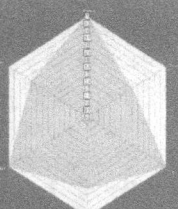

Eva Allen has the ability to manipulate water. She usually uses it for the purpose of advanced traversal. Eva is an elite operative with a feisty attitude and a quick wit. She was engaged to Simon Miller before they both lost their lives in the great compromise.

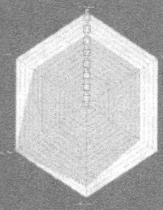

DILLAN SNYDER

Atlas Operative **Shift**

Height: 6'1　　Intelligence: 6　　Durability: 7
Weight: 195lbs　Strength: 6　　Fighting Skill: 8
Eyes: Brown　　Speed: 6　　　Energy Projectile: 6
Hair: Brown

Dillan Snyder has the power of telekinesis and is former United States Military. He is an expert marksman with a personality that's as cold as the blade of his dagger. Dillan has combat mastery in many forms of combat. Dillan has a strong sense of duty and it is his duty to protect the world.

SCOTT MCMILLAN

Atlas

Height: 5'8
Weight: 145lbs
Eyes: Blue
Hair: Brown

Intelligence: 6
Strength: 5
Speed: 5

Durability: 4
Fighting Skill: 5
Energy Projectile: 0

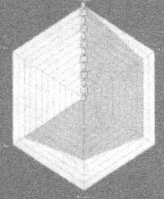

   Scott McMillan has enhanced eyesight that rivals any bird. He is also team 407's personal pilot. Scott joined Atlas right out of college. He became a transportation specialist because both of his parents were former pilots. Scott does his job tirelessly no matter the outcome.

TRISTEN REYNOLDS

Redemption Survivor

Height: 5'6
Weight: 115lbs
Eyes: Blue
Hair: Brown

Intelligence: 5
Strength: 4
Speed: 7

Durability: 5
Fighting Skill: 4
Energy Projectile: 6

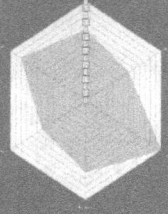

Tristen Reynolds is an orphan boy with the power to harness and manipulate light itself. He joined his brother's gang Redemption when he came of age. Tristen struggles with being courageous. He is a gifted free runner with little combat experience. Although his life was hard, Tristen is a good natured person. After his brother's death Tristen finds himself motivated by revenge.

TYRELL MARTINEZ

Nova Commander Quake

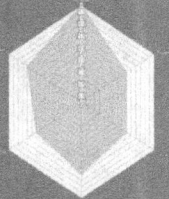

Height: 5'10	Intelligence: 8	Durability: 6
Weight: 165lbs	Strength: 5	Fighting Skill: 5
Eyes: Green	Speed: 5	Energy Projectile: 6
Hair: Blue		

Tyrell Martinez has the power to absorb people's abilities. He is a self taught scientist turned militant leader. Tyrell is very manipulative and can flawlessly talk his way out of a situation. He is a shell of his former self, this tends to keeps his followers on edge around him. Tryell is a master strategist and is usually two steps ahead of Atlas.

CORDELL WELLINGTON

Nova

Height: 5'11   Intelligence: 7   Durability: 5
Weight: 150lbs Strength: 4   Fighting Skill: 4
Eyes: Maroon   Speed: 5   Energy Projectile: 9
Hair: Mahogany

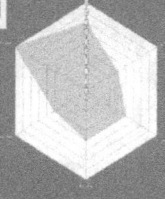

Cordell Wellington is a legendary mystic with mastery in both the light and dark artes. He is cold and calculating, he always keeps his composure even in the face of adversity. Cordell is the second in command of Nova. He is the only person Quake truly trusts. Cordell doesn't usually engage in close quarter combat, he relies on his magic to overpower and out match his foes.

KYLE TURNER

Nova Operative **Stargazer**

Height: 6'0   Intelligence: 7   Durability: 6
Weight: 175lbs   Strength: 6   Fighting Skill: 8
Eyes: Red   Speed: 7   Energy Projectile: 7
Hair: Brown

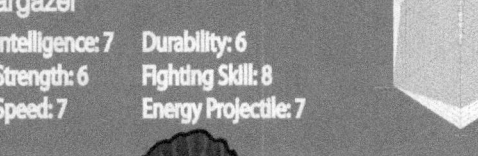

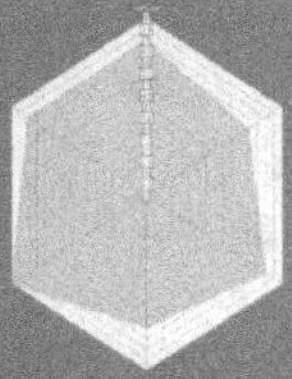

Kyle Turner is a very powerful darkness elementalist with a deep lust for destruction. Not much is known about him outside of the fact that he is a very troubled individual. Kyle was at one point the best operative at Atlas, but fell victim to Quake's manipulation. He has an unhealthy hatred for David and wants nothing more than to destroy him. Kyle is Quake's best operative but also one of his greatest burdens.

REBECCA, ALEXIS, JENNIFER MARTINEZ
Nova Operative Mirror Sisters

Height: 5'4 Intelligence: 7 Durability: 4
Weight: 115lbs Strength: 3 Fighting Skill: 7
Eyes: Green Speed: 7 Energy Projectile: 0
Hair: Green, Blue, Pink

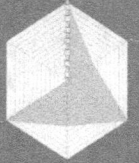

Alexis

Rebecca

Jennifer

Rebecca has the power to mimic people's appearance, Alexis has the power to copy herself seemingly an infinite amount of times, and Jennifer can make copies of people. They are highly gifted meta-humans and the first successful subjects of Project Acceleration. Having the bodies of fifteen years old, the skills of seasoned warriors, and the will of their father Quake, the Mirror Sisters are highly dangerous.

ALBERT SULLIVAN

Nova Operative **Twister**

Height: 6'0	Intelligence: 4	Durability: 6
Weight: 175lbs	Strength: 5	Fighting Skill: 4
Eyes: Blue	Speed: 6	Energy Projectile: 7
Hair: Blonde		

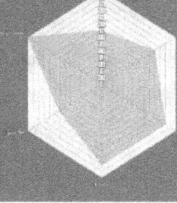

Albert Sullivan is a destructive wind elementalist who enjoys the carnage of destruction. What he lacks in brains he makes up for in effectiveness. Albert is by far one of Nova's most dangerous operatives. This is not only due to his mindless destruction, but also his lack of regard for collateral damage. He possesses a basic knowledge of combat, thus he usually leaves strategy to his teammates and goes for total destruction.

BRODY WARD
Nova Operative **Screech**

Height: 6'5
Weight: 210lbs
Eyes: Red
Hair: Green

Intelligence: 6
Strength: 7
Speed: 5

Durability: 8
Fighting Skill: 8
Energy Projectile: 7

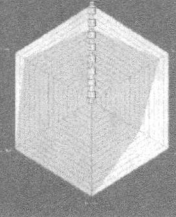

Brody Ward possesses the power to emit high frequency supersonic vibrations. The frequency is so intense that it harms Brody himself, therefore he wears a special mask that pumps a continuous dose of a nerve numbing sedative into his body. Brody is a dangerous person, his skills have earned him the position of leader of a group of Nova's most dangerous operatives. It's known as Delta unit.

WESLEY THOMAS

Nova Operative Rampage

Height: 5'8(7'0)
Weight: 130lbs(580lbs)
Eyes: Blue(Yellow)
Hair: Brown

Intelligence: 5
Strength: 8
Speed: 8

Durability: 8
Fighting Skill: 3
Energy Projectile: 0

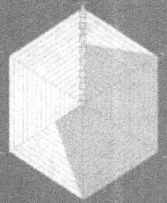

Wesley Thomas has the ability to undergo a full body metamorphosis, turning into the unstoppable beast Rampage. Normally weak and frail, when Wesley transformers he is virtually indestructible and inhumanly strong. Wesley must be kept separated from his teammates as it is not uncommon for him to lose himself to the primal rage. Pound for pound Wesley is one of Nova's most deadly operatives.

GREGORY O'NEAL

Nova Operative Hardwyre

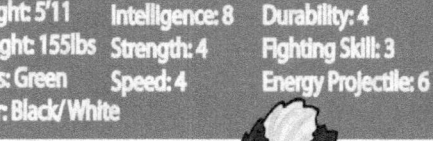

Height: 5'11	Intelligence: 8	Durability: 4
Weight: 155lbs	Strength: 4	Fighting Skill: 3
Eyes: Green	Speed: 4	Energy Projectile: 6
Hair: Black/White		

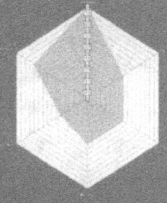

Gregory O'Neal is a low level lightning elementalist with the gift of hacking. He is awkward and outspoken. Gregory oversees all of Nova's projects and programs, like Project Acceleration. He has very little combat experience and very rarely leaves the island.

HAYDEN ELLIOT

Sadist

Height: 6'0   Intelligence: 6   Durability: 5
Weight: 185lbs   Strength: 6   Fighting Skill: 5
Eyes: Brown   Speed: 4   Energy Projectile: 0
Hair: Black

Hayden Elliot is a narcissistic sociopath with the power to reconstruct his limbs into weapons. He fought his way to leadership of his group of Sadist. Hayden has a twisted sense of reality and is feared by more than just his crew. He doesn't carry a firearm because he considers himself to be the ultimate weapon. Hayden and his crew are infamous on the streets of Chicago.

BRAD SIMMONS

Sadist

Height: 6'5   Intelligence: 5   Durability: 8
Weight: 265lbs Strength: 7   Fighting Skill: 4
Eyes: Blue   Speed: 3   Energy Projectile: 0
Hair: Brown

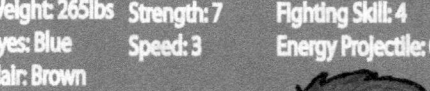

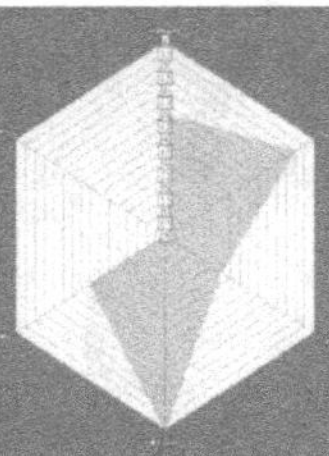

Brad Simmons has the power to absorb all types of energy. He was once married and has a daughter. His daughter was taken from him, his search for her led him to Chicago. There he linked up with Sadist. He agreed to help Hayden secure Chicago with hopes of getting some answers. Brad is bold and intimidating, his size alone strikes fear into the eyes of his victims.

THOMAS ROBERTS JR.

Sadist

Height: 5'5 Intelligence: 6 Durability: 4
Weight: 130lbs Strength: 4 Fighting Skill: 4
Eyes: Green Speed: 3 Energy Projectile: 7
Hair: Blonde

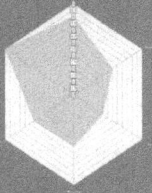

Thomas Roberts Jr. is a young runaway with the power of pyrokinesis. Thomas is very snarky and unkind, he is prone to bouts of verbal disrespect. He found a family in the Sadist; one that he never felt like he had back home with his parents and sister. He is not that brave therefore he uses his powers to great effect so that he seldom has to see actual combat.

About the Author

Michael Williams

has a passion for writing. Growing up he struggled with both reading and writing, however he always possessed an abundance of creativity. While in High School he developed a love for Art so much so that he slowly taught himself how to draw. After his doodles became recognizable as characters he started to name them. Eventually he decided to pull all his characters together and create his own world much like his biggest inspirations Marvel and DC.

Although his writing skills left to be desired, over the years he taught himself how to be a better writer and storyteller. He briefly became a Writing Teacher for a year, where he taught his students how to tap into their inner storyteller. He ended up starting a company with his brother doing what they both love…storytelling. His first novel; The Chosen: Breaking Bonds is the first of a series of books that are filled with characters who have evolved from sketches and doodles to fully realized characters with storyline, purpose, feeling, and conflict.